W9-AYZ-999

OCT __ 2015

KHCPL MAIN
220 North Union St.
Kokomo, Indiana 46901-4614
765.457.3242
www.KHCPL.org

KOKOMO-HOWARD COUNTY
PUBLIC LIBRARY

the NIGHT SISTER

Center Point
Large Print

Also by Jennifer McMahon and available from Center Point Large Print:

The Winter People

**This Large Print Book carries the
Seal of Approval of N.A.V.H.**

the NIGHT SISTER

JENNIFER McMAHON

KOKOMO-HOWARD COUNTY PUBLIC LIBRARY
KOKOMO, INDIANA

CENTER POINT LARGE PRINT
THORNDIKE, MAINE

This Center Point Large Print edition is published in
the year 2015 by arrangement with Doubleday,
an imprint of The Knopf Doubleday Publishing Group,
a division of Penguin Random House LLC.

Copyright © 2015 by Jennifer McMahon.

All rights reserved.

The text of this Large Print edition is unabridged.
In other aspects, this book may vary
from the original edition.
Printed in the United States of America
on permanent paper.
Set in 16-point Times New Roman type.

ISBN: 978-1-62899-721-7

Library of Congress Cataloging-in-Publication Data

McMahon, Jennifer.
The night sister / Jennifer McMahon. — Center Point Large Print
edition.
pages cm
Summary: "A suspenseful tale set in rural Vermont that probes the
bond between sisters and the peril of keeping secrets"
—Provided by publisher.
ISBN 978-1-62899-721-7 (library binding : alk. paper)
1. Large type books. I. Title.
PS3613.C584N54 2015b
813'.6—dc23
2015023887

A long time ago, I tried to convince my younger brother that on some nights, while he was sleeping, I turned into a monster. This is for you, Tom.

2013

Amy

Amy's heart hammers, and her skin is slick with sweat.

Focus, she tells herself.

Don't think about the thing in the tower.

Amy knows that if she thinks too hard about it she won't be able to do what needs to be done.

She looks down at the photo, the old black-and-white print she's kept all these years, hidden away in the drawer of her bedside table. It's been handled so much that it's cracked and faded, one of the corners torn.

In it, her mother, Rose, and her aunt Sylvie are young girls, wearing crisp summer dresses as they stand in front of a sign that says *World Famous London Chicken Circus.* Each girl clutches a worried-looking hen, but that's where the similarities end. Amy's mother is wearing a scowl beneath tired eyes, her hair dark and unkempt; Sylvie is radiant, the one who was going to grow up and go to Hollywood. Her blond hair is movie-star perfect; her eyes are shining.

Someone had scrawled a date on the back: June 1955. If only Amy could travel back in time, talk to those two girls, warn them what was coming. Warn them that one day it would all lead to this moment: Amy alone and out of options, on the verge of doing something terrible.

She bites her lip and wonders what people will say about her once she's gone.

That she was broken inside, a woman with a screw loose. (Aren't all women like that, really? Little time bombs waiting? Especially women like her—surviving on monthly boxes from the food pantry, dressing her children in ragged, second-hand clothes that never quite fit.)

What went wrong? they will whisper to each other while fondling artichokes and avocados in the produce aisle of the grocery store.

What kind of monster was she? they might ask after a few glasses of wine, as they sit in tidy living rooms, gathered for book club.

But these people know nothing of true monsters. They will never have to make the choices Amy has made.

The fluorescent lights in the kitchen buzz and flicker. Amy takes a deep breath, looks out the kitchen window. Beyond the gravel driveway, past the two ruined motel buildings with their sagging, swaybacked roofs, the tower leans precariously. Made of cement and stone, it was built by her grandfather all those years ago as a gift for her grandmother Charlotte. Her own Tower of London.

Amy thinks, as she often does, of that long-ago summer when she was twelve. Of Piper and

Margot and the day they found the suitcase; of how, after that, nothing was ever the same.

Where was Piper now? Out in California somewhere, surrounded by palm trees and glamorous people, living a life Amy couldn't even imagine. Amy suddenly longs to talk to her, to confide in her and ask for forgiveness, to say, "Don't you see this is what I have to do?"

She thinks that Piper and Margot might understand if she could tell them the whole story, starting with the suitcase and working forward.

But mostly what she wishes is that she could find a way to warn them.

She glances at the old photo in her hand, takes a black marker from a kitchen drawer, and hastily writes a message along the bottom, over the chickens and patterned summer dresses. Then she tucks the photograph into her back pocket and goes to the window.

The clock on the stove says 12:15 a.m.

Down at the tower, a shadow lurches from the open doorway.

She's out of time.

Moving into the hallway, she latches the deadbolt on the front door (silly, really—a locked door will do no good), then stops at the closet and grabs her grandfather's old Winchester. Rifle in hand, she climbs the stairs, the same stairs she's climbed her whole life. She thinks she can hear young Piper and Margot following behind her, whispering, warning her, telling her—as they did all those years ago—to forget all about it, that there is no twenty-ninth room.

Amy takes each step slowly, willing herself not to run, to stay calm and not wake her family. What would Mark think if he woke up and found his wife creeping up the steps with a gun? Poor, sweet, clueless Mark—perhaps she should have told him the motel's secrets? But no. It was better to protect him from it all as best she could.

The scarred wood beneath her feet creaks, and she thinks of the rhyme her grandmother taught her:

When Death comes knocking on your door,
you'll think you've seen his face before.
When he comes creeping up your stairs,
you'll know him from your dark nightmares.
If you hold up a mirror, you shall see
that he is you and you are he.

Jason

The call came in at 12:34 a.m.: a woman reporting that gunshots and screams were coming from the old Tower Motel.

Jason was putting on his coat, but froze as he listened, dread creeping into his chest and squeezing his heart like an icy hand.

Amy.

Even though he'd already punched out, and even though he heard Rainier and McLellan were on their way to check it out, Jason decided to swing by on his way home. It couldn't hurt to take a look, he told himself. He knew he should leave it, should just get in his truck, drive home, and crawl into bed beside Margot. He should put his arm around her, rest his hand on her belly, and feel the baby kick and turn in her sleep.

But there was what he *should* do and there was what he *needed* to do. And as soon as the call came in, he knew he needed to go out to the motel. He needed to see if Amy was okay.

He was at the motel in ten minutes, his headlights illuminating the faded and rotting old sign: *Tower Motel, 28 Rooms, Pool, No Vacancy.* As he turned up the gravel driveway and drove past the crooked tower and decrepit motel rooms where, as a boy, he used to hide out, he felt strangely faint; then he realized he wasn't letting himself breathe.

Idiot.

Amy's house was at the top of the driveway, perhaps twenty yards beyond the low-slung buildings of motel rooms. Rainier and McLellan's cruiser was parked in front of it, and the front door of the house stood open. Every light in the house was on, making it look too bright and all wrong somehow—like something you weren't supposed to stare directly at, something dangerous, like an eclipse.

He'd been here just a week ago. Amy had called him at the station, out of the blue, saying she really needed someone to talk to, and would he come? He was taken aback; other than saying a quick, impersonal hello when they ran into each other around town, they hadn't talked, *really talked,* since high school.

"I can come on my lunch break," he'd answered without hesitation.

Some part of him knew it was wrong, how eager he was to see her, how he had lit up like a Christmas tree because he was the one she'd turned to. He'd thought of how disappointed Margot would be when he told her, so he decided he wouldn't tell her. What she didn't know wouldn't hurt her, and it wasn't so terrible, was it? He was just going to see an old friend, to help out—where was the harm in that? Still, guilt whined around his head like a nagging, persistent mosquito. *You have a wife you love and a baby on the way,* it said. *What do you think you're doing?*

Now, as he stood in the open doorway, he heard what sounded like a low groan. His skin prickled. Unholstering his gun, he stepped into the front hall; a closet door stood open, revealing a row of shiny rain slickers and grubby sweatshirts hanging over a jumble of shoes. Jason spotted small, sparkly pink sneakers; a large pair of worn work boots that had to belong to Amy's husband, Mark; the leather flip-flops Amy had been wearing last week when she met him at the door. "Jay Jay," she had said as she embraced him, somewhat clumsily, sloshing coffee out of her mug. "I'm so happy you're here."

Now he looked around the house. The living room was to the right, the kitchen to the left, and a staircase directly in front of him. Everything smelled musty, vaguely ruined. Wallpaper hung off the walls like torn pieces of skin. The dull brown carpet (had it been white once?) was full of stains and burns, worn through to the floorboards in places.

He hadn't noticed any of this last week.

Jason's radio squawked. Doug Rainier was upstairs—Jason heard his shaking voice both in the house and, a split second later, as a mechanical echo over the radio. "Three victims," he was saying. "All dead." Then, quietly, "Oh God. Oh, shit."

Adrenaline flooded through him, even before his brain fully understood Rainier's words. He ascended the stairs two at a time, right hand on his gun.

Amy.

Where was Amy?

The scene at the top of the stairs nearly brought him to his knees. He had to grab hold of the wall to keep from going down.

He'd never seen anything like it.

Never seen so much blood.

A gunshot hadn't done this.

There were gory red tracks everywhere in the hall. Doug Rainier was on his knees near one of the victims, retching violently. Jason staggered toward them. The victim was facedown, her long blond hair splayed out around her head. There was a rifle beside her, and she lay in what looked like a small lake of blood. The smell of it, sharp and metallic, hit him hard, filling his nose and mouth.

"Oh Jesus." Jason breathed out the words and let himself sag against the wall.

She was facedown, but he knew it was her and he knew that she was dead. Her right arm was tucked beneath her chest, but her left was outstretched. A piece of paper rested near her elbow. He leaned in a bit—no, not paper, an old photograph. It was a black-and-white image of two little girls, and written across it in black

16

marker was the phrase "29 Rooms." He blinked; a part of him knew it must mean something, must be a clue, but what he found himself focusing on instead was Amy's hand, pale and waxy. Her engagement ring and wedding band glinted up at him, just as they had last week, when she'd reached across the kitchen table to take his hand.

"There's no one else I can tell all this to, Jay Jay," she'd said through tears. "I swear, I think I'm going crazy."

"Hawke?" a voice called. Jason looked up and saw Bruce McLellan looming in the doorway of the bedroom at the opposite end of the hall. "What the fuck are you doing here?" Jason couldn't speak, couldn't breathe, couldn't take his eyes off Amy.

"Do you remember, Jay Jay, back when we were kids, how you used to write me notes in secret code?" she'd asked, and he'd nodded. Of course he remembered. He remembered everything.

"Sometimes I'd pretend not to understand them," Amy said. "But I always did. I always knew just what you wrote."

"Hawke, I need you in here—now!" McLellan barked, and Jason turned from Amy at last, to walk down the hallway like a ghost version of himself, there and yet not.

As Jason entered the bedroom, he realized this was Amy's old room. He remembered standing in the shadows of the driveway as a boy, looking up at her dormer window, hoping to catch a glimpse of her.

Now Jason did a quick sweep of the room's contents: a fluffy pink throw rug in the middle of the wide, white-painted floorboards; a dresser with a small collection of glass and plastic jungle animals displayed on top; a disheveled bed with a twisted polka-dotted pink-and-purple comforter, its pillows and stuffed animals spilling onto the floor.

McLellan was standing in the center of the room, his gun clenched in both hands. He nodded down at the floor. A trail of small, bloody prints led to an open window.

"Out there," he whispered, his face red and sweaty. He sounded boyish, frightened. "On the roof."

Jason nodded and walked slowly across the room with his gun in front of him, hands trembling.

He put his back against the wall on the left side of the open window, and listened. He heard a low moaning. A whimper. From out on the roof.

Sirens wailed in the distance. Backup would be here soon. He could wait. But what if someone was out there, hurt?

"London Police Department!" Jason shouted. "We know you're out there. I need you to come inside and keep your hands where I can see them."

There was scrabbling, a scuttling noise, but no one appeared.

"I'm going out," he mouthed without sound. McLellan nodded and stayed where he was, his gun locked on the open window.

Holding his gun, Jason ducked through the opening and stepped out onto the roof. Immediately he dropped into a crouch and swiveled right, then left, scanning the rooftop.

A pair of eyes glinted in the dark. A flash of blond hair.

He felt the gun slip from his grasp, heard it hit the roof and slide off with a clatter. Amy? It couldn't be, but there she was, looking just like she had when he first met her, all skinny legs and wild hair.

Suddenly he was twelve years old again: a gangly, awkward boy staring at a girl who held all the secrets he'd ever dreamed about.

"Hawke?" McLellan called from inside. "What's going on out there?"

Jason blinked and looked at the little girl again, his eyes adjusting to the dark. Like Amy, but not Amy. Amy's daughter. She was squatting down next to the crooked chimney with crumbling mortar, one hand resting on it for balance. Her blond hair was in tangles; her lips were trembling, eyes wild with fear. She had on pale pajamas that shimmered in the moonlight.

"Remember me? I'm Jason," he said, holding out his hand. "And I'm going to get you out of here."

Piper

Piper was frowning at the giant sinkhole that had appeared in her tiny backyard.

She had put a lot of work into this yard, pulling up the sickly grass and relandscaping with drought-tolerant plants: sedum, purple sage, sheep fescue, deer grass, desert mallow. A crushed stone path led to a small patio shaded by an avocado tree, where she sometimes sat with a good book and a glass of sauvignon blanc.

Now it was all falling into the earth. The neighbors were there, gawking and expressing alarm (how big could the sinkhole get? would it swallow the neighborhood?). Her sister, Margot, was there, too, so hugely pregnant she waddled around off balance, like a drunk penguin.

Jason was not there, a fact that irked Piper but did not surprise her.

"Be careful," Piper warned her sister as the avocado tree was swallowed up, and knew right away that she shouldn't have spoken; thoughts and words have power, and if you allow your worst fears to form fully, you run the danger of bringing them to life.

As if on cue, Margot stumbled too close to the edge. Piper reached for her, but it was too late. The hole, which had been growing ever wider, threatening to swallow everything, took her sister deep down into the earth, so deep that they couldn't even hear her scream.

In the distance, alarms rang. But they sounded funny. More like music.

Piper opened her eyes, found herself in her own bed.

She rolled over, looked at the clock: 4:32 a.m. Across the room, her phone was playing Madonna's "Like a Prayer"—Margot's ringtone.

"Oh my God," Piper gasped, jumping out of bed—the baby. It was seven-thirty in Vermont, and Margot wouldn't call this early unless something was really, truly wrong.

Piper snatched up the phone she'd left on the dresser.

"Margot?" Piper said, half expecting it to be Jason on the other end with terrible news. The worst news of all, even—*we've lost them both.* She shuddered as she recalled her sister slipping into the sinkhole, felt herself reaching for her, her hands grabbing nothing but air.

"Piper," Margot said, and Piper felt a weight lift from her chest. But she felt it return when she heard the strain in her sister's voice as she continued: "I'm sorry to wake you. Something's happened."

"The baby?"

Margot was eight and a half months pregnant. It was her third pregnancy. The first had ended in a miscarriage at sixteen weeks, and the second in a stillbirth at thirty weeks—a baby boy they had named Alex. Margot and Jason were trying again, though Margot had said that if she lost this baby, that was it. No more. She simply couldn't bear it.

"No, no. The baby's fine."

"Jason?"

"No, not Jason. It's Amy. She . . . Oh God, Piper, it's awful." Margot was crying.

"Jesus, what happened?" Piper asked. She flipped on the light and blinked at the sudden brightness. The room around her came to life—the queen-sized bed with its snowy duvet, the old rocking chair in the corner, the maple dresser with the mirror hanging above it. She caught sight of her own reflection; her face was pale and panicked, and her white nightgown made her seem like an apparition, gauzy and ethereal, not quite there.

Her sister snuffled and sobbed, and at last was able to speak in partial sentences, voice shaking.

"Last night . . . they're saying Amy shot and killed Mark and their little boy, Levi, and then herself out at the motel. Lou—that's her daughter?—she's alive. The police found her crouched on the roof. She climbed out a window and hid there. . . . I can't imagine how she . . . what she . . ." Margot trailed off.

Piper said nothing. She couldn't move. Couldn't breathe.

After a moment, Margot went on:

"She didn't just shoot them, Piper. They were . . . all cut up. Butchered."

Margot started to cry and gulp again. Piper forced herself to take deep breaths. Behind the shock and gut punch of loss, another feeling was there, worming its way to the surface: fear.

Piper looked over at the framed photo she kept on her dresser: Amy, freckle-faced and smiling as she stood between Piper and Margot, her arms draped heavily over each of their shoulders. They all looked impossibly happy, grinning up from the bottom of the empty swimming pool, white roller skates with bright laces on their feet. This photo had been in her bedroom at home when she was growing up, in her dorm room at college, and in every apartment and house she'd lived in since.

"When was the last time you talked to Amy?" Margot asked at last, the phone crackling, her voice staticky, like it was coming in from a far-off radio station.

"It's been a while," Piper said, feeling light-headed, queasy. And guilty. Margot had urged her, over the years, to reach out to Amy, to try harder. But Amy had made it clear after that summer that she didn't want to remain friends. They hadn't lost touch completely—she and Amy sent each other occasional Christmas cards with impersonal messages and, in Amy's case, stiff-looking school photos of her kids posed against colored backdrops. They were friends on Facebook, and now and then promised each other that they'd get together soon. But when Piper made it back to London to visit Margot every couple of years, the time always seemed to fly by—Amy had to work, or the kids were sick, or Piper was just there for a couple of days to help paint the nursery. Whatever the excuse, she and Amy never got together. *Next time,* they promised each other. *Next time.*

Maybe Margot was right—she should have made more of an effort. She should have called Amy to check in from time to time, to ask how the kids were, how Mark's job was going, to talk the way women talked. After all, she'd let herself imagine it often enough. She had an ongoing imaginary conversation with Amy that had gone on for years. In her mind, Amy was the first person to get all the big news: each of Piper's relationships and breakups; the steady rise of the video-production studio she and her friend Helen had started six years ago; her scare last year with the lump in her breast that turned out to be benign. But the reality was, Piper never actually picked up the phone. It was easier, more comforting, to go on talking to the Amy in her head—the Amy of her childhood, not the adult version with two children whose names she could never quite remember and a husband that Piper knew only through Facebook photos.

She stared harder at the photo on the dresser, tried to remember that particular day, but all that came back was the sound the wheels of their roller skates had made on the bottom of the pool, the smell of Amy's Love's Baby Soft, and the way Amy's arm around her made her feel invincible. Who had taken the picture? Amy's grandmother, most likely. The image was tilted at an awkward angle, as though the earth were off its axis that day.

"There's something else," Margot breathed into the phone, voice low and shaky. "Something that Jason said." Jason was one of the half-dozen officers in the tiny London Police Department. In a town where the biggest crimes were deer jacking and the occasional break-in, Piper could imagine how they were handling a gruesome murder-suicide.

"What was it?" Piper said.

"He said they found an old photo with . . . at the scene."

"A photo?" For a crazy second, Piper imagined that Margot was talking about her photo, the photo on the dresser.

"Yeah. It sounds like the one we found that summer. Remember?"

"Yes," Piper breathed. She remembered it too well. Amy's mom and her aunt Sylvie as kids, in old-fashioned dresses, cradling fat chickens against their chests. It had been taken years before

Sylvie disappeared. So—a different photo, of different girls; a different innocent childhood.

"Well, someone had *written* something on it. None of this is being talked about on the news," Margot went on. "Not yet. No one in the department can figure out what it means. The theory is that Amy was just crazy. Jason asked me if I had any idea what it was about, and I said I didn't. But I think he knows I was lying."

Piper felt her throat getting tighter. She swallowed hard, and made herself ask the question. "What did it say?"

There was a long pause. At last, her sister spoke. "'29 Rooms.'"

"Oh Jesus," said Piper. She took in a breath, felt the room tilting around her. Suddenly she was twelve again and skating around at the bottom of that old pool with the cracked cement and peeling paint. Up above, Margot was going in backward circles around the edge, and Amy was whispering a secret in Piper's ear—breath hot, words desperate.

"I'll be on the next plane," promised Piper. "Don't do anything. Don't say a word to anyone. Not even to Jason. Not until I get there. Promise?"

"I promise," Margot said, her voice sounding far off, a kite bobbing at the end of a long string Piper was barely able to hold on to.

1955

Mr. Alfred Hitchcock
Paramount Pictures
Hollywood, California

June 3, 1955

Dear Mr. Hitchcock,
My name is Sylvia Slater, and I am
eleven years old. I live in London,
Vermont, where my family runs the
Tower Motel on Route 6. I get top
marks in my class and my teacher,
Mrs. Olson, says I am already reading
and writing at a high school level.
Daddy is teaching me to help with the
bookkeeping, and sometimes he even
lets me write the daily tallies in our big
ledger.

I want to be an actress when I grow
up. Or maybe even a movie director,
like you. Are there any girl directors?
My sister Rose, she says she doesn't
think there are, but she's only eight.

I don't mind telling you, Rose is a
little odd. She watches me all the
time and it's starting to bother me.
Mama says Rose is just jealous. My

father says Rose has an overactive imagination. I honestly can't imagine what goes on in her head. She runs around the motel in torn dresses, tangles in her hair, and her best friend on earth is a sad old cow we have named Lucy. And yet she has the nerve to tell me I'm silly for wanting to be an actress one day.

I've started keeping a movie scrapbook filled with pictures I've cut out of famous actors and actresses. Sometimes I show my uncle Fenton what I've pasted in my book. You're his favorite director. He's seen every single one of your pictures. It was his idea that I write to you, because I have an idea for a movie. But I have to warn you, it's really scary.

My Oma, she's my mama's mother, came to visit last year all the way from England. Oma told me and Rose terrible, frightening stories. Rose loved the stories, but I hated them. They gave me nightmares.

She told one story that I'll never forget, because she swore it was true. It's the scariest thing I ever heard.

Mr. Hitchcock, before I tell you any

more, there is something I need to know:

Do you believe in monsters?

Sincerely yours,
Miss Sylvia A. Slater
The Tower Motel
328 Route 6
London, Vermont

Rose

Rose watched her sister, Sylvie, pull back the curtain that they'd strung up along the clothesline at the side of the house before stepping out onto the stage. "Ladies and gentlemen," Sylvie announced in a booming voice. "Welcome to the one and only World Famous London Chicken Circus!"

She dropped the needle onto the phonograph, and "Sh-Boom, Sh-Boom" by the Crew Cuts began to play. As Sylvie began to sway back and forth, with each graceful step her blond curls bounced. They were pulled back from her face with simple white barrettes. She'd put her hair in curlers before the circus, because she thought it made her look like Doris Day.

Rose wiped the sweat from her forehead and hauled back the curtain to reveal their audience: Mama and Daddy, Uncle Fenton, Bill Novak the fish man, a shy young couple driving up to Nova Scotia for their honeymoon, and a New Jersey family of four—two parents, one boy, and one girl—who were all on their way to a week of camping in Maine. It wasn't the largest crowd they'd performed for, but not the smallest, either. It certainly wasn't bad for a Thursday—tomorrow and Saturday, when the motel was full, they'd have their biggest crowds. The size of the crowd didn't matter, though: she and Sylvie would do the circus for even a single guest. Daddy said to make every performance count, even if there was just one man watching.

"You never know who that one man might be," he told them. "Maybe he's a talent scout. Or a reporter. Maybe he has a hundred friends back home who he'll tell all about the show and motel."

Daddy was sitting in the very front row, leaning forward, elbows on his knees, watching intently through his one good eye, the other squinting at them, able to discern only their shadows. He wore his buttoned white shirt rolled up at the sleeves, and kept a pack of Lucky Strikes in his pocket, along with a pen and pencil and little notepad. His hair was cut short and slicked back with Brylcreem.

Daddy was the most handsome man Rose knew. Sylvie said he looked just like Cary Grant, who she loved to read about in the papers and magazines guests left behind. She'd talked Daddy into getting a subscription to *Life* and studied each issue cover to cover as soon as it arrived in the mailbox each week. On the cover of this week's issue was Henry Fonda in his new picture, *Mr. Roberts.*

Rose knew that if it came to London—and if the picture was approved by Mama and Daddy—Sylvie would persuade Uncle Fenton to take her to the Saturday matinee. Fenton loved the movies, too, and went as often as he could. He and Sylvie would have long, animated conversations about directors and stars, and sometimes he'd describe the movies she hadn't been allowed to see to her, scene by scene. It was Fenton's idea that Sylvie start a movie scrapbook, and she spent hours going through magazines and newspapers, cutting out pictures of her favorite stars and pasting them into her book. She also took notes— making lists of movies she'd seen, movies she wanted to see, and even ideas she had for making movies of her own.

Sometimes Rose got to go to the Saturday matinees with Sylvie and Fenton, but most of the time, she was pronounced too young and was left behind to help Mama with cleaning and mending. To be honest, Rose didn't mind much. Sometimes Mama would tell her the story of how she met Daddy, and that was kind of like a movie, too.

Rose liked to imagine it. There they were, her parents, up on the big screen. Daddy was in an English hospital bed, rumpled and wounded but still handsome after his plane had been shot down, and Mama looked like an angel in her stiff white nurse's uniform as she changed the bandages over his injured eye.

"I'd all but given up on myself," he'd tell the girls when they asked for his version of the story. "The last thing I wanted to do was go back home and be a half-blind farmer. I was feeling like my life was just about over until your mother came along. Charlotte, your mama, was the most beautiful girl I'd ever seen."

Rose would always smile at this part, imagining her mama young and pretty, drifting onto the scene, and changing everything—Mama, who was what Daddy called a rare beauty. When he said this, Rose would picture him off in the jungle, coming upon a one-of-a-kind orchid high up on the edge of a waterfall, carefully uprooting it, putting it in a pot, and carrying it home, hoping he had what it took to help it flourish.

"I asked your mama where she was from. 'Here in London,' she said. And I laughed and said, 'Wouldn't you know it? I'm from London, too.'"

"I think it's so romantic," Sylvie would say. "The boy from London meets the girl from London. Like it was meant to be."

"Life could be a dream, if I could take you up in paradise up above," the Crew Cuts doo-wopped now, as the record spun on the little portable player Sylvie had brought out from their bedroom.

"Introducing Miss Matilda, the star of the show," said Sylvie, and she led the plump Rhode Island Red onstage with her handful of raisins. Matilda followed Sylvie over to the wooden structure they'd built with two poles placed four feet apart, each with a platform and a ladder leading up to it. This was the high-wire act, although instead of a wire they had a narrow board, because they hadn't been able to teach a chicken to walk across rope.

With Sylvie's encouragement, Matilda climbed the ladder on the left, made her way across the narrow top board, then to the other platform, and down the ladder. When she reached the bottom, she rang the little bell that hung there by hitting it with her beak.

The crowd applauded, smiling. Sylvie had Matilda do her bow, which got more applause. Sylvie looked up and smiled, her hair coming loose from her right barrette, a few wisps falling into her eyes. The boy guest was at the edge of his seat, his eyes dreamy, the way people's eyes often got when they watched Sylvie. She had the same effect on people that she did on chickens: they watched her intently, eager to do whatever she asked them next.

Sylvie might be able to entrance the chickens and the whole rest of the world, but Rose Slater was immune to her sister's charms. That didn't mean Sylvie didn't try.

Uncle Fenton had given Sylvie a book—*Mastering the Art and Science of Hypnotism*—for Christmas, and she'd studied it cover to cover, underlining passages and making notes in the margins. Fenton had thought that she could use some of the techniques on the birds, but Sylvie had taken it further, insisting on practicing on Rose.

"Keep your eyes on my finger; feel yourself getting sleepier, sleepier still. I'm going to count backward from ten; when I get to one, you'll be fast asleep, but you'll hear every word I say."

It never worked, really, but Rose pretended. She followed Sylvie's finger, lowered her eyelids, spoke and moved as if she was in a trance state. She said goofy things, clucked like a chicken, did whatever Sylvie commanded. It was great fun, fooling her sister, letting Sylvie think she was in control. Rose loved knowing that she had the power to ruin the game, to pop open her eyes and confess that she'd been faking all along. And there would be Sylvie, the clever daughter, the beautiful, graceful girl, waving her dumb finger through the air for nothing.

Rose herself was just the opposite of Sylvie: awkward and thick-limbed, with dark, easily tangled hair. She was the kind of kid people glanced right over, a short and clumsy shadow lurking behind Sylvie and occasionally sticking out her tongue when she was sure no one could see.

As Sylvie and Matilda hammed it up for the audience, Rose busied herself setting up the next act: Petunia was a Barred Rock who Rose had taught to balance on a metal roller skate as it was pulled across the stage on a string. The best part was her costume—a little gingham dress and a pillbox hat that Rose bobby-pinned to her feathers.

"We're on, girl," Rose whispered to the hen,

giving her a good-luck stroke. She grabbed a handful of raisins from the Sun-Maid box and went to work, leading Petunia across the stage as the skate's metal wheels rattled.

Uncle Fenton whistled appreciatively. He was not actually their uncle, but a distant cousin of Daddy's and much younger: he'd just turned nineteen. He was wearing his usual outfit—a stained white T-shirt with a pack of cigarettes rolled up in the sleeve, blue work pants and heavy black boots. In his back pocket he always kept a thin paperback book, something he'd picked up at the five-and-dime: science fiction or crime, sometimes a Western. Uncle Fenton was Daddy's helper, the fix-it man at the motel, and he lived in a trailer behind the house that Daddy helped him pay for. When Fenton wasn't reading, repairing something, or cutting the grass, he was building himself a motorcycle out of parts he'd been collecting. Sometimes the girls would go help him, and he'd promise that once he got it running he'd take them for a ride—maybe even add on a sidecar, so they could all three go.

Now they got Sunshine, a big, glossy black hen, from the cage behind the back curtain, and all three birds were dancing, moving back and forth, spinning in carefully choreographed circles, banging into each other clumsily, while the girls led them on with raisins; all the chickens wore hats and silk scarves.

"And now for the grand finale," Sylvie announced. "I will use the power of hypnosis to put all three chickens to sleep. I need absolute quiet from the audience. Watch, and you will be amazed."

Rose held Matilda and Petunia firmly in place next to one another. Sylvie held Sunshine down with her left hand; with her right, she used a white stick (she called it her "magic chicken wand") to twirl circles in the air in front of them, then drew lines on the ground, a straight line drawn again and again in front of each hen. The birds watched the white stick, eyes focused on the line it made in the dirt, and gradually relaxed, holding perfectly still. One by one, Sylvie picked the birds up and flipped them onto their backs, where they lay with their eyes closed, feet in the air. The crowd oohed and aahed. Sylvie gave a proud smile, then snapped her fingers and said in a loud voice, "Awaken!" All three birds jumped up, righted themselves, and ran wild.

"Tah-dah," she said, taking a long, deep bow, chicken wand still clutched in her right hand.

Mama looked down and picked at the hem of her dress, pulling a thread loose. But Daddy banged his hands together and gave the girls an enthusiastic grin. Uncle Fenton laughed out loud, slapping his knees. The young newlyweds applauded politely, then headed back down to their room. The housewife from New Jersey reached over and took her husband's hand, and he looked at her and smiled a *can-you-believe-this* smile. Their wedding rings glinted in the sun. The little girl turned to her brother and said, "We need to get some chickens when we get home." The parents laughed.

"Good show, girls," Daddy said. He pulled the little notebook from his pocket and jotted down something. Daddy was always getting wonderful ideas—ideas that would make money, make the motel bigger and better and more efficient; ideas that could change the world.

"I'll go start dinner," said Mama, her wary eye on the hen in Sylvie's arms. Mama was not a big fan of the chickens. She thought they were dirty and not all that bright, and sometimes worried out loud about the diseases the girls might catch from them, like salmonella. Secretly, Rose wondered how you could get a sickness from a chicken that would turn you into a fish, and what exactly would happen—would you grow gills? Scales? Not be able to breathe on land?

"It's my paper night," Mama reminded them. Every Thursday, after dinner, the girls had to clean up the kitchen and get their own selves off to bed, so Daddy could watch the office while Mama had her newspaper meeting. She and some of the members of the Ladies Club of London put out a weekly paper—*The London*

Town Crier—full of news, recipes, and advertisements. Mama was the editor, and each Thursday night they planned the next week's issue.

Sylvie wandered over to Lucy the cow's pen, and let the guest kids pet Petunia while Daddy talked to their father, the two men huddled close, smoking. They were talking about the highways being built all over, how soon there would be one running right by London, going from White River Junction all the way up to the Canadian border. Daddy shook his head, said in a low voice, "It's no good for this town. No one will come through on Route 6 anymore."

The boy who was petting Petunia moved closer, so that the toes of his Keds were practically touching Sylvie's sandals. His hand brushed hers, and she smiled.

"How do you do it?" he asked. "Hypnotize the chickens?"

"It takes a lot of practice," Sylvie told him.

"Can you hypnotize people?" he asked.

"Of course," she said. "I do it to my sister all the time."

"Will you do me?" His eyes glistened, his whole body thrumming with excitement at the possibility.

"I don't know," Sylvie said. "Maybe."

The boy's little sister was reaching through the cedar fence rails to pet Lucy. Nailed to the fence was a sign Daddy had painted:

41

LUCY, THE STATE COW, WAS BORN IN THE
FALL OF 1943. IF YOU LOOK ON HER
LEFT SIDE, YOU WILL SEE SHE HAS A
SPOT IN THE SHAPE OF THE GREAT
STATE OF VERMONT.

Now Lucy gave the little girl's hand a lick with her enormous tongue. The girl laughed.

"She was born the same day as my sister, September 16, 1943," Rose said. "Sylvie and that cow are as good as twins." Rose leaned in to rub Lucy's lucky spot, her hand covering the whole state of Vermont. "Daddy says when Lucy was born he had a vision. He saw the motel, the tower, the pen for Lucy. He knew people would come. And he was right. Because here you are."

"Did your daddy build that big tower?" the girl asked, turning from the cow to look down the driveway. The tower was thirty feet tall, twelve feet across, built of stone and cement.

"He built it the year I was born," Rose said. "He did everything himself: mixing the concrete, batch after batch, in a wheelbarrow, hauling rocks down from the hillside."

"It was a gift for our mama," Sylvie explained. "She's English, and he wanted to give her her own Tower of London so she wouldn't be homesick."

The boy smiled at this. "This place is amazing. I can't believe you get to live here. You've got the tower, the pool, the whole motel."

"And Lucy," Rose added.

"She's soft," the girl said, rubbing her hand over the cow's fur.

"If I lived here, I'd never want to leave," the boy said.

"I know," Rose said. "We're real lucky."

"I'm going to leave one day," Sylvie said, bending to set Petunia down. The chicken began to peck at the dusty ground. "I'm going to go to Hollywood when I grow up."

"Hollywood?" Rose snorted. "You're going to *Hollywood?*"

"What for?" the boy asked.

"To be in the movies," Sylvie said.

The boy smiled. "I'll bet you'll be a big star," he told her.

Above them, a monarch butterfly fluttered through the air. No one seemed to notice it but Rose. She stepped away from the fenced cow pen and toward the butterfly. It hovered over Sylvie, then landed lightly on her shoulder.

The boy smiled. Sylvie caught sight of it and laughed. "Isn't it lovely?" she said.

"Yes," the boy answered, not looking at the monarch.

Rose reached out her finger, willing the monarch to her. *Choose me,* she thought with all her might.

When the butterfly didn't come, Rose made an impatient grab for it, tearing one of its paper-thin wings.

"Rose!" Sylvie hissed. "Look what you've done! How could you be so careless?"

Sylvie ran off toward the house, cradling the wounded butterfly, calling for Mama. But Rose knew that, for all Mama's healing powers, there was nothing she could do for the ruined wing.

The boy from New Jersey turned away in disgust, his chance with Sylvie lost, probably forever. He took his little sister by the hand and dragged her off toward Room 12, ignoring her protests that she wasn't done petting the cow. Now Rose was alone with Lucy. She stroked the cow, her fingers making circles in her familiar, dusty fur.

"She's wrong," Rose told Lucy, glancing over her shoulder to watch her sister bang through the front door of the house. Rose wasn't careless. She cared too much, that was all. She cared so much that sometimes she was sure her heart might explode from the pressing ache of it.

Rose

The next evening, the motel was nearly full. Only one room was still vacant: Room 28, all the way at the end of the new building.

Rose was sitting with Mama in the office. Daddy had run out to do an errand after dinner and wasn't back yet. When Rose asked Mama where Daddy had gone, Mama's lips tightened and she said, "He's just out, Rose. He'll be back when he gets back."

Rose didn't mind. She loved these times, when it was just her and Mama, alone. Sometimes Mama would read to her from the paper, or tell her stories about when she was growing up back in England. Rose tried to picture Mama as a little girl; she imagined a neat, stern-faced child who ran the neighborhood doll hospital and never once broke any rules.

Rose was tired. Her eyelids kept drifting closed as she stared at the bright office light. The screen door was closed, June bugs and moths thumping into it. *The sign said* Vacancy, they seemed to say. *Can we come in?*

It was well past bedtime now, but Mama said Rose could stay up a little while longer, just in case another guest showed up. Rose wanted to be the one to run down to the road and flip the sign to *No Vacancy.*

She loved to be there when people checked in, road-weary, blurry-eyed. She'd slide the little manila registration card across the desk to them, watch as they wrote down their names, addresses, number of people in their party, car make and model, license number. Rose loved to see where they were from: Staten Island, New York; Portage, Pennsylvania; once, they had an older couple from Christmas, Florida. Imagine, a town called Christmas!

Sometimes they'd mention where they were traveling to: New Hampshire, Maine, all the way up into Canada. There were even people going to see the ocean, which Rose had seen only once, when Mama and Daddy took the girls to Hampton Beach a few years ago. They'd gone in the winter, because when you're motel people you can't go anywhere during the busy season. Sylvie had run up and down the shore, collecting rocks, shells, and bits of driftwood, oohing and aahing about how beautiful it was, how lovely it was to lick your lips and taste the salt of the ocean. Rose stood shivering on the beach, thinking only that the ocean looked cold and dark and seemed to go on forever. She tried to imagine the beach crowded with swimmers and sunbathers stretched out on towels, the smell of hot dogs and candy apples in the air, but it was no good. It was like standing on the empty stage long after the school play was over and all the costumes and sets had been packed away.

Rose loved the names of the cars people arrived at the motel in—Dodge Coronet, Hudson Hornet, Studebaker Starliner—the heavy steel bodies, the sparkling chrome grilles, the tires spinning through the gravel of their driveway, tires that had been turning for hundreds of miles, been to places Rose could only imagine.

The cars, Daddy said, got bigger and faster each year. Rose imagined one day cars would be more like rocket ships, like in one of Uncle Fenton's science-fiction books. You'd be able to blast off and go from London, Vermont, to Christmas, Florida, in less than an hour. Maybe even all the way across the ocean, to London, England, where Mama was from.

Down at the road now, a car went by. Rose could see the taillights fading away. They turned the corner and were gone, moving toward downtown London. Soon they'd be passing the Texaco, Woolworth's, London Town Library, Congregational church—everything shut down, locked up tight this time of night.

There was talk, lots of talk, about how the interstate highways were coming. Her teacher, Miss Marshall, said that President Eisenhower was promising bigger, better roads that would connect the whole country. Rose liked the sound of this (though she would never tell her father, who got red in the face whenever the word "highway" was mentioned), of being able to follow a highway from here all the way to the other side of the country. A highway built for all those beautiful cars to rumble along, engines purring, tires spinning so fast they were just a blur. Not quite like rocket ships, but a step closer.

Sometimes she dreamed of machines. Of cars and rockets. Of the big machines that would build highways: of bulldozers and graders, mechanical shovels and steamrollers. She dreamed they were coming this way, tearing up the land, dynamiting rocks, making a smooth blacktop surface for cars to race along. Coming closer. Closer. Rumbling, chugging.

"Where's your sister?" Mama asked, and Rose looked up and rubbed her eyes.

"Up in our room. She's got a headache."

"Poor thing," Mama said, and Rose nodded sympathetically.

"Maybe this butterfly isn't just a butterfly," Sylvie had said to Rose just after dinner, when they were alone in their room, looking at the broken-winged butterfly on Sylvie's nightstand.

"What do you mean?"

"Don't you remember Oma's stories?" Sylvie had asked, her eyes growing wide.

Rose nodded. She did remember. She remembered that Sylvie had been frightened to death by Oma's stories, so Oma had stopped telling them to her and shared them only with Rose.

Oma had come to visit last year. They'd spent

weeks getting ready: cleaning the house from top to bottom, setting up a cot in Mama's sewing room, asking excited questions about what she was like, this grandmother they'd never met, coming all the way from England.

"This is your grandmother," Mama had announced as the old woman climbed out of the backseat of Daddy's car, shouldering a large patent-leather pocketbook, wearing loose white gloves stained yellow at the fingertips.

She took the girls in, studying them from head to toe, turning them, touching their faces and hair. Then, apparently finding them acceptable, she gave them each a kiss on both cheeks. "You call me Oma," she said, her accent different from Mama's. When Rose asked Mama about it later, she explained that her mother was German but she'd married a Londoner.

"How come we've never met her before?" Rose had asked.

"Because she's a busy woman. And crossing the Atlantic is no small feat. Especially since Oma hates to fly. She came in a boat."

Oma sucked on horehound candy, wore sweaters she'd knitted herself, and taught the girls to make apple cake.

One morning, Rose woke up with her hair in tangles. Oma clucked her tongue and went to work brushing it out.

"Perhaps you've been visited by a mare," she said.

"A mare? Like a girl horse?" Rose asked.

Oma shook her head. "Your mother hasn't told you girls about mares?"

Rose and Sylvie shook their heads.

"Mares are human during the day, but at night, they change into all different creatures. One minute, they're a person; the next, they can be a cat, a bird, or a butterfly."

Sylvie, listening from her own bed, said, "That's made up. It's another of your fairy tales."

"You think so?" Oma said, continuing to gently work the tangles out of Rose's hair.

"Are they good?" Rose asked.

"Sometimes. But sometimes they turn into terrible monsters with teeth and claws. They come to you in the night, give you bad dreams, tie knots in your hair, suck your breath away. If you're not careful, they'll swallow you whole."

Later, Rose wished Oma hadn't told them about mares. Not because she was scared, but because of Sylvie. Her sister had been so frightened that she started having nightmares.

One morning, when Mama was comforting Sylvie after one of her bad dreams, Sylvie told her about Oma's stories, about how, ever since, she couldn't stop thinking that every person she met, every animal she saw, might secretly be a mare.

"Even though I know it can't be true," Sylvie said, sniffling. "It couldn't be true, right, Mama?"

Mama was furious with Oma.

"I will not have you poisoning the minds of my children," Mama had hissed at Oma. She said it had been a mistake to invite Oma at all. Rose tried to eavesdrop on the argument from the top of the stairs after she and Sylvie had been sent to bed early, but caught very little of it. Oma left the next day and went back to England.

Rose was mad at her mother for sending Oma away, but mostly she blamed Sylvie—if Sylvie hadn't been such a scaredy-cat tattletale, Mama would never even have known.

Oma sent Rose a few cheerful letters from England, letters Mama always opened and read before giving them to Rose. Oma told Rose she was knitting her a sweater for Christmas and asked what color she would like. Rose wrote back, "Red, please," and told her how much she missed her.

But Rose never got the sweater. Just before Christmas, Mama got a call from a cousin in England. Oma had been killed in an accident.

Rose was devastated. Oma was the only adult who had ever seemed to prefer her to Sylvie, who had ever thought she was the special one. It just wasn't fair.

She thought of Oma often—of the stories she told when they were alone together, the walks they had taken through the woods behind the motel. "Everything out here is alive, Rose," she had said, her hand wrapped around Rose's. "Can't you feel it?"

Rose thought about that still: how everything seemed to have a life of its own, not just the trees and mushrooms in the forest, but things like highways and buildings and cars. A car was coming up the driveway now, its headlights winking in the dark. At first, Rose thought it was Daddy in their Chevy Bel Air. But the shape of the car and the sound of the engine were all wrong.

"Looks like we might have a full house after all," Mama said as the car pulled up and parked outside the office. A man got out and stood up, stretching. (They almost always stretched.) A woman with a pale kerchief over her hair waited in the car.

The car was a Nash Rambler. Rose could tell, even from in here. Rambler. Rambling. Rambling Rose, like in the song Perry Como sang: "She's a beauty growing wild." Mama and Daddy had the record. Sometimes Daddy sang it to her, his own little Rambling Rose.

The man came into the office, shuffling a little, blinking at the shock of bright lights. His white shirt was wrinkled; his eyes were bloodshot from driving too long.

"Good evening. My wife and I need a room for the night," he said.

"You're in luck," Mama said. "We have one room left. Four dollars a night."

"Perfect," the man said. Rose slid him the registration card, then slipped out from behind the desk.

"I'll go flip the sign, Mama," she said.

"Good girl," Mama said. "Then head on up to bed."

"Yes, ma'am," she said, giving Mama and the man a little curtsy as she left, because she knew she had to be especially good, especially polite, in front of guests. No matter what was happening, they had to play the perfect family, Rose had to be a perfect child.

"Turn on the charm, girls," Daddy always said. "Make them want to come back and see us again."

"Cute kid," the man said, as he leaned against the desk to fill out the form.

"Yes," Mama said. "She's a good girl."

Good girl. Good girl. Good girl.

Rose skipped down the driveway (she was right—the man did drive a Rambler) and to the sign, where she stepped forward, into the light, and flipped it so that the *No* showed. She stood for a minute, bathed in light, as if onstage with the Tower Motel backdrop behind her. She did a little dance, a few ballet moves Oma had taught her—slide, step, slide, pirouette, curtsy. She thought of Sylvie saying that she was going to leave one day and run off to Hollywood to be a star. *Not me,* Rose thought as she danced. *I'm going to stay right here forever.*

Mr. Alfred Hitchcock
Paramount Pictures
Hollywood, California

August 11, 1955

Dear Mr. Hitchcock,
   Sometimes a butterfly is not just a butterfly.
   This is what Oma taught me.
   You know the worst thing I learned from her?
   You can be a monster and not even know you are one.
   They look like us.
   They think they are us.
   But really, they've got a monster hiding inside.
   If that's not a good idea for a movie, I don't know what is.

Sincerely Yours,
Miss Sylvia A. Slater
The Tower Motel
328 Route 6
London, Vermont

Rose

Rose was having the dream again. A dark, formless beast had overtaken her, pinned her, crushed her from all sides until she got smaller and smaller—the size of a doll, then as tiny as a teardrop. She did her best to fight it, but in the end she was powerless.

Wake up, she told herself. *Time to wake up now.*

She opened her eyes. The broken-winged butterfly was in an old canning jar on Sylvie's bedside table. It banged silently against the glass, a shadow in front of the curtained window. Rose watched it struggle in the dim light of early dawn, her heart pounding, her lungs unable to draw a breath.

She was sure she was awake, and yet her body was completely paralyzed. The air was heavy with a rank, wild-animal smell.

Rose listened hard. She was sure she could hear something breathing nearby—a rasping, grunting, guttural sound—but there was nothing there.

Or was there? Out of the corner of her eye, she saw a flicker of movement, a shift in the darkness. And there was the feeling she had, this deep sense that something else was in the room, something evil that meant to do her harm.

Her eyes darted around, but found only the

familiar landscape of the small bedroom she shared with Sylvie. And yet, it was also terribly unfamiliar, off-kilter, bathed in a greenish glow, as if the moonlight itself was somehow the wrong color. Rose opened her mouth to scream, to call for help, but she couldn't make a sound.

Am I dead? she wondered.

Concentrating with all her might, Rose tried to sit up—just to wiggle her pinkie—but the only thing she could move was her eyes.

She looked past the butterfly in the jar to Sylvie's twin bed. She willed her sister to wake up, open her eyes, and save her, but she realized now that Sylvie's bed was empty. The covers were thrown back, the pillow indented where Sylvie's head should be.

A horrible thought came over Rose: A mare had come. And it had gotten Sylvie first.

There it was again—the rotten, wheezing stink of rancid meat breath and damp fur, so strong she could taste it in the back of her throat. She heard a low, quiet sound, almost like a growl; felt it vibrate through her whole body. She still couldn't see anything—it was hiding in the shadows, under her own bed, maybe even. She was sure that, whatever this was, it had rows of sharp teeth—and if she was able to look in those teeth, she would find shreds of her sister's white nightgown.

Please, Rose thought. *Please, go away. Spare me. Please.* And then she thought of part of the little prayer Mama had both girls say each night before bed: "Angels watch me with the night, and wake me with the morning light."

And just like that, she could move again. She gasped, and air rushed into her lungs. The foul animal smell dissipated. She sprang from her bed without daring to look underneath, scampered down the hall to her parents' room, and flung open the paneled wooden door.

"What on earth?" asked Mama, squinting into the moonlight spilling from the hallway.

"Something was in my room," Rose said, panting. The windows were shut, the shades drawn. The air in her parents' room was dusty and still, and smelled of Daddy's cigarettes and Mama's Jean Naté. Daddy's work shirt was hung up on the back of a chair, its arms limp at its sides; in the dark, this made the chair look strangely human, as if it would start walking across the wooden floorboards on its four legs.

"Another bat?" asked Mama, sitting up in bed, her pale nightgown glowing. Beside her, Daddy stirred, sat up, and groaned—they'd had a bat in their room in the early spring, and he'd had to chase it out with the broom. He reached for the clock. It was a little before 5:00 a.m.

"No. Not a bat. I . . . I don't know what it was," Rose admitted.

A monster. A monster who followed me from my dreams. One of Oma's mares.

"I could hear it, smell it, but I couldn't see it. I couldn't get up, couldn't move at all. I think . . ." Did she dare say it? "I think maybe whatever it was got Sylvie."

Her father made a dismissive chuffing sound.

"Shhh," Mama soothed. "You're all right now."

"Go back to bed," Daddy said, voice gruff and sleepy. "It's too early for any of your stories, Rose."

Daddy always said Rose had quite an imagination, which was his kind way of saying that she liked to exaggerate, to make things up just to see if she could get away with it.

"I can't," Rose said. "Didn't you hear me? There was something there. Something in the room with me. And Sylvie is gone!"

"There was nothing in your room," Daddy said, turning over. "You had a bad dream, that's all."

Rose shook her head. She wasn't a scaredy-cat like Sylvie with her nightmares.

"But it wasn't a dream," Rose insisted. "And I'm not making it up. It was real."

"I'm sure your sister's in her bed," said Mama, voice low and calm.

"But she *isn't*. I think a mare got her."

Mama turned on the bedside light with an irritated snap.

"A *mare?* How many times must I tell you girls? Oma's stories were just that: stories." She jumped out of bed, pulled on her robe, and marched down

58

the hall. She returned in less than a minute and reported, "Sylvie is right in her bed, where she should be." She slipped off her robe and climbed back into her own bed. "And, I might add, where we all should be. Off you go."

"But she wasn't there a minute ago, I swear," Rose said.

"Oh, for God's sake," Daddy said with a groan, sitting up. "I'm going to go put some coffee on."

He thumped out of the room in his striped pajamas, hair rumpled. *Be careful,* Rose wanted to call after him. *It's out there still.*

Rose crawled in beside her mother; Daddy's spot was still warm. She snuggled up next to Mama, laid her head on Mama's shoulder.

"Ah, my poor girl." Mama sighed. "You really are scared silly. I wish to God Mother hadn't filled your head with all that nonsense."

Rose heard water running in the kitchen, and the sound of her father flipping on the old wooden Philco radio. Daddy hummed along to the tune. The door of the new Frigidaire opened, then closed.

While Mama stroked her hair, Rose recalled a conversation she'd had with Oma.

"Does Mama know about the mares? Does she believe?"

Oma smiled. "Indeed she does. But she would never admit to it. For some people, Rose, it's easier to pretend the things that frighten us most don't exist at all."

"It's dead," Sylvie said, plunking the glass jar with the butterfly on the coffee table, right in front of Rose.

Rose was sitting on the couch, hugging a pillow tight against her chest. The monarch's body lay on top of the bed of leaves, perfectly still. Rose gazed at it through the glass, which magnified the monarch's wings, brilliantly orange and veined with black. They reminded her of the stained-glass windows at church. Rose imagined a church of the butterflies where they worshipped meta-morphosis. Caterpillar, cocoon, pupae, butterfly.

"You killed it. I hope you're happy," Sylvie said, hands on her hips as she glared down at Rose.

Rose bit her lip and hugged the pillow tighter. She remembered how much she'd wanted the butterfly to come to her, to choose her. If Oma were here, she would understand. "I didn't mean to."

Sylvie looked at her a minute. "Maybe you did and maybe you didn't. Maybe you meant to and didn't even realize it."

"That makes no sense." Rose picked up the jar and looked inside, willing the broken creature to move, to flutter its wings.

"Neither does killing a butterfly."

Sylvie sat in their father's wingback chair, not taking her eyes off Rose.

"Where were you, anyway?" Rose asked

accusingly, watching her sister through the glass jar.

"Where was I when?" Sylvie snapped. Her face was distorted by the glass, all mixed up with the bright-orange colors of the butterfly. For once, she was not the beautiful one, but something strange and hideous—an orange-faced monster.

"Earlier this morning, just before five," Rose said, putting the jar back down on the coffee table; Sylvie looked normal again, her hair neatly combed, tangle-free. "I woke up and you weren't in bed."

"Of course I was in bed, Rose." For half a second, Sylvie looked worried, panicked almost, but then her expression changed into her best poor-crazy-little-sister look. "Where else would I be?"

"But your bed was empty. Your pillow . . ."

Sylvie held up a finger and waved it back and forth the way she'd learned in her hypnosis book. When she spoke, it was in her slow, wavering hypnotist voice. "Follow my finger with your eyes. That's right, good. Now feel your eyelids getting heavy, heavier still; it's a struggle to keep them open."

Rose played along, following her sister's finger with her eyes.

"Go ahead and close them, Rose. That's right. Let yourself go deeper. Deeper still. The only thing you're aware of is the sound of my voice.

You're going to listen to what I tell you. You're going to understand that each word I speak is the absolute truth. Nod if you understand."

Rose nodded.

"My bed was not empty," Sylvie told her. "I was there the whole time."

Rose slumped her shoulders forward, tried to look relaxed and like she was at her sister's mercy.

"Now tell me what you saw this morning," Sylvie commanded, her voice low and soothing.

"Your bed was not empty," Rose repeated, voice dull and robotic. "You were there the whole time."

"Very good," Sylvie said. "And that's the way you'll remember it from this moment on. Do you understand?"

"Yes," Rose said.

"Good girl. On the count of three, you will open your eyes. One, two, three."

Rose opened her eyes. Sylvie sat in the chair across from her, curling her hand into a tight fist and smiling. The butterfly lay in the jar on the coffee table between them, its orange color seeming impossibly bright for something dead.

"Do you think Mama will put blueberries in the pancakes this morning?" Sylvie asked brightly, glancing toward the kitchen, as though nothing unusual had happened.

Rose's heart began to thump madly. She was

surer than ever now that her sister had been out of bed last night; for some reason, Sylvie really didn't want Rose to know it. This was the first time Rose could ever remember Sylvie keeping a secret from her, and Rose didn't like it. Not one little bit.

2013

Piper

Piper wheeled her carry-on through the terminal, passing rows of plastic seats, a crêpe restaurant, and a kiosk selling overpriced neck pillows and eye masks. Once she exited through the double doors out into the main corridor, she searched the small crowd for Margot. In the final weeks of her pregnancy, Piper figured Margot would be impossible to miss. She recalled the image of her sister from last night's dream: Margot teetering at the edge of a hole, off balance.

Piper blinked away the vision. She saw a couple embracing, a mother welcoming a college-age son home, a man in a suit holding a sign that said *Walker Party,* a cop scanning the crowd. No Margot. Piper was reaching into her bag for her cell phone when she felt a hand on her arm.

"Piper?"

She turned. The cop had approached.

"Jason!" she said, realizing that the police officer was none other than her brother-in-law. It was more than the anonymity of the uniform—he looked thinner and much older than he had when she'd last seen him, two Christmases ago.

Sometimes it was nearly impossible to remember him as being the same boy who'd followed the girls around that long-ago summer, a gangly kid, all arms and legs, with shaggy hair and pockets full of bugs. The boy who once wrote Amy love poems in secret code. Now and then she caught a glimpse of him in a boyish smirk, a shrug that made him look twelve again.

"It's so good to see you," she said, and he gave her a stiff hug. He smelled like spicy aftershave and cigarette smoke. "But where's Margot?"

"Couldn't make it," Jason said, and looked away, his jaw tense. There were dark circles under his bloodshot eyes. He looked like he hadn't slept in a week. "Come on," he said, "let's get you home. We'll talk in the car."

Jason took charge of the small suitcase, and Piper struggled to keep up as he led her through the airport to the parking garage.

They climbed into an old Ford Ranger pickup and rode with the windows rolled up, no AC. The sun beat down through the windshield and the cab was stuffy and hot, but Jason seemed oblivious; he didn't even break a sweat. In spite of the heat, and the apparent lack of shock absorbers or much of a suspension system, Piper was grateful he'd come in his own vehicle and hadn't picked her up in a police cruiser. Did London even have police cruisers? She couldn't recall.

Piper didn't get home much. Margot usually came to her in L.A., thrilled to get away from their hometown for a week or two, to do all the touristy things: the tar pits, the Chinese Theatre, the Santa

Monica Pier. She loved to study the architecture—
Piper was continually amazed by her sister's love
for all things Art Deco, which couldn't be more
different from the old mills, farmhouses, and
granite sheds of Vermont that Margot had
dedicated her life to saving and preserving.

Jason rarely came to California with Margot—
too hard to get time off from the force, he said.
Piper was always relieved when Jason didn't join
Margot. It wasn't that she disliked him, but she
never felt entirely comfortable around him,
always felt she had to be on her best behavior, had
to prove her place as the wise older sister. God
knew that Jason had grown up with a different
Piper, the big sister who did wild things, got
Margot in trouble again and again, whether
bringing her to her first keg party or introducing
her to pot.

The worst of it was, when the girls were in high
school, Piper had thought Margot's dating Jason
was basically the stupidest idea she'd ever heard.
Even told her, "You know, with him you'll always
be second best. The consolation prize. He's been
in love with Amy his whole life, and you'll never
be able to change that."

She cringed now at the thought of saying
something so cruel (even if it was absolutely true)
to her own sister. Piper had no idea what, if anything, Jason knew about her unwanted relationship
advice—but Piper knew, and that was bad enough.

Jason drove out of the airport parking garage and paid the attendant. His hands gripped the wheel tightly, his gold wedding band glinting in the sunlight coming through the windshield. He stayed silent.

Piper began to worry.

"Jason," she said at last, "is Margot all right?"

He kept his eyes on the road. "She fainted this morning. I brought her in to the doctor, and they said her blood pressure is too high—it could be dangerous for her and the baby. She's got something called pre-eclampsia. He's ordered bed rest until she delivers. And depending on how she's doing, he might decide to induce her early." He delivered the news in his cop voice—no sign of emotion: *Just the facts, ma'am.*

"But she's okay?" Piper asked, her own voice squeaky and panicked.

"As long as she rests, listens to the doctor. We're only two weeks away from the due date, so hopefully it won't be much longer."

Margot was one of those people who hated to sit still and always had at least five projects going at once. Being confined to bed must feel like a prison sentence.

"She must be miserable," Piper said.

Jason nodded, keeping his eyes on the road. They came to an intersection with a gas station and a Friendly's restaurant. Jason turned right, and they passed big box stores and chain restaurants.

He eased the truck into the left lane and headed for the highway on-ramp. It hadn't been like this when Piper was a kid: back then it was all farmland and houses.

"Piper," he said, sounding solemn and coplike. "I know this . . . situation with Amy has got to be a blow. The whole town's reeling, and Margot's taking it really hard. I remember how close you three were when you were kids."

Of course. Of course you do, Piper thought, unbidden. *Because you were there, watching from the shadows, spying, always trying to catch Amy's eye. But you never really did, did you?* She shook off her own cruel thoughts, realizing that he had paused and was waiting for an answer. She nodded, not knowing what she was expected to say.

"I don't want you upsetting Margot with any talk about Amy. I don't want her to read anything more about it in the paper or watch the news."

"Okay," Piper agreed. "Before we get there, is there anything you can tell me? Anything about what happened?"

"It's an ongoing investigation, so no."

"Is there a chance Amy didn't do it? Any chance at all?"

Jason sighed. "I don't want to believe it, either. But all the evidence points to her."

"It's just so hard to imagine—you know?—that Amy was capable of doing something like this."

71

He shook his head, glassy eyes focused on the road ahead. "I guess you never know what someone's capable of."

"The little girl," Piper said. "Amy's daughter? Is she okay?"

"As okay as can be expected, considering we found her hiding out on the roof, her whole family dead inside."

"God, how awful," Piper said.

"She was just like a statue out there in her pajamas, blood on her feet. God, she looked so much like Amy out there—like Amy back when we were kids." Emotion finally began to creep into his words—his voice rose and cracked. "Anyway, when I found her out there, she wouldn't move. I had to carry her back inside. She could barely talk at first, couldn't stop shaking. A state of shock—that's what the doctors said."

"Poor thing," Piper said, trying to remember the girl's name. She'd never met her, but had gotten updates about Amy's kids from Margot, seen the pictures and news Amy posted on Facebook. Piper was embarrassed to ask Jason, not wanting to admit how out of touch she'd become with her once-upon-a-time best friend.

They drove the rest of the way mostly in silence, their few attempts at small talk quickly dying. Eventually, she and Jason both gave up and just stared out at the scenery. When the exit for London came up, Piper remembered Amy's telling her once that it was the highway that ruined the motel:

"Before the highway came, people just came through along Route 6. There was so much traffic then. My grandma Charlotte said they had guests every night, and were full most weekends. My mom and her sister, Sylvie, they had a full audience for their crazy chicken circus. People came to see Lucy the cow. Once the interstate opened, people stopped coming, just zipped right on by. There was no reason to come to London anymore."

Piper got that. When they moved to London after her parents got divorced, Piper felt like she'd been dropped in the middle of nowhere—a regular ghost town, full of closed shops and restaurants that were now boarded-up buildings with sagging roofs and broken windows. Even now, as they drove through town, she wondered what would bring anyone here, how her sister could possibly have stayed. Margot worked for a nonprofit historical-renovation organization; her job was to give out grants so that historic buildings could be maintained. She was always talking about how London was undergoing a renaissance—young families were buying some of the gorgeous old houses and fixing them up; a developer had bought a bunch of the buildings downtown, and there were plans for a yoga studio, a coffee shop, and a brew pub. But Piper didn't see signs of any of this actually coming to fruition and thought her sister's optimism at times bordered on delusional thinking.

The storefronts along Main Street were still mostly closed. A few were open: an antiques shop, the London House of Hair Salon, and a Dollar Store. The old Woolworth's still stood; though there were boards over the windows, through the cracks you could see the lunch counter. There were two gas stations (one that advertised Mrs. Cluck's famous fried chicken), a tiny library in a stone building, the Congregational church, and a VFW post. At the edge of the downtown sat the granite fire-and-police-department building. Jason cast an eye toward it and gave a guy in a uniform a wave.

They bumped along the road, which was full of potholes and frost heaves, badly in need of repair. They were following a school bus, and Piper saw a girl looking out at them through the back window. Her friend whispered something in her ear, and the girl turned, laughing. Piper remembered riding in the back seat with Amy, getting off at the motel, running up the washed-out gravel driveway toward the kitchen, where Amy's grandma Charlotte would be waiting for them, a cigarette between her lips and *Guiding Light* on in the living room, the volume up as loud as it could go so she wouldn't miss anything as she moved from room to room. She'd have a plate of cookies waiting—biscuits, she called them in her English accent.

"My grandparents were both from London," Amy told her once with a grin. "London, England, and London, Vermont."

But the school bus did not slow this time. It sped past the motel sign, which now leaned backward, as if it had been struck by a truck at some point. Piper read the familiar words as she and Jason drove past—*Tower Motel, 28 Rooms, Pool, No Vacancy*—but now the letters had faded from red to a pink so pale you could only just read them. Beyond the sign, on the other side of the drive-way, was the crumbling tower. The kids in the yellow school bus all turned their heads to look up the driveway, still full of police cars and vans. Piper held her breath.

"Jesus," she hissed out as she let the breath go, looking beyond the news trucks to the tower. It had been in terrible shape when she was a girl but was even worse now, leaning so precariously to the right that it looked as though it were reaching toward the house. Most of the stone battlements at the top had crumbled or fallen off. There were two boards and a *No Trespassing* sign nailed over the doorway, and the word *Danger* had been spray-painted on the wall above the arch.

Piper's skin went cold. Jason had slowed to a crawl.

"Sorry," Jason said. "I guess we should have come the back way."

"No," Piper said, "it's fine."

But it wasn't. It wasn't fine at all.

"Margot might have mentioned it," Jason said, gripping the steering wheel a little more tightly. "But Amy left a note . . . well, not a note, really, just something written on an old photo. It said, '29 Rooms.' Does that mean anything to you?"

For the first time since he had picked her up at the airport, he looked directly at her, his brown eyes studying her, watching for a reaction. And once more, she was twelve again, being grilled by the pesky kid who followed Amy around like a puppy dog—a boy who was a laughingstock, not just to Amy but to them all.

She paused for a moment, pretending to search her memory, then shook her head slowly.

"No," she told him, holding eye contact, her face a mask. She wished, with all her might, that they'd never found that goddamn photo; that she had never heard of the twenty-ninth room, had never seen it with her own two eyes. "It doesn't mean anything at all."

Jason was quiet for a moment. She had no idea if he believed her.

"The photo itself," Jason went on at last, "we figured out it's Amy's mother, Rose, and Rose's sister, Sylvie, when they were kids, about eight and twelve. Sylvie, she went missing not long after she graduated from high school. Did Amy ever talk about her?"

Piper shrugged. "Once or twice, maybe. She said Sylvie ran away. Went off to Hollywood, maybe."

And, for half a second, she was sure she could feel Amy's hot breath against her cheek, hear her singsong voice as she whispered in Piper's ear:

"Liar, liar."

Piper

Margot and Jason's bedroom was painted ivory with sea-foam trim. Like the rest of the house, it was decorated with framed antique photos of a London long gone—a shot of downtown showing the old A&P market, a photo of an old dairy farm along Main Street.

Margot was propped up in bed against fluffed pillows like an invalid queen, surrounded by everything she could want or need within reach: a stack of paperbacks and baby magazines, bottled water, the TV remote, cell phone, a pile of protein bars and apples. There was also a collection of old, yellowed newspapers in plastic sleeves. She was reading one, with a masthead across the top that said *The London Town Crier.*

She tossed aside the paper she was holding and squealed, "Piper! You're here!" as though she hadn't been expecting her sister at all.

Piper plunked herself down on the bed and they embraced. Piper felt Jason's gaze boring into her back.

"What's with all the old papers?" Piper asked. "Don't tell me it's for work!"

Margot gave a sly smile. "Not exactly. A little side project I took on for the historical society. I'm organizing a collection of old *Town Crier*s for display. They were published here in town by the ladies' auxiliary in the fifties and sixties. It's amazing stuff, really. If you read between the lines, you get this incredible history of the town."

Margot's face lit up whenever she spoke about London's history. Piper relaxed; she hadn't realized just how worried she'd been about her sister on the drive from the airport until she saw her with her own eyes. Margot was stuck in bed, hugely pregnant and quite a bit puffier than usual, but she was still Margot, getting excited about a stack of dusty old papers.

Piper picked one of the papers up and scanned the front page. It was dated March 12, 1952. The lead story was about the talent show held at the high school. There was also a recipe for Mrs. Minetti's famous three-bean casserole.

Piper glanced at the photograph of a farm on the wall to the left of the bed. There was something familiar about it. She studied it for a moment before realizing it must be the old Slater farm that sat on the Tower's land before Amy's grandfather tore down the barn and built the motel. She recognized the house and the hill behind it. It was strange to see it as a blank landscape dotted with Holsteins, no sign of the crumbling stone tower or rows of motel rooms.

It seemed an odd, even unsettling choice of a photo for Margot to hang in her bedroom, especially now. Piper looked away, not wanting to draw attention to the photo or her realization of what it was.

"Can I get you anything, hon?" Jason asked, reaching down to take Margot's hand.

Margot shook her head. "No. Piper's here now. You can go back to the station. I'm sure they need you there."

He stood in the doorway, hesitating, shuffling his feet like a little boy.

"Okay," he said at last, "but you call me if you need anything. Anything at all. And, Piper," he said, locking her in a gaze, "remember, what Margot and the baby need is rest. And calm."

"Got it," Piper said. "I'll take good care of her, Jason. I promise." She gave him a warm, convincing smile, but his steely gaze told her he wasn't buying it.

He came over and gave Margot a gentle kiss on the cheek.

"If you get a headache, or get nauseous, have double vision, or any kind of pain, call the doctor."

"Of course," she said. "Now go. All your worrying is raising my blood pressure!"

He gave a sheepish nod and left the room. They heard him in the kitchen, filling a travel mug with coffee. Piper noticed another collection of photographs on the dresser. There was Margot and Jason's wedding picture, both of them looking so young and happy; one of Margot and Piper as little girls, sitting under a Christmas tree; and one of their mother, the day she graduated from law school. Their mother had gone on to work as a public defender, then opened her own practice. She'd died at forty-six of a brain aneurysm. Probably had been there for years, the doctors said—just bad luck, or possibly untreated hypertension, that caused it to rupture one spring day as she crossed the parking lot of Garden World, her cardboard tray of pansy and petunia seedlings spilling to the asphalt.

Piper turned away, her stomach twisting in that old, familiar way when she thought about how unfair life could be. It wasn't right that their mother—who had never smoked, barely drank, worked hard but not too hard, always chose the nonfat everything, took her vitamins, went to Jazzercise religiously even when Piper and Margot had teased her—hadn't been at Margot's wedding, wouldn't be here to see the birth of her grandchild.

There were no photos of Piper and Margot's father. He'd remarried not long after the divorce, moved to Dallas, and started a whole new life, complete with four new children—including a set of identical twins—with his new wife. When Piper and Margot were kids, there were court-mandated visits twice a year, but as time went by, a mutual understanding seemed to develop that this second family was his real family now; Piper and Margot and their mother had just been a trial run. Now they were down to awkward phone calls at Christmas. Piper wasn't sure Margot had even told him he was going to be a grandfather.

Jason called out one more "Goodbye," then went out the front door and started his truck in the driveway.

As soon as he was gone, Margot took Piper's hand.

"You know, it was Amy who gave me this box of newspapers," Margot confessed, her voice low and conspiratorial. "She stopped by my office last week. It was a surprise, really—I hadn't spoken to her in ages, and she just showed up in my office. She'd found the papers up in the attic at the house. Apparently, her grandmother—you remember Charlotte?—was the editor of the *Town Crier.*"

Piper thought of poor old Grandma Charlotte shuffling around in her billowing housedress, doing her best to keep the house going, to take care of Amy—both of her own daughters gone—a ghostly shadow of the woman who had spent the early part of her life running the motel her husband had built.

"No kidding?" Piper said, picking up the paper again; she knew she shouldn't be encouraging this, but she couldn't dim her own curiosity. Still, she needed to try. For Margot and the baby.

"Hey, look at this: the secret ingredient in

Mrs. Minetti's three-bean casserole is diced frank-furters. Talk about gross!"

Margot was undeterred.

"Amy *also* wanted to talk about the possibility of getting a grant to help save the motel! She'd been taking some business classes at the community college and had this idea to reopen the motel with a retro theme. She'd actually written out a really solid business plan."

"Wow," Piper said, setting the old newspaper back down. "Ambitious."

"Yeah," Margot said. "And this was just *last week,* Piper. Tell me, does that sound like a woman getting ready to go on a killing spree? To kill her whole family and then herself?"

Piper shook her head uncertainly. Margot went on.

"I mean, I know she had some other stuff going on—her mom, for one."

"Rose? What happened with her?"

"From what little Amy said, it sounded like some kind of dementia. It's so awful. Remember how Rose was never really around when we were kids? But then, a few years ago, Rose shows up at the motel and moves back into the house. She isn't drinking, and seems totally fine. According to Amy, she and Lou really bonded. I saw them around town together all the time—at the market, going for ice cream. Amy and her husband worked a lot, so Rose was with Lou and Levi after school every day. It was like Rose had a second chance—she wasn't a mother to Amy growing up, but she was grandma of the year."

Piper nodded, suddenly remembering a recent batch of photos Amy had posted on Facebook—an older woman sitting with the family, opening gifts on Christmas morning; the same woman playing dolls with a little blonde girl who must be Lou. Piper hadn't recognized Rose—she'd never met her, had only ever known Amy's mother as the little girl in the photograph standing beside her sister, Sylvie, clutching a chicken. But she could see it now.

Margot continued. "Then Amy says that, all of a sudden, her mom got confused, paranoid, not sure what was real and what wasn't. They just couldn't risk it—not with the kids. So they put her in a nursing home about a month ago."

"Terrible," Piper said. "Does she know? About Amy and her family?"

Margot let out a breath. "Jason said that a couple of officers went to talk to her early this morning, to tell her what had happened out at the motel. According to them, she didn't say a word. Acted like they were invisible."

"That's so sad."

"Maybe. But maybe she's got it easy. She doesn't have to deal with what's happening."

Piper looked up at the photo of the old Slater farm and noticed that there was a figure standing by the barn in the back left corner. She couldn't tell if it was a man or a woman, only a shadowy smudge in the shape of a person.

Margot looked up at Piper, her eyes suddenly brimming with tears. "If only we'd tried harder. We should have been there for her. Should have stayed close. I think that maybe, when she came to my office, she was reaching out to me—to both of us."

"What?"

"She asked about you. Wanted to hear what you were up to. She seemed . . . I don't know . . . kind of nostalgic. Like she missed us."

Piper shook her head; she could no longer act like none of this was striking a nerve.

"*Missed us?* She didn't want anything to do with us after that summer, Margot. She made that clear. She's the one who cut all ties, and acted like she barely recognized us."

She remembered passing Amy in the halls at school, how Amy would avoid catching Piper's eye, making a point to look anywhere but at her. How Amy walked right by Piper on the school bus every morning and afternoon, calling to her new friends at the back of the bus, and ignoring that Piper had saved her a seat.

"But she needed us," Margot said, wiping at her eyes with the back of her hand, "and we weren't there. Maybe this . . . this *nightmare* wouldn't have happened if we'd tried harder."

"That's insane. How can you think that?"

Margot was crying hard now. "I never understood," she said, "how you could turn your back on her so easily."

This was too much. Piper wanted to scream, *I'm not the one who turned my back,* but she just bit her lip. She recalled what Jason had said about keeping Margot calm, not letting her get worked up. She was doing a wonderful job so far.

"Look at you," Margot sobbed. "You don't even seem upset by what happened. It's like you don't care at all."

It was true that once Amy broke things off and started to ignore their calls, Piper was too hurt and furious to keep trying. It seemed . . . pathetic to keep calling and leaving notes, begging Amy to talk to her, to keep saving Amy a seat on the bus. If Amy didn't need Piper, Piper sure as hell didn't need Amy. Amy had slammed the door shut, but maybe Piper went ahead and added a few locks for good measure.

Piper took a deep breath and put her hand on her sister's arm. "Of course I care, Margot." *Too much,* she thought. That was always the problem, wasn't it? She smiled at her sister and added gently, "It's just that one of us has to keep her shit together. And at the moment, it's me."

Margot laughed weakly.

"I flew all the way out here as soon as I heard

86

about Amy, didn't I? But, honestly, right now my biggest concern is you and the baby."

"I appreciate that," Margot said. "I do. It's just that I haven't been able to stop thinking about it, and God knows I can't talk to Jason about it. And that *message* . . . Written on that old photo of Rose and Sylvie, the same one we found in the suitcase that summer, for Christ's sake," Margot said.

"I know," Piper said.

"I can't help thinking that someone—or something—is out there. That you and I are in terrible danger." Margot rubbed her stomach. "The baby, too."

Piper shook her head, leaned in to stroke her sister's hair. "We're fine. We're together. We're safe. And there's nothing out there trying to get us. What happened to Amy . . . it's terrible, horrific, but it has nothing to do with you and me."

"But Amy left that message for *us,* Piper—because we'd understand it. Whatever happened out at the motel that night has something to do with what we found!"

Piper felt the hair on the back of her neck stand up.

"Margot," Piper said, "seriously, I'm sure the cops are right—Amy was depressed, or mentally ill, and something just snapped inside her. It happens."

Margot shook her head and scooted back on

the bed so she was taller against her backrest of pillows. "Jesus, Piper! You don't really believe that, do you? You don't really believe that Amy would be capable of something like this? Her own husband and son?"

"Other than generic Christmas cards and Facebook, I haven't seen or talked to Amy in years. I don't know her at all."

She felt a lump growing in her throat.

Margot plucked at the covers. "You're wrong." Her voice was calm now, low and serious. "You knew her better than anyone ever did."

The statement hung in the air between them; for the first time, Piper wondered how much her younger sister truly knew about everything that had gone on between her and Amy that summer.

"But we were kids then. People change. I've changed." She swallowed hard. Had she changed that much? Does anyone, really? "I can only imagine Amy had, too."

"Changed enough to become a killer? A crazy person who would *slaughter* her own family? And then blow her brains out?"

"I don't know. . . . I—"

"Yes, you do!" Margot shot forward in bed, puffy face growing redder.

"Relax, Margot," Piper said, squeezing her sister's arm. She had to be the big sister here, the right kind of big sister, the kind she'd seen in movies and read about in books. The older sister

88

who was selfless, wise, who knew just the right thing to say. She owed it to Margot, to the baby, to do the best she could.

Margot leaned back against her pillows obediently, but her face was set stubbornly. "You *do* know. So we have to figure out what really happened up at the motel and what it means."

"We? You're not figuring out anything," Piper said. "You're going to do what the doctor and Jason say and stay in bed and watch cooking shows and read articles about proper breast-feeding technique and cloth diapers versus disposables."

"Right. Which means it's all up to you," Margot said, eyes glittering.

"And what exactly am I supposed to do?"

Margot bit her lip. "Maybe you can talk to Amy's daughter."

"What makes you think the kid will talk to me at all?"

"Jason said she seems really stunned, like she's in shock still. She keeps repeating her story like a robot. But maybe . . . maybe if you give her some kind of hint that you know her mother didn't do this . . . maybe she'll open up and tell you what she really saw and heard that night."

"I don't know—"

Margot gripped Piper's hand tight. "Please. Do it for me. And for Amy."

Piper blew out a breath. She remembered being

in the tower with Amy, Amy's hand gripping her own, pulling her farther back, into the shadows.

"Okay. I'll try," Piper said reluctantly. "But if Jason finds out what I'm up to, that you and I are even talking about Amy or her family, he'll have me on the next plane home—you should've heard the lecture I got on the ride here."

"I know. We'll have to be careful. Keep everything secret. But we're good at that, aren't we?"

Margot gave Piper a bittersweet smile.

And just like that, Piper realized she'd already failed. She was not being the responsible older sister. Here they were, back in their old roles, sharing secrets, chasing trouble: foolish girls once again on a wild-goose chase, Amy egging them on, taunting them, saying: *I dare you.*

1989

Piper

"Jason Hawke and I kissed," Amy whispered to Piper. "With tongues."

"Ew!" shrieked Margot. She leapt up and skated off to the deep end of the empty swimming pool, the wheels of her skates rattling against the pocked and flaking blue concrete. Margot, who was only ten, always lost patience with truth-or-dare when things got good and turned to crushes and kissing. Her hair was in messy pigtails that stuck out from beneath her helmet, and her eyelids were coated with the neon-blue eye shadow Amy had put on her earlier. They'd have to wash it off before they went home or their mom would have a fit. Margot wore the knee and elbow pads Mom had bought for her. She'd bought them for both girls, but Piper never wore hers. She didn't because Amy didn't. Amy didn't even own any.

Amy's little transistor radio was resting on the edge at the shallow end of the pool, tuned to WQVT, "All hits, all the time." Guns N' Roses' "Sweet Child of Mine" started—one of Amy's favorite songs. Amy liked any song where the singer poured his soul out—even some of her grandma's old Perry Como and Frank Sinatra records. Totally cheesy, but somehow, when Amy sang along with them, she made them seem cool.

"What was it like?" Piper asked, leaning closer. Amy smelled like Love's Baby Soft and strawberry lip gloss. She had on a tight *Ghostbusters* T-shirt and ragged cutoffs.

Amy smiled impishly and tucked a chunk of her pink bangs—dyed with Jell-O—behind her triple-pierced ear. She had neon-blue eye shadow on, too, along with a big streak of silver that went all the way up to her eyebrow. She looked like she'd just stepped out of an MTV video. The little sister of Cyndi Lauper, maybe, but Amy thought Cyndi Lauper sucked, so Piper would never mention the resemblance out loud.

"Come on, I'll tell you," Amy said, undoing the rainbow laces on her white skates. Piper did the same, and both girls slipped on their flip-flops and climbed the ladder out of the pool. It was the end of summer—there were only two more weeks until school started—and both girls' legs were bronze from the sun. Amy's were long and lean, the legs of a dancer, like one of the Rockettes Piper had seen when her mom took her to Radio City Music Hall.

"Where are you going?" Margot asked, scowling. She hated to be left out, but often was, because she was really still a baby even though she pretended not to be. Her pigtails stuck out like antennas from under her helmet, making her look like an angry beetle.

"Be right back," Amy said. "Stay here."

Piper and Amy hurried across the concrete patio that surrounded the pool, over the crabgrass that had pushed its way up through the cracks, and past the line of broken lounge chairs that led to the motel office, with its steeply peaked roof. A red *Closed* sign hung in the window, and all the dusty plastic blinds were drawn. Attached to the office on the right were Rooms 1 through 14; 15 through 28 were in a second building, around back.

All of the motel rooms were now sealed up like little tombs, even though the keys with their blue plastic tags still hung on the metal rack behind the office desk. Sometimes the girls would sneak into the rooms, which had been left unchanged since the motel closed in 1971. The beds were covered in brown-and-mustard paisley spreads, and dull turquoise carpeting full of cigarette burns and years' worth of unidentifiable stains was underfoot. There were prints of yellow and orange marigolds in heavy frames. The old color TVs had been sold, but the tables that had once held them remained, along with bureaus and nightstands, some of which still contained mildewed copies of Gideon's Bible. Their finishes were nicked and scratched, covered in circular water stains—the ghostly images of wet glasses left by guests long gone. Some of the bathrooms still had soap wrapped in paper, but most of the soap had been chewed through by mice. There were ashtrays in all the rooms, and sometimes when Piper went in she swore she was breathing 1971 air—it smelled like dust and cigarettes and long-faded perfume. Like ghosts, if ghosts had a smell.

The roofs in some of the rooms had begun to leak; the ceilings were water-stained and mildewed, the plaster crumbling in places. Some of the rooms still contained matchbooks and notepads printed with the Tower Motel name and logo—a simple drawing of the castlelike tower that stood at the base of the driveway by the road.

Amy's grandma had shown them pictures of the tower being built. Her gnarled fingers, stained yellow from nicotine, pointed at the curled black-and-white photos glued in an old album.

"He always said he built the tower for me," Grandma Charlotte would say. "But we knew the truth. He did it because he wanted to. Because he thought it would bring people in from all over, make us rich and famous."

The pictures were not all that exciting: Amy's grandfather wanted the tower to be a surprise, so he'd built large staging around it, sheathed in boards and tarps so that no one could see what he was doing. At last, in the final photo, the great unveiling: Clarence Slater stood, a dashing figure in a suit and hat, dark hair slicked back, one eye squinting slightly. He was holding his wife's hand; Grandma Charlotte was young and beautiful then, not the disheveled old woman Piper knew now. They posed with the painted wooden sign he'd put up in front of the tower, angled to catch the eye of drivers on Route 6: *Come See the Famous Tower of London.*

Piper and Amy stepped over the remains of the sign, which had been knocked over years ago and lay in rotting pieces amid clumps of grass, mullein, and chicory, strewn with cigarette butts and fast-food wrappers thrown out the windows of passing cars. Then they paused just outside the tower.

Amy and her friends were not supposed to go inside. Her grandma said it was dangerous, with its crumbling walls and sagging floors.

"It's a death trap," Grandma Charlotte had said over and over, voice rusty, breath sour. "You steer clear of it," she warned, giving an uncharacteristic shake of the finger to emphasize just how serious she was. "One of these days, someone's going to fall straight through the floor and end up in hell."

Grandma Charlotte took care of Amy when Amy's mom, Rose, wasn't around (which, as far as Piper could tell, was pretty much all the time—she'd never laid eyes on Rose, not once in the whole year she'd known Amy). Amy said that her mom had mental problems. And she drank. Grandma Charlotte explained once, "My poor Rose was never the same after we lost Sylvie. She blamed herself. Never got over it. Some people are made stronger by loss. Others are broken by it."

Sylvie was Amy's aunt, her mom's older sister, and she had run away when she was eighteen. Went off to California to be a movie star—that's what Amy said. She packed a suitcase and left a note in her typewriter, saying goodbye and that she'd be in touch soon. They never heard from her again. Amy's middle name was Sylvia, after her long-missing aunt.

Piper felt kind of bad for Grandma Charlotte—an old woman left alone to raise a wild kid like Amy. Her husband, Clarence, had died not long after the motel went out of business, back before Amy was even born. Grandma Charlotte said he'd died of a broken heart, which Piper figured meant a heart attack.

Grandma Charlotte was thin, her sallow skin sagged, and her hair had gone white. She had two long silver hairs coming off her chin, and Piper longed to pluck them. The house was always a wreck (despite the fact that Grandma Charlotte never seemed to stop tidying), and sometimes they'd catch her just staring out the kitchen window down the driveway, a lost and vacant look on her face.

"What's she doing?" Piper asked.

"I dunno," Amy said. "Looking for my mom or Sylvie, maybe. Or for motel guests? I think she still half expects that old bell wired from the office to the main house to ring, even though it's been broken for a zillion years."

Sometimes Amy's grandma got confused and called Amy "Sylvie." Piper heard her do it once in a while.

"Come here, Sylvie, and let me braid your hair."

"I'm Amy, Grandma," she'd say, sounding uncomfortable and impatient. "Sylvie's gone."

"So she is," Grandma Charlotte would say, running her gnarled fingers through Amy's golden-blond hair. "She was my good girl. So are you."

Now Amy pulled Piper through the arched doorway and into the cool shade of the tower. Piper held her breath, waiting for the walls to collapse around her. Inside, it was dark and smelled like damp cement, rotten leaves, and something acrid and spoiled. The wooden planks covering the floor were spongy beneath their feet. There were no windows on the first level, and the only light came from the narrow doorway.

Years' worth of dry leaves crunched beneath their feet. Piper could also make out a Milky Way wrapper, and a crushed Budweiser can. Far off, she could hear the sound of Amy's radio playing up at the pool; the music drifted down like fog, the song unidentifiable.

"Do you really want to know what it was like?" Amy asked, her face nearly lost in the cool shadows of the tower. "Kissing Jason?"

"Yeah," Piper said, her palm sweaty as Amy

held it tightly, gave it a squeeze. Piper had never kissed anyone, but she thought about it all the time. She stared at the lips of all the boys she knew, studying their shape and the way they moved when the boys talked. She tried to imagine their lips touching hers, wondering if it mattered whether or not they had the soft, peach-fuzz beginnings of a mustache. She wondered if it tickled, and how you arranged your heads so that noses didn't get in the way.

Jason Hawke was in their grade, a scrawny boy who lived practically next door to Piper and Margot, in one of the condos on the back side of the hill Amy lived on. His hair was a little too long (but not long enough to be cool), and he was always creeping around with a magnifying glass, trying to show them how neat tree bark or a little green beetle looked through it. Margot said she felt bad for him, because he seemed lonely. Piper thought he was just a geek. A few months ago, he'd given Amy a note written in secret code. She hadn't even tried to decipher it, which had seemed a terrible disappointment to Jason.

"I'll show you," Amy said, and before Piper could say anything or even think about what was going to happen next, Amy's lips were on hers, slick with lip gloss. Her small tongue probed gently at Piper's mouth, coaxing it open. Piper opened her lips and tasted strawberry lip gloss and the moist heat of Amy's breath. Piper made a soft moaning sort of sound, an I-surrender-to-this-and-whatever-might-happen-next sigh, and leaned into the kiss. The tower around her seemed to shift and spin a little. Piper was sure it was going to come crashing down on them right then, at that very moment.

Then she sensed movement, actual movement —not from the tower, but from a shadow that passed over them. She looked up. Someone was there, in the doorway, watching. She froze, jerked away.

The shadowy figure backed up into the light, and Piper saw his face.

"Jason?" Piper heard Margot call; she must have been coming up the driveway that led toward the tower. "Have you seen Piper and Amy?"

Jason bolted from the doorway without answering, and disappeared outside.

"Hey! Wait a sec," Margot called. They could hear her footsteps running after him. Then both their footsteps stopped.

Piper and Amy held very still and listened. Piper leaned back against the wall; the stones felt cool through her T-shirt.

"Where are you going?" Margot asked.

"Home," Jason said.

"So did you see Piper and Amy?" Margot asked.

Piper crouched lower in the shadows and looked over at Amy, but couldn't read her expression. She didn't look worried or stressed, that was for sure. If Piper had to guess, she'd say Amy seemed mildly amused.

"Nah," Jason said.

"Want to help me look for them?" Margot asked.

"Can't," Jason said.

"Are you going to be around later?" Margot asked. "You were going to show me the telescope you got. Remember?"

"Not tonight," Jason said. "Maybe another time."

"It's just that I was thinking of asking for one for my birthday, and I wanted to see yours. To see if maybe that's the exact kind I should ask for."

"It's a Tasco. My mom got it at the hobby shop." Footsteps crunched on the gravel again, fading, like they were heading up the hill. Jason going home.

"Okay, see ya!" Margot called. Jason didn't answer.

"I think your little sister has a crush on Jay Jay," Amy whispered.

"Does not," Piper said.

Margot was close now; they could hear her footsteps approaching the doorway of the tower.

"Piper? Amy?" she called, her voice echoing.

"Shh," Amy hissed, finger to her lips, smiling. "Come on." Still holding Piper's hand, she led her to the ladder. Piper followed Amy up to the second floor, trying to move up the splintery ladder as silently and gracefully as Amy. They crouched below one of the three long slit-shaped windows.

It was darker up there. Amy squeezed Piper's hand. Piper tried to slow her breathing. She wondered why they were bothering to hide; it seemed kind of mean, but exhilarating at the same time.

Piper reached with her right hand, and touched Amy gently on the face. Amy turned and looked at her, smiling a conspiratorial smile, and then the smile faded. Amy looked so serious it made Piper's stomach hurt.

"You're a better kisser than Jason Hawke," Amy whispered, leaning close.

"He saw us," Piper said, her stomach tightening.

"So what?" Amy shrugged.

"So . . . he might tell or something."

"He won't," Amy said.

"How do you know?" Piper asked. She imagined it: going back to school in a couple of weeks and everyone talking, whispering, the whole middle school buzzing with the news that Piper and Amy were—what—freaks? lezzies? Good God.

"I just do," Amy said. "He didn't tell Margot now, did he? Jay Jay is nothing to worry about. Relax. It's fine."

But it didn't feel fine.

"Piper?" Margot was in the tower now. "Are you guys in here?"

Below them, they heard Margot tentatively start to climb the ladder.

"Come on," Amy whispered, tugging on Piper again, and they moved toward the next wooden ladder, the one that led up to the rooftop deck that was ringed with castlelike battlements. And what were they going to do once they were up there? It's not as if there was any place to hide. Maybe they'd flap their wings and fly off the edge.

Amy was giggling, one hand slapped over her mouth to quiet herself. It was all a game to her —the kiss, Jason seeing them, hiding from Margot.

"Come on, you guys," Margot called. "I know you're up there. I hear you!"

Amy pulled harder on Piper, urging her silently toward the ladder. As Piper did a clumsy gallop, her right foot plunged through the floor like it was made of graham crackers. Piper tumbled forward, her hand slipping out of Amy's.

She screamed, partly with the scraping pain on her shin and partly from the feeling of falling, the fear that she would go all the way down (all the way down to hell, maybe, as Grandma Charlotte had warned). But she didn't. Something stopped her. She looked down and discovered that there were two layers of boards: the floor she had just fallen through was nailed to the top of the rafters, and the ceiling below was nailed to their underside. The boards on the ceiling had held.

"Whoa!" Amy said, turning back, reaching to pull Piper out. "You okay?"

"I think so," Piper said, lifting her leg out gently and scooting back away from the rotten spot in the floor. Her shin was bleeding, and there was a two-inch-long splinter of wood poking out of the skin like a jagged and bloody thorn. Looking at it made her head swim. She imagined it went all the way down to the bone.

"Oh, *man,*" Amy said, looking at Piper's leg. She tucked a strand of pink hair behind her ear and leaned in for a closer inspection.

"We should get your grandma," Piper said, carefully keeping her eyes away from her leg. Grandma Charlotte had been a nurse in the war: Piper had seen pictures of her in a crisp white uniform standing before rows of hospital cots. Even though it had been over forty years since she'd tended wounded soldiers, Piper was sure she'd know what to do. When you've seen guys with their legs blown off by land mines, surely you could handle a splinter—even a giant one.

"No way," Amy said. "We can*not* tell her we were in here. She'd never trust me again. We can totally handle this. Trust me."

"But I . . ."

"Shh," Amy said. "Close your eyes."

Piper closed them a little, but not all the way.

Amy reached for the splinter, expertly grabbed

it between her fingernails, and gave it one quick tug. Piper wanted to scream a thousand bad words, but it hurt too much for her to do anything more than give a guttural cry.

"Got it," Amy said. Piper opened her eyes to see Amy holding the bloody sliver of wood, triumphant. It seemed to glisten and shimmer in the dim light.

Piper's stomach did a flip.

"What happened?" Margot asked. Her head had appeared at the top of the ladder, and she was now peering into the room.

"Don't come in here," Amy ordered. "It's not safe. The floor's rotted out."

"You okay?" Margot asked, eyes worried.

"Fine," Piper said, using the bottom edge of her T-shirt to dab at the dark blood seeping out of her shin. "I'm totally fine," she said through gritted teeth. "And you have to swear not to tell Mom about this. She'd kill us. We'd never be allowed over here again."

Margot nodded. Her eye shadow sparkled in the light coming through the slatted window. "I know that. You think I'm stupid, but I'm not."

"You're lucky you didn't go all the way through," Amy said, stooping down to inspect the hole. "That would have been a nasty fall."

All the way to hell, Piper thought, nodding in agreement.

"Come on, you guys," Margot urged, in a voice

as small and whiny as a mosquito. "You shouldn't stay up here."

For once, Piper agreed with her little sister, and stood up on shaky legs. Her right shin throbbed and was sticky with blood.

"Wait a sec," Amy said. "There's something in here." She leaned down for a better look, then got on her belly and reached into the hole in the floor to shove her hand way back.

"Be careful," Piper warned, worried that the floor wouldn't hold her weight and she'd go tumbling in, headfirst, like Alice down the rabbit hole.

Amy pulled out a small olive-green hard-sided suitcase.

"What is that?" Margot asked, leaning in for a better look.

Amy said nothing. She turned the suitcase on its side and popped open the clasps by the handle with a loud click. Then she paused, held her breath, and gently swung the top up.

Inside was clothing, neatly folded. Amy pulled out a gingham dress, some stockings. Then a little coin purse stuffed with a thick roll of bills: tens, twenties, fives. Tucked into the bottom of the coin purse was a pair of old earrings with green stones, and a pearl necklace.

"Whoa," Margot said. "I bet those are real emeralds and pearls!"

Amy studied them a minute, then placed them

back in the purse and continued unpacking the suitcase.

Beneath the clothing was an old scrapbook, with the letters "SAS" in neat black calligraphy. Amy pulled it out carefully and began to thumb through it. The brittle pages were pasted with photos of old movie stars cut from newspapers and magazines. Piper thought she recognized a couple of them, but they weren't anyone who was popular now. Some of them had names neatly printed under-neath: Gary Cooper, Rock Hudson, Audrey Hepburn, Doris Day.

Amy dug around in the suitcase again, and pulled out a photograph in a frame this time: two girls. One was a stunningly beautiful older girl with a narrow face, straight blond hair, and haunting eyes; the second girl seemed a shadow of the first, with dark, unkempt curls, and circles under her heavy-lidded eyes. Both girls wore stiff dresses, smiling into the camera with faces that looked equally stiff, as if the photographer had grumbled a warning, "Smile now, damn it." Each was holding a chicken cradled carefully in her arms, and they stood in front of a painted sign: *World Famous London Chicken Circus.*

"It's my mom and Aunt Sylvie," Amy said. She thought a minute. "This has to be Sylvie's suitcase. The one she took with her when she left."

"But why's her suitcase still here, then?" Margot asked as they stared down at the now disheveled pile of clothing inside. It gave off a musty smell, the scent of things long forgotten.

Amy picked up a dress and held it so that it waved gently, like a flag, like a moth fluttering. If Piper squinted her eyes, she could almost see the blond-haired girl from the picture wearing it; she was smiling, but under the smile, her eyes flashed them a warning glance.

Put it back, she seemed to say. *If you know what's good for you, you'll walk away and forget you ever found it.*

Jason

Jason was still trying to make sense of what he'd seen in the tower. He kept playing it back in his mind, a broken loop of tape that always ended with Piper looking up and seeing him, just as Margot called his name. And then he thought of Amy. Would she be mad? Was she looking for him right now, ready to wring his neck, to make him swear to forget what he'd seen?

After slipping away from Margot, he'd gone home and played Nintendo for a while, but he couldn't concentrate. He'd sneaked back through the woods to the motel just in time to catch the girls coming out of the tower, arguing. He stopped where he was, crouched behind a thick maple tree.

Piper was limping, her leg bleeding.

"We need to tell your grandma what we found," Piper said.

"Maybe call the police," Margot chimed in.

"No," Amy ordered. "Not until we know what it means."

Jason clung to the tree he hid behind.

Call the police? What had they found?

When the girls went into the house, Jason circled around the woods to the motel units and let himself into Room 4.

Room 4 was his favorite to hide in, because the

lock was broken and he didn't have to stop at the office for a key. He'd even hidden some things under the bed: binoculars, an old Coke bottle full of water, a flashlight (just in case he ever came after dark, which he hadn't been able to pull off yet), and a bag of sunflower seeds. Jason's mom didn't believe in junk food, so she fed him bird food instead: nuts, seeds, dried fruit.

In addition to these supplies, he kept his treasures there, too. Things of Amy's he'd found lying around by the pool: a half-full bottle of Coppertone, a single silver hoop earring, a pair of knockoff Wayfarer sunglasses with red plastic frames. He'd added other relics he'd found around the motel: a book of Tower Motel matches, a page of motel stationery, and a brass key-ring with a single skeleton key that he'd found hidden at the back of a desk drawer in the office.

Sometimes he made believe that he lived at the motel. That he'd just come in after a long day. He'd kick off his Nikes and lie back on the musty bed with its moth-eaten paisley spread, look around the room, and think how good he had it. His own room. His own bathroom, albeit one where the water didn't turn on anymore and the bathtub was full of broken tiles. Mostly, what he thought of was Amy. Of how, one day, she'd be his girlfriend. He was sure of it. His mom always told him that if you wanted something badly enough you just had to visualize it; if you pictured yourself having it already, soon it would be yours. His mom was big into things like visualization and positive affirmations. There were little sayings taped to the mirrors all over their condo with statements like "I am living my dream" and "Wonderful things are on their way to me." Jason wasn't too sure about the power of these tactics: even though she said, "I am wealthy beyond my wildest dreams," twenty times a day, his mom still had her minimum-wage job over at the nursing home, cleaning drool and pee off old people.

Still, he visualized Amy being his girlfriend. He concentrated so hard on it that his head hurt. And maybe, just maybe, the power of positive thinking was working after all: yesterday Amy Slater had actually kissed him. And it wasn't just a stupid half-second little peck—it was a real kiss. Their tongues had touched (which was kind of gross, yet thrilling at the same time), and at the end she'd given his lower lip a little nibble. Okay, maybe more than a little nibble. When he looked in the mirror this morning, it still looked slightly puffy and purplish. But he didn't mind. He kept working his tongue over the swollen place on his lip, remembering what her teeth had felt like.

It had all been so surprising that he half-wondered if it had really happened. If he had really found Amy roller skating by herself at the bottom of the pool yesterday, and if she had invited him down.

"Come here," she said, in a way that was really more of an order than an invitation. "You got any cigarettes?"

Jason shook his head.

"Of course not," Amy said, disappointed, but not altogether surprised; she rolled away, her back to him.

"But I can get some," Jason called after her.

She stopped short and spun neatly back to face him, grinning. "Really?"

"Sure," he said. "No problem."

She laughed, skating forward like a rocket, then skidding to a dead stop, her face inches away from his nose.

"When?" she asked.

"Umm . . . tomorrow? I can bring them tomorrow. If that's okay, I mean."

"That's just perfect," she said, smiling. She stared hard at him, cocking her head first to the left, then to the right, studying him from different angles. "Hey, did anyone ever tell you you're kind of cross-eyed?"

"Um . . . no," he stammered. He felt his face flush.

"No one has a perfect face," she said. "Not even supermodels. Did you know no one's face is symmetrical? The left half of our nose is totally different than the right. Like here," she said, putting a finger on the left side of his mouth, "this side might be just a little bit bigger than the other, or turn down a little more. I guess we're all kind of like messed-up jack-o-lanterns."

Then she leaned in and kissed him, despite his crossed eyes and his face that didn't match up.

And if it wasn't for the swollen lip, he might be able to tell himself he'd imagined the whole thing after all. It had happened so quickly and was over too fast. She'd skated off, saying, "Toodle-oo, Jay Jay. Don't forget the cigarettes next time."

And he hadn't forgotten the cigarettes. He'd gone home and nabbed a pack from his brother's carton of Marlboros. As soon as his mom left for work this morning, he'd thrown on one of his brother's Ramones T-shirts.

"I didn't know you were into the Ramones," Amy might say.

And he'd say something like "There's a lot about me you don't know." Or maybe, "I'm full of surprises."

No. That was too stupid, even for him.

He'd gone to the motel, seen only Margot at the pool, and headed down to the tower to look for Amy and give her the cigarettes. That's when he'd seen them. And smushed the cigarettes when he involuntarily clenched his fist in shock.

Now, as he lay on the bed in the musty darkness, he pulled the crushed cigarette pack from his pocket and wondered what the girls were up to, what they'd found in that old crumbling tower. He took out a cigarette. Still smokable.

Maybe he could leave them for Amy some-where. It would be a way to say, *No hard feelings.* That he wasn't weirded out by what he'd seen in the tower.

But where should he leave them?

Somewhere he was sure she'd go.

The pool? No, her grandma sometimes went out there to sit in one of the old sagging chairs. She'd see the cigarettes, and then Amy might get in trouble.

The tower.

He'd leave them in the tower!

Would she know they were from him? Probably. Maybe he should leave a note, too.

He jumped up, went to the desk. Found a pencil stub and an old piece of Tower Motel stationery.

He thought and thought about what to write. Should he say anything about what he'd seen in the tower? Should he remind her of their kiss yesterday in the pool? Tell her that he thought about her all the time? That, whatever it was she'd found, she could tell him—she could trust him?

Maybe he should write her in code?

No. In the end, he decided simple was best.

She'd appreciate that more than anything stupid and sappy.

Finally, he wrote his note:

Cigarettes as promised.
Hope to see you soon.
—J

He peeked out the window and saw it was all clear. He opened the door slowly, listening, looking both ways. The girls still hadn't come out of the house.

He darted across the driveway and went straight for the tower. As he ran, he thought he saw movement in the shadows that gathered around the doorway.

Had he missed the girls somehow? Were they back there? If they were, it was too late now: they'd have seen him. He'd play it cool, tell Amy he had something for her. He kept going, got to the doorway, and peeked in.

"Hello?" he called.

Nothing. No one.

But he couldn't shake the feeling that there had been someone there. He could almost smell it in the air.

"Anyone there?" he called again, looking up at the ceiling. He could climb the ladder to check the two floors above him. But, somehow, he couldn't make himself.

He set the cigarettes and note down in the center of the ground floor and ran back outside, across the driveway, and to Room 4.

Piper

"Grandma," Amy cooed in her sweetest voice, "tell us about Aunt Sylvie."

They were all sitting at the Slaters' kitchen table, sharing a can of Pringles and some flat Pepsi. They'd tucked the suitcase back into the floor of the tower. Piper and Margot thought they should bring it right to Grandma Charlotte, but Amy didn't agree. "Not just yet," she said. "Not until we know more. We don't know what it means yet, and I don't want to go upsetting my grandma for no reason. She can get pretty freaked out by anything having to do with Sylvie."

So the girls had left the suitcase in the tower and come back into the house, where they'd gone straight into the bathroom to fix Piper's leg. Amy dumped peroxide on it, which sizzled and hissed dramatically but didn't sting, just like Amy promised. Then Amy covered the wound with gauze and medical tape. They told Amy's grandma that she'd fallen while roller skating.

"You girls should be more careful," Grandma Charlotte said vaguely.

Piper was trying not to think about how badly her leg was throbbing. Over and over, she saw the sliver Amy had pulled out, a pointed wooden

117

dagger that she was sure had gone all the way to the bone.

The potato chips tasted like salty cardboard. She took a sip of soda, remembering, with a warm rush, the feel of Amy's lips on hers.

The room felt hot. She wiped at her face with her hand.

Margot gave her a worried look. Mouthed, *You okay?*

Piper scowled at her little sister. Of course she was okay.

"Tell us about the day Sylvie ran away," Amy said.

Amy's grandma stood at the kitchen sink, her back to the three girls. Their sweaty skin stuck to the vinyl chairs.

Grandma Charlotte was wearing a light cotton housedress that billowed around her thin frame like a blue-flowered tent. Her gray hair, tinged with yellow, hung in limp wisps. A cigarette was burning low in the ashtray while Grandma Charlotte worked at the dishes in the sink. Piper watched the cigarette burn down on its own, like a fuse. Soon the filter would start to burn, filling the kitchen with its chemical stink.

"My Sylvie was a good girl," Grandma Charlotte said.

"But she ran away," Amy said. "Why?"

Grandma Charlotte's face twitched silently, but then she shook her head. "I guess we'll never know," she said, pulling off the yellow rubber gloves to reveal gnarled hands.

Piper thought of the photo they'd found in the suitcase: Two girls. One plain and chunky with dark, tousled hair; one blonde and beautiful. Both lost in their own ways now. Amy looked nothing like her mother. Amy, Piper suddenly realized, looked more like her aunt Sylvie, radiant and blonde.

Piper glanced at Margot. She was listening politely, like the good girl she always was, sitting straight up in her chair. Piper felt a brief surge of anger; if her little sister hadn't been there, hadn't come into the tower looking for them, then she never would have run and fallen through the floor. They would never have found the suitcase. Piper wished it had stayed hidden. She had a terrible feeling about the whole thing. It had started small at first, like a toothache, but now it traveled through her, pulsed along with the pain in her shin. When Piper glanced down at the bandage now, she saw the pink bloodstain soaking through—it was shaped like a butterfly.

"Sylvie left a note, didn't she?" Amy asked.

Her grandmother sighed. "You know the story. And you know I don't like to talk about it. Neither does your mother. If . . . *when* she comes back, you mustn't ever bring it up. It upsets her."

"I know," Amy said. For a second, Piper thought Amy looked like she might start crying.

Piper thought of how little Amy ever said about her mom.

"She's a drunk," Amy had told Piper once, when Margot wasn't around. "Grandma says that she can't help it. Something's broken inside her, and the only way she knows how to make it feel better is by drinking. But I think she's just plain crazy, drunk or not. One time, when I was real little, I woke up and found her standing over my bed. She was holding this big old chain and looking crazy. I started screaming and crying—I was sure she was going to kill me. Grandma came and asked her what she was doing. Mom kept saying she 'needed to know.' I have no freaking idea what she was talking about. Then she just turned and left. She took off, and we didn't see her for almost a year that time."

Piper thought it was awful and sad, to have a mother who was alive but who, for whatever reason, couldn't be your mother. She wondered where Amy's mom was, and if she thought of Amy every day or if she forgot all about even having a kid.

"Please, Grandma," Amy said as she pushed back from the dining-room table. "Just tell me one more time. You found a note Sylvie left, right?"

Her grandmother blew out a breath, then nodded, closing her eyes, like it was easier to tell the story in the dark. "I woke up that morning because your mother was crying, just howling away like it was the end of the world. I went into their room and saw Sylvie's bed was empty. Your mother was so upset she could hardly speak. The closet was open, and most of Sylvie's clothes were gone. Then I found the note. It was stuck in her typewriter. On her desk."

"What did the note say? Do you remember?"

"It said she couldn't stay here anymore. And that she loved us and hoped we'd understand. She promised to get in touch as soon as she got settled."

"But she never did, right?" Amy asked.

"No." Amy's grandma flinched slightly. "Not a word."

"Are you sure? Are you sure Mom never heard from her?"

"I'm sure."

"Do you think that's where Mom goes?" Amy asked, voice low. She picked at some skin around her thumbnail. "When she's not here? Do you think maybe she's off looking for Sylvie?"

"Oh, sweetie," Grandma Charlotte said, coming to stand behind Amy and putting her arms around Amy's shoulders. But Amy only stiffened, sat up straighter.

"Do you still have the note?" she asked. "The one Sylvie left?"

Amy's grandma narrowed her eyes. "Why does it matter?"

"What'd you guys do with all her stuff? The things she left behind?"

Her grandmother turned back to the sink and pulled the plug out of the drain. "I don't know. There wasn't much. Some of it might be in the attic, I think. Your grandfather and I, we cleaned out their room, packed everything of Sylvie's into a trunk. We thought it would help poor Rose. She was so destroyed by Sylvie's leaving. We thought it might be better if she wasn't surrounded by all of those things—reminders of her sister everywhere."

The last of the dirty dishwater went down the drain with a terrible, wet sucking sound.

The attic smelled like dust and mice. Piper was sure she could hear faint scuttling sounds off in the shadows, feel beady eyes upon her. She hoped it was only mice and not something larger, something more dangerous.

Was it more than rustling?

Was that faint breathing she heard coming from the darkest corner, the place where no light touched?

"I don't like it up here," Margot complained.

"So go back home. Nobody's stopping you," Piper said. She wanted to get the hell out of there, too, but no way would she admit that to Amy.

Margot flashed her a no-way, not-without-you look. Their mom was working, and then she had class—she was going to law school part-time. She was doing it for all of them, she repeated, again and again. She could have a good job, make some real money, make a difference in the world—wasn't that what her daughters wanted from her?

Not really, Piper always wanted to say. What she wanted was to have a mom who was more like a mom, someone to be there when they got home from school, to cook real dinners instead of Hamburger Helper and frozen lasagna. A mom who wouldn't order Piper to stay with goody-two-shoes Margot all day, no matter what. It pissed Piper off a little—it was like being an unpaid babysitter.

"Aw, your little sister's not so bad," Amy would always say. "She's actually pretty cool."

Amy sometimes said she wished she had a kid sister, or any brothers or sisters, for that matter. She said it stank to be an only child—a mistake.

"My mom told me once that's what I was," she'd confessed to Piper. "That she'd never wanted kids. She got pregnant by accident. Never even told me the guy's name."

Piper had thought that was a cruel thing to tell a kid, even if it was the truth.

"There's a lot of crap up here," Amy said now, blowing dust off another cardboard box. She'd already opened half a dozen of them and found nothing useful—baby clothes, old *Life* magazines, stained tablecloths, and chipped china.

There was an old couch covered by a sheet, a broken treadle sewing machine, a wooden wardrobe that was empty except for a few mothballs, and a steamer trunk with a tiny suitcase resting on top. Amy reached for the little square suitcase and undid the latches.

"Cool! It's a typewriter," she said, pulling off the cover to reveal a gunmetal-gray typewriter with green keys. *Royal,* it said in silver letters on the front. And on the back, *Quiet De Luxe.* "Holy crap, I bet this was Sylvie's typewriter! The one she wrote her goodbye note on!" She punched a few keys, and the arms with the letters moved up and got stuck, tangled together. Amy hefted the typewriter to the floor and opened the trunk. "Jackpot," she said.

Inside, they found clothes: a wool winter coat, saddle shoes, a couple of dresses and cardigans, a few slips, three white nightgowns. There was a bowling trophy, a certificate for winning the London High spelling bee: *Presented to Sylvia Slater on the thirteenth day of March, 1959,* it said in ornate calligraphy.

"I guess this is definitely Sylvie's stuff," Piper said.

"The things she left behind," Amy said, staring down as she pulled things out of the trunk.

Piper wondered what she would choose to take with her if she ran away.

Amy—you'd take Amy.

Idiot, she thought to herself.

Amy unpacked the trunk. A handful of books were tucked into the bottom corner: *Grimm's Fairy Tales*, a book called *Beauty, Glamour and Personality* that seemed to be a hair-and-makeup guide, some dress patterns, and then, all the way at the bottom, a stained and worn hardcover: *Mastering the Art and Science of Hypnotism.* Amy lifted it out and opened the cover.

"Check out the inscription."

To Sylvie, the world's greatest chicken hypnotist, with love from Uncle Fenton, Christmas 1954

"Who's Fenton?" Piper asked.

"I guess he was my mom's uncle or something? He lived in that old trailer out back for a while."

Piper had never paid much attention to the trailer. It sat in the overgrown field just behind Amy's house, blending in with all the other junk back there: a decaying pickup truck without tires, a half-built motorcycle, a rusted oil tank, a tractor missing the seat, and a bunch of television sets with the picture tubes busted to shit.

"Fenton's a weird name," Margot observed.

"I think it was a family name or something," Amy said. "I don't know much about him. There are a couple of pictures of him with my mom and Sylvie and my grandparents. He worked at the motel, like the fix-it guy. My grandfather was the idea man, but Fenton put all the ideas into place. Grandma told me once that after Fenton left, everything started to fall apart. I bet if I ask Grandma about him she'll tell me more."

"You ever been inside the trailer?" Piper asked.

Amy shook her head. "It's got a huge old rusted padlock on the door. The ceiling's caved in. It's been deserted forever. But it might be worth checking out, if we can find a way in." She flipped through the hypnosis book. "Check this out! Sylvie underlined parts, wrote notes in the margins."

She held out the book, and Piper saw that at the bottom of page 75, Sylvie had written in neat cursive: *"9/23/55: Attempted post-hypnotic suggestion with Rose. Success! Will continue to experiment."*

"What's post-hypnotic suggestion?" Margot asked.

"It's where you tell someone to do something when they're hypnotized, then they do it some time later, after they're not hypnotized anymore," Piper said. "I don't think they have any idea about it."

"That seems kind of mean," Margot said.

Amy closed up the trunk but held on to the book. "It might be mean," Amy said, "but it's also really cool, having that kind of control over someone. I mean, who knows what you might be able to get them to do."

"Remind me never to let you hypnotize me," Piper joked.

Amy smiled. "Oh, come on, you know you're dying to let me try," she said, looking right into Piper's eyes. "Who knows what I might get you to say or do? You'd be under my complete control."

"No way," Piper said, looking away, her face burning as she wondered what it might feel like, to give yourself over to another person so completely, whether you meant to or not.

Jason

Jason had been sitting by the window in Room 4, watching the house and tower, for hours now. He'd seen Piper and Margot leave the main house and head for home, walking around the pool and to the path in the woods. But Amy never came outside. He'd waited and waited, and now it was too late. He had to go. His watch said 6:05. His mom would kill him if he wasn't home for supper. And he had to pee. Tempting as it was, he couldn't use the toilet in Room 4—no way to flush it.

He opened the door, looked right and left, listened. Heard only the wind in the trees. A truck going by on the road.

He planned to run behind the building and circle around to the path through the woods. If he really booked, he'd be home in five minutes. But once his feet hit the driveway, that wasn't the way he went.

He sprinted back across the gravel to the tower, just to check.

"No way," he said aloud as he peered in at the wide-planked wooden floorboards, "no freaking way."

The pack of cigarettes and note were gone.

Which was impossible.

He'd been watching the tower.

No one had gone in or come out.

"What are you doing here?"

He spun, saw Amy coming down the driveway toward him.

"Nothing, I . . . I left you some cigarettes. Did you get them?"

"Cigarettes? No, I never saw any cigarettes."

"I put them in the tower earlier this afternoon."

She moved close, stuck her head in the tower. "Well, where are they?"

"Gone," he said. "I left them right there just a couple hours ago. If you didn't take them, who did?"

"I dunno. Someone must have come along and picked them up."

"But no one went in or out of the tower! I was watching!"

"Watching?" She looked from the open doorway to his face, which suddenly felt like it was on fire. "Stay out of the tower, Jay Jay," she snapped.

Jason nodded. Took a step back, away from Amy, toward home. "But I just wanted to give you the—"

"I don't want to catch you anywhere near this place. It's off limits. Piper nearly died falling through the floor in there today. It's not safe. Got it?"

"Whatever you say," he told her, and she smiled, tousled his hair.

For once, he'd done the right thing.

2013

Jason

Jason sipped his black coffee while Piper flitted around the kitchen. She whipped eggs and milk, dunked slices of crusty bread, then gently placed them in the cast-iron skillet, where they sizzled and spat in butter. A huge fruit salad sat on the counter in a cut-glass bowl he and Margot had gotten as a wedding gift and only used for special occasions.

Margot was in bed, resting, just the way she was supposed to be.

He was still a joke to Piper. He saw it in the way she watched him, waiting for him to screw up in some way, to let Margot down. There was something slightly amused—mocking, even—in the way she looked at him and spoke to him, as if he were still an awkward little boy.

Piper had lied to him about not knowing what "29 Rooms" meant. It meant something to her; to Margot as well. He could see it there, a flicker of recognition, perhaps a twitch of fear. He could understand Piper's not telling the truth, but Margot had never lied to him before. Maybe she'd break down and tell him. He wouldn't push her, though. He didn't want to risk upsetting her, raising her blood pressure.

Jason bit the inside of his cheek. He wished he could smoke a cigarette, but he never smoked in front of Margot (though sometimes she smelled it on him) and wouldn't dream of lighting up in the kitchen. He'd wait till he was in his truck.

He blamed the smoking on Amy. Hadn't his first cigarette ever been from a pack he'd stolen to give to her? And later, when they were in high school, the two of them smoked together all the time, even sharing cigarettes. There was something so intimate about it, almost more intimate than when they slept together.

They were never exactly going out. They didn't do the things other couples did: going to the movies, holding hands in the halls at school, hanging out at Dairy Cream on Friday nights and sharing a chili dog and a banana split.

"I don't believe people are meant to be monogamous," Amy told him once, after sex. It was when they were lying together in the dark, smoking, that Amy would share all her secrets and dreams. All the walls came down, and she would talk to him about anything and everything. "Do you?"

"I dunno." He shrugged, although inside he wished that she'd be his girl and wear his ring and do all that other sappy bullshit that other couples did.

It was Amy who encouraged him to ask Margot to the junior prom. This was after Amy had turned him down flat—no way would she be caught dead at any prom.

"You should ask Margot. She's been madly in love with you since she was in, like, third grade."

He shook his head. "Maybe you and I can meet up and have our own un-prom night."

"Jay Jay," she said chidingly, "I'm telling you: ask Margot. Sooner or later, you've gotta get a real girlfriend. You've got to do stuff like go to prom and take a girl out on an actual date. That's what normal people do."

"Maybe I don't want to be normal," he said.

She scowled at him. "Yes, you do."

And now here he was, normal, and the thing of it was, Amy had been right: being with Margot, having a house, a steady job, a baby on the way, all of that felt right and made him happy, like he had his own solid place in the world at last.

Sometimes the fierceness of his love for Margot caught him off guard, left him breathless. There had been a lot of moments like that lately, when he'd just look at her, imagine the baby, *his baby,* growing inside her, and think about how soon they'd get to meet their baby, and they'd all be a family. And his job was to protect them, keep them safe.

When he decided to join the London police, shortly after they got married, Margot hated the idea.

"Jesus Christ, Jason. What if you get yourself shot? I'd rather not be a widow in my twenties."

"In London?" He laughed. "Nothing bad ever

happens here. I don't think there's ever even been a murder."

He thought of this now, as he sipped his coffee. The crime scene was vivid in his mind: Amy laid out on the floor, all torn up, with a rifle at her side. They'd found a kitchen knife in Mark's hand. The theory was that they had fought, and he stabbed her to try to defend himself before she shot him in the chest. Then, they figured, she'd shot herself.

But something wasn't right.

Just last night, Tony Bell, the chief of police, told him that Amy's injuries were not from that knife.

"So it was another weapon?" Jason asked.

Tony shook his head. "Medical examiner says they've never seen anything like it. It looks more like claw marks. And the other two victims— the husband and the boy—had them as well, in addition to the gunshot wounds."

The clank of a plate startled him. Piper turned now, presenting him with a pile of French toast and fruit salad—the raspberries bleeding onto the cantaloupe, the green grapes like pale eyes staring up at him.

"Oh, no thanks," Jason said, gulping down the last of his coffee and standing. "Looks delicious, but I've gotta run."

He went into the bedroom. "I have to go into work early," he announced.

"Not again," Margot said, giving him a sympathetic smile from her spot on the bed as he leaned down to kiss her goodbye. "You look exhausted. You're working too hard," she said.

Suddenly he was desperate to tell her everything: That he wasn't going into work early. That he was driving to the Foxcroft Health and Rehab to see Amy's mother because, a week ago, Amy had called him and asked him to come out to the motel. That Amy had told him something crazy her mother had said, something he hadn't been able to stop thinking about since last night, when Tony said it looked like Amy was not stabbed but clawed.

But here came Piper, breakfast tray in hand; and there was his sweet, fragile wife, who would be crushed if she knew he'd gone to see Amy and kept it from her.

Why? she would ask. *Why would you go see her and not tell me?*

It was a question he'd asked himself over and over. A question he was afraid to let himself answer. The secrets he kept made him feel rotten, poisonous; they were a dark, growing thing, a cancer deep inside.

"Hey, didn't you go out with Amy back in high school?" McLellan had asked him the other morning, as the medical examiner's team carried Amy's body out of the motel in a bag.

Jason's whole body went rigid. "No," he said. "Not really."

"Are you sure? I remember you two being an item. You even took her out to Belmont Bridge once, I swear."

Jason felt his face heating up. He remembered parking the car (his mom's old Impala) at Belmont Bridge, where all the kids went to park, get a little stoned, have a few beers, and fool around. He remembered the radio playing low—probably a mixtape Amy had brought: Smashing Pumpkins, Throwing Muses, Nirvana, all those bands Jason pretended to like but didn't. He didn't care, though, because Amy's hand was on his thigh, her fingers moving up, spider-crawling the way they did, moving back and forth, teasing, pretending they might not go where he most wanted them to go.

Jason swallowed hard as he looked at the black body bag being loaded into the van. "We might have gone on a date or two. To the movies or something. But it wasn't anything big. I barely remember."

McLellan lit up a cigarette, his face bathed in the flashing blue lights from the police cruisers in the driveway. He said no more, deciding to let it go. As far as Jason knew, he hadn't mentioned it to anyone else working the case. And Jason decided it was best to keep to himself his little trip out to the motel to see Amy the week before, too. If he told them, there would be questions, and even if it was clear he'd done nothing wrong, it still wouldn't look good: Officer Jason Hawke, married man with a pregnant wife at home, sneaking off to see an ex-girlfriend. London was a small town, and people had long memories. Even though Amy had settled down, plenty of folks remembered her teenage Bad Girl years. Word would get around. Margot would find out. He didn't want any of that to happen.

Now, as he drove toward the nursing home, he went over that last visit with Amy for the hundredth time, trying to recall each detail.

She'd walked him into the kitchen, poured some coffee.

"You look good," she told him, and his face reddened. "Fit. Healthy. How's Margot?"

"Great," he said.

"And when's the baby due?"

"About three weeks."

Amy turned her coffee mug around, finger looped through the handle. Surely she didn't call him all the way out here to ask about Margot and the baby? Maybe he should follow her lead, ask about Mark and the kids. But he couldn't bring himself to.

"So you said you needed to talk?" he said.

"Yeah. Sorry. I don't really know how to start. I just didn't know who else to turn to. I feel like I need . . . I don't know . . . a sane, rational person's perspective. Someone who can be objective, no matter what."

Jason laughed. "So you called me?"

Amy smiled. "You've always been the most rational human being I know. You take everything in. Weigh evidence carefully. You don't let emotions get in the way of your thinking."

He shook his head. She was so wrong. That he was sitting here in her kitchen was proof. He knew he should leave—make some excuse and go. But he couldn't. The fact was, some small part of him had been waiting his whole life for this moment: for Amy to call him up, to say she needed him. Pathetic.

"You heard we had to put my mother in Foxcroft?" she asked.

"No. I'm sorry to hear it. What happened?"

He had never actually met Rose Slater, but he'd seen her plenty around town since she'd been back and Margot had filled him in a bit. When they were all growing up, Rose hadn't been around much; Amy never talked about her, but word was she had a drinking problem, maybe had been in a mental hospital. Then, after years of being God-knew-where, she'd made a reappearance just after Amy's daughter was born and had moved back into the house; she helped Amy and Mark with Lou, and in time with baby Levi. Margot said that Amy was thrilled to have her mom back in her life and that she was turning out to be a wonderful grandmother. There were murmurs about where Rose Slater had been all those years, how she could have gone and left her daughter to grow up alone with old Charlotte in that creepy motel. But soon, according to Margot, all the gossip turned positive: *Isn't Rose looking well? She must have been in some fancy rehab out west. Maybe she got religion. Did you hear she's running the elementary-school bake sale? And she's a troop leader for the Girl Scouts now! Just goes to show, anybody can turn it around.*

"Did she fall or something?" Jason asked. "My grandmother broke her hip and had to spend some time in the nursing home, but once she was well, she went back to her own place, and—"

"My mother didn't break her hip," Amy said abruptly. She stood up, went to the counter, and grabbed a pack of cigarettes. Once she had shaken one out, she held the pack out to him.

"Sure," he said, though he'd hardly smoked since high school—just the occasional pack when he was feeling stressed or working too many hours.

She sat back down, handed him a cigarette, lit it for him, and put the ashtray on the table between them.

"So what happened?" he asked.

"She suddenly went crazy," Amy said. "Some kind of dementia, the doctors think."

Jason drew smoke into his lungs, and let it out slowly. "But I thought things were good. I heard she was doing real well."

"She was! She was doing amazing. It was like . . . like I finally had a mom, you know? Like other people. But then, a couple of months ago, she started saying really weird stuff. Talking absolutely crazy."

"Like what?" Jason asked.

"Oh, like, she said that there are *monsters*." She laughed, but didn't seem amused. "Actual monsters, with teeth and claws and shit, and that we might have one here at the motel. She said if we didn't do something soon, something terrible would happen."

"Wow," Jason said. "Was she drinking?"

"I don't think so. I never saw her anyway, never smelled it on her. She was really freaking me out. Scaring the kids. Sometimes they'd wake up in the middle of the night and she'd be there in their rooms, standing next to the bed, watching them sleep. Mark asked her what in God's name she was doing, and she said she was protecting them. Standing guard. Keeping us all safe from the *monsters*." Amy did dramatic air-quotes with this last word.

"Sounds terrible. I'm so sorry," Jason said.

Amy nodded. "We took her to the doctor. They admitted her to the hospital, did all kinds of tests, but they didn't find anything physical, nothing they could do, blah, blah, blah, so they discharged her. Mark didn't want her to come back home— felt it wasn't safe to have her around the kids. So

142

we got her into the nursing home. They're taking good care of her."

"Probably for the best," Jason said.

Amy pulled another cigarette from the pack and lit it with the tip of her first smoke, which was still burning. Her hands were shaking.

"Here's the thing," she said. "The thing I haven't told anyone, not even Mark." She sighed mightily, clearly steeling herself for what she was about to say. "I'm starting to think maybe my mother *isn't* crazy. That maybe . . . maybe . . . she was right."

Jason stubbed out his own cigarette. "Right about what, exactly?" He kept his voice low and level, the way he was trained to do when talking to the emotionally disturbed. But surely she couldn't be serious? She wasn't about to tell him that monsters were real?

She reached across the table and took his hand. "There's no one else I can tell all this to, Jay Jay," she said quietly. Her eyes were brimming with tears. "Maybe I'm crazy, too, but I really don't think—"

"Mama?" a voice chirped from behind him.

Amy jerked her hand away, wiped at her eyes. "Lou? What are you doing home?"

Jason turned and saw a little girl in the doorway to the kitchen, shouldering a heavy-looking pink backpack. Jason guessed she was eight or nine. She was an exact replica of her mother in miniature, only brighter, more sparkling, dressed

143

143

in pink and purple glittering clothes and sneakers.

"We got out early 'cause of a teachers' meeting. I brought home a letter about it last week, *remember?*" She sounded vaguely irritated, like maybe Amy forgot such things all the time.

"I guess not," Amy said, sighing. "Sorry, love."

Lou regarded Jason. "Who's this?"

Amy stood up. "This is my friend Jason. But you can call him Jay Jay. Jay Jay, this is my daughter, Lou."

"I didn't know you had a friend who was a policeman," Lou said.

"And I didn't know your mother had such a pretty little girl," Jason said, smiling at Lou.

Lou looked at Jason. "I'm not little. I'm ten. That's double digits."

Jason nodded. "You're right. Ten is big."

"Are you a friend of my dad's, too?" she asked.

"Sure," he said. He looked at his watch. "I've gotta get back to the station. It was great to meet you, Lou. Thanks for the coffee, Amy. I can see myself out."

"Thanks for stopping by," Amy called. "We'll talk again soon. Give my love to Margot."

"I know who you are," Rose said, peering at him with dark eyes. "And I know why you've come."

Her silver hair was pulled back in a tight braid. Her skin was porcelain white and remarkably free of wrinkles—just the vaguest hint of crow's-feet.

144

She was sitting up in bed; across the room was a TV, tuned to a shopping channel. The room smelled like talcum powder and bleach, but underneath there was something else—musty and fetid.

Jason couldn't wait to get the hell out of the Foxcroft Health and Rehabilitation Center. He was thinking it was a mistake to have come at all. The nurse at the desk had told him that Rose had her good days and bad days, that she'd been confused and agitated. They'd caught her wandering the halls at night, not knowing where she was, so they'd put an alarm on her bed for her own safety. They'd also upped all her medications, in an attempt to keep her calm and comfortable.

"Why have I come, then?" he asked, sounding too much like an annoyed little boy. He was wasting his time. The woman was demented—even the nurse said so. Years of hard-core drinking and whatever else she'd been into had pickled her brain, interrupted the firing of synapses.

But didn't he owe it to Amy to check?

He kept replaying what Amy had said that afternoon: "I'm starting to think maybe my mother isn't crazy. That maybe . . . maybe . . . she was right."

Rose sat up in her metal hospital bed, drew in a breath, and let it out slowly. "You're here because you want to know what I know."

"Great," Jason said, spreading his hands, palms upturned. "So enlighten me. What is it you know?" Jason asked.

She looked him up and down. "I'd like to tell you, Jason. Really, I would. But I'm not sure you're ready to hear it."

Jason took a step back toward the doorway. The wild, mischievous look in the woman's eyes told him everything he needed to know. She was bonkers. Maybe Amy had been, too. Hereditary delusional thinking. Madness in the family.

"Nice seeing you again, Mrs. Slater." He tipped his hat in that way that older people seemed to like, and started to back out of the room.

"Miss," she said.

"What's that?"

"I never married. Amy's father, he was nothing. A no one. Not worth the time of day, much less a lifetime commitment. 'Slater' is my maiden name. It's *Miss* Slater."

"Yes, ma'am. I apologize."

"Do you know anything about my granddaughter, Jason? Where they've put her?"

"She's fine," Jason said. "She's safe."

"Safe!" Rose repeated incredulously.

"I just stopped in to say hello," Jason said. "Gotta get to work. You take care, now."

He turned his back to her, started to leave.

"Jason," she called when he got to the door and was about to make his escape back down the

hallway, past the nurses' station, out the front doors, and into the fresh air. God, he couldn't wait to breathe that air. He half-thought of pretending he didn't hear her. How easy it would be to just keep on walking, quickly, with purpose; he'd have to concentrate on not letting it turn into an I'm-getting-the-hell-out-of-here jog.

"Yes?" He turned, caving. His mother had raised him to respect his elders, to be polite, always: the sadder the shape someone was in, the more compassion they deserved. Besides, this wasn't just any senile old lady. This was Amy's mother. She deserved more than a brush-off, crazy as a loon or not.

"Aren't you going to ask me if I know what '29 Rooms' means?"

The photo with the message hadn't been released to the media. No one was supposed to know about it but the cops working the case.

He looked intently into her eyes, black like pools of ink. "Do you?"

She grinned. "Do you believe in monsters, Jason?"

"No, ma'am," he told her.

"Neither did my daughter," Rose said, cocking an eyebrow. "And look what happened to her."

1955

Mr. Alfred Hitchcock
Paramount Studios
Hollywood, California

September 9, 1955

Dear Mr. Hitchcock,
It's me again: Sylvia Slater from London, Vermont. I hope you've been getting my letters.

I don't think I've told you yet, but I can hypnotize people. I actually started with hypnotizing chickens (they're pretty easy) and now I practice on my sister Rose. She's more difficult, but I think I'm making progress.

My uncle Fenton gave me a book last Christmas, *Mastering the Art and Science of Hypnotism*, and I've studied it from cover to cover.

To be good a good hypnotist, you must project self-confidence. You must have a strong will and a belief that you will succeed. Self-doubt will bring failure. I think this is true not just with hypnosis, but with anything you try, even acting or making movies. Don't you agree?

My book says that once you've mastered the art of hypnosis, you can make a good-hearted man do something truly evil, or make a cruel person perform an act of kindness.

I have been testing this out with Rose, trying to make her a little more friendly with me, a little more agreeable in general. But the thing is, she has a stronger will than I thought. I will keep trying.

Sincerely yours,
Miss Sylvia A. Slater
The Tower Motel
328 Route 6
London, Vermont

Rose

Rose was excited to be out after dark, past bedtime on a Friday night. She and Sylvie were walking down Main Street in Barre with Uncle Fenton, who was doing his best James Dean impression, catching the eye of every teenage girl they passed. He had bought them both chocolate malted milk shakes in waxy paper cups.

It was raining. Rose and Sylvie shared an umbrella, while Fenton let the rain fall on him, small beads collecting on his freshly oiled hair and leather jacket. Main Street was crowded, thick with people of all sorts; they'd had to park the old Chevy pickup truck on the other side of town and walk in.

"What's happening?" Rose asked. "Is there a festival or something?"

"It's a surprise," Fenton reminded her. "It's something big. Something your sister's going to love."

What about me? Rose wondered. *Will I like it, too?* Her teeth had started to ache from the cold, sweet milk shake. Her toes felt pinched, because she'd worn her good Sunday shoes. As exciting as it all was, she was getting tired and cold.

Sylvie, on the other hand, danced through the crowd, face flushed with excitement.

"Hey," Fenton called to her, "you stick with your little sister, here. I don't want anyone to get lost. Your parents would never let me take you out again."

Reluctantly, Sylvie came back and took Rose's hand, squeezing it a little too tightly before pulling Rose along like an uncooperative dog. *Pest,* her grip seemed to say.

Fenton had asked Mama if he could take Sylvie into Barre. "It's a once-in-a-lifetime thing," he'd said. Mama agreed, but insisted they bring Rose along, too. Though Sylvie had protested, Mama was firm.

Now, up ahead, bright lights swept across Main Street and the sidewalk. All Rose could think of were the stories her father told of spotlights over Europe during the war, used to light up enemy aircraft.

"Are we at war?" Rose asked, suddenly frightened. Was that why everyone was out on the streets? Was there a squadron of German bombers on the way, ready to destroy Vermont? An atomic bomb could do that, Rose knew. Her daddy had told her about them, about what had happened when the United States bombed Japan, leaving a mushroom cloud where a city had been.

When a bomb like that hits, her daddy told her, there's nothing left; people just turn to vapor. It sounded like something out of one of Fenton's science-fiction books, not anything that could happen in real life. She tried to imagine it: a whole human being, flesh and blood and bones, turned to vapor, a puff of greasy smoke, something you could take into your lungs and hold there.

Without warning, Sylvie grabbed her sister's jacket, jerking her back.

"What's happening?" Rose asked, angry and frightened. She'd been pulled off balance, had nearly fallen on the wet sidewalk. The worst part was, Fenton hadn't noticed and was now far ahead, lost in the thick crowd in front of the Paramount Theater.

Sylvie tugged Rose back out of the street, into a small, dark alley between two brick buildings. Was she right? Were they at war, and here was brave Sylvie, saving her young sister from disaster? Rose started to duck down, to cover her head with her arms, but Sylvie pulled her up.

"Look," Sylvie said, turning Rose's head so that she was facing across the street.

"What?" Rose asked.

"Don't you see him?" Sylvie asked.

Rose stared a minute, scanning the crowd through the drizzling rain. On the other side, amid the jostling strangers, stood a familiar figure: their father in his long black coat, hat cocked on his head.

Friday night was his bowling night, and he'd left the house before they did, carrying his black bowling bag. But now here he was on Main Street in Barre, and Rose saw he wasn't alone. There was a woman with him, holding his arm, leaning in to say something to him. She had red hair and wore a green coat with matching hat. Whatever she said made their father shake his head, then smile.

"Who is that?" Rose asked.

"Daddy."

"Well, I know that!" Rose snapped. "But who is he with?"

Sylvie didn't answer.

The woman their father was with leaned in and kissed him on the cheek.

Rose blinked, and blinked again, more slowly, watching them go in, then out of focus as her eyelids closed.

Now it was almost as if a bomb really did go off. The pavement seemed to shift, and there was a dull roaring in her ears. She dropped the paper cup, and the top flew off, what was left of her milk shake flying everywhere, covering Rose's good shoes and tights.

"Come on," Sylvie said, tugging Rose back into the throngs of people, heading for the theater. "Before he sees us." Sylvie pulled Rose along.

"There you are!" Fenton called, pushing through people to get to the girls. "Good grief, I thought I'd lost you. I was about to start panicking. Where were you?"

"Sorry, Uncle Fenton, we got caught up in the crowd," Sylvie said.

"Well, you're just in time. Look—they've arrived."

"Who?" Rose gasped, wondering for a split second if he could possibly mean Daddy and the red-haired woman.

A platform had been set up in front of the Paramount Theater, and spotlights illuminated the sidewalk and street. A string of shiny new cars with a police escort had pulled up out front.

"What's happening? Who's here?" Sylvie asked, perched on tiptoes.

Rose struggled to see over the heads of the people in front of her, and Fenton, seeing her distress, lifted her up and put her on his shoulders, though she was really much too big for such things. But she didn't mind. From up there, she had a perfect view.

From the lead car stepped a large, jowly man, with close-cropped gray hair, wearing a black suit. He stopped and waved at the crowd. A woman from the car joined him: she was young and beautiful in a dark-blue dress with a deeply scooped neckline. A mink stole was draped over her shoulders.

"Oh! It can't be! It can't be, but it is!" Sylvie exclaimed.

"Who is it?" Rose asked.

"It's Alfred Hitchcock," Fenton said. "One of the most famous movie directors in the world. And see that actress with him?" Fenton said.

"She's the star of his new picture. Her name's Shirley MacLaine. Beautiful, isn't she?"

Shirley MacLaine waved graciously to the crowd, smiling, her pearl earrings glistening in the spotlights.

"They're from Hollywood," Sylvie gasped as the director and actress were ushered through the crowds toward the platform. Sylvie pushed in closer to the street, as if being magnetically pulled toward the cars.

"The movie's called *The Trouble with Harry*," Fenton explained. "They're having the world premiere tonight, here, because it was filmed up in Craftsbury. A little taste of Hollywood right here in Vermont. You remember this, Rose. This here is something you're going to be telling your grandchildren about—the day Alfred Hitchcock came to Barre for a movie premiere."

Sylvie had made her way through the crowd to the base of the podium, where a man was introducing Alfred Hitchcock and Shirley MacLaine.

Rose watched in fascination as Sylvie stood—eyes wide, face strangely blank, slack-jawed—staring up at the director and movie star, as if, for just this once, she was the one hypnotized.

Mr. Alfred Hitchcock
Paramount Studios
Hollywood, California

September 30, 1955

Dear Mr. Hitchcock,
Tonight, my uncle Fenton brought me
and my sister Rose to Barre, and we
stood in the crowd along Main Street
and watched you and Miss MacLaine
go into the Paramount Theater.

It was the most exciting thing that's
ever happened to me in my whole
entire life. I stood next to the
platform. You and Miss MacLaine
were close enough to touch.

My daddy always says that there
are moments in our lives, moments
that change everything.

I never understood what he meant
until tonight.

When I saw you and Miss MacLaine
earlier, I knew, I just knew, that one
day, whatever it takes, I would come
to Hollywood and be in the movies.

The idea hit me so suddenly and so
hard that I actually couldn't breathe

for a minute. There I was, standing along Main Street, with my uncle and little sister behind me, and I couldn't get any air. I saw everything in a whole new way. Like I'd been living this upside-down life, and suddenly things were right-side-up and the whole world in front of me made sense.

Rose was talking to me, but she sounded far off, like a bug. Little and buzzing and insignificant. Even Fenton, marvelous as he is, seemed to fade away.

I tried to talk to you, to shout up and say that I was the girl who'd been writing you the letters, but there were so many people, and it was noisy. I was sure I would be crushed. You looked at me, though. I'm sure of it. And for that one second I wondered if you knew I was the girl who'd written you from the little motel in Vermont.

Fenton has promised to take me to see *The Trouble with Harry* if Mama and Daddy will allow it. I've seen quite a lot of movies, but none of yours. Not yet. But from now on, I'll find a way to see them all, even if I have to sneak into the theater through the back door (something Fenton told me some of the boys do when they don't have money to go to a show).

I wanted you to know all this. And I wanted to thank you. Because, even though we didn't really meet, seeing you, just standing outside the Paramount tonight, has given my life new direction.

I hope that one day, when I am in Hollywood, I can meet you to thank you in person.

Sincerely yours,
Miss Sylvia A. Slater
The Tower Motel
328 Route 6
London, Vermont

Rose

"You awake, Sylvie?" Rose asked.

They were both in their twin beds. The radio, a new Zenith Daddy had given Rose last Christmas, played on the bureau between them, Bill Haley and the Comets rocking around the clock. Sylvie loved to fall asleep listening to the radio. She said sometimes the music followed her right into her dreams.

"Mmm-hmm."

"What do you think it means—Daddy and that lady?"

Sylvie was a quiet a minute; the radio announcer came on, telling the weather. Frost warning. Chance of showers tomorrow.

"I'm not sure," Sylvie said at last. "But I know one thing—he didn't mean for us to see them together."

"But who is she?"

"I've never seen her before," Sylvie said.

"I feel like I have," Rose said, thinking. There was something familiar about her—the red hair, the coat she was wearing. Had she been a motel guest? A friend of Mama's from town? "We should ask Daddy about her."

"No!" Sylvie said, exasperated. "We should pretend it never happened. Pretend we didn't see

162

anything. Most of all, we shouldn't say a word about it to Mama."

"But . . ."

"No 'but's. Do I have to hypnotize you to make you forget? Because I will."

Rose cringed, ducked beneath her covers. "No. I won't say anything. I'll forget all about it."

The thing is, Rose thought as she lay there in the dark, listening to Frank Sinatra now, the more you concentrated on trying to forget something, the more you couldn't get it out of your head.

"Fairy tales can come true," Frank promised, his voice soft and velvety, like the inside of a fancy jewelry box.

"Try not to worry," Sylvie said, her voice gentle again. "Really. It'll all be okay." She sounded like she was trying to convince herself as much as Rose.

Rose fell asleep and dreamed she was walking in a cornfield. At first, Oma was with her, holding her hand. Then she was alone again. She kept walking, going down row after row, trying to find her way out. Sylvie was there, too. Rose could hear her, but couldn't see her.

"Sylvie?" she called.

She heard a rustling up ahead and moved forward, through the leaves of corn that scratched at her skin and cut into her face. The corn seemed alive, angry, and Rose didn't want to be there anymore.

A crow was perched on an ear near the top of a stalk of corn just ahead of her, its black reptilian toes clinging, claws digging into the green husk. Rose froze. There was something familiar about the crow. It looked right at her, and she was sure she knew it somehow.

Then the crow cocked its head and winked one glistening, black eye.

"You're getting very sleepy," the crow said, only it was Sylvie's voice inside the crow's caw. "You couldn't open your eyes now even if you tried."

I can speak the language of crows, Rose thought, excited.

"Poor Rose," the Sylvie crow cawed. "Always looking for ways to be special. But you're just an ordinary girl. A plain, ordinary girl. No talents at all."

When Rose opened her eyes, she instantly remembered where she had seen the red-haired woman, the one who had kissed Daddy's cheek. She'd been here once, at the house. Rose remembered coming home from school one day in the spring when Sylvie had to stay late for band practice. The woman was coming out of the house with Daddy.

"This is your mama's friend Vivienne," Daddy told her, and Rose got the sense that he was mad at her for being there—that they were in a hurry and Rose was holding them up.

"Pleased to meet you," Rose said, and the woman smiled and took Rose's hand. She wore a lovely hat with bits of lace worked in, and a green sweater set that matched it perfectly. Her cheeks were powdered, and her eyes were rimmed with smudged, coal-black liner. She was beautiful. Almost as beautiful as Mama.

"I hear you're quite a talented girl," Vivienne said.

"No, ma'am," Rose answered. "You're thinking of my sister, Sylvie. I don't have any talents."

"We've all got talents, dear," the woman said, smiling. "Some are more hidden than others. The trick, you see, is finding them."

"Yes, ma'am," Rose said.

Daddy seemed flustered. He whispered something to Vivienne, then took her arm and guided her down the steps.

"Nice meeting you," Rose called after her.

"I'm sure we'll see each other again," Vivienne said. "Maybe then you can tell me what talents you've discovered."

Rose went inside, calling for her mother. But her mother wasn't home. There was a note on the table saying she'd gone to the market and would be back soon. "Help yourself to a slice of pie," it said.

"I met your friend," Rose said when Mama came through the door half an hour later, balancing two paper sacks of groceries from the A&P.

"Who?"

"Vivienne. When I came home, she was just leaving with Daddy."

"Ah," Mama said, eyes narrowing. "Vivienne." Then she turned and starting putting the groceries away, shutting the cupboard doors a little too hard.

"Sylvie?" Rose called out in the darkness. "Are you awake?"

Her sister did not answer. The radio was still on, but the station had gone off the air, leaving nothing but static, humming like an insect in the middle of the room.

Rose crept past it to Sylvie's bed, planning to shake her sister awake.

"Wake up," she said. "I remember! I remember where I know the lady from."

But her sister's bed was empty; Rose's hands grasped only the covers, still warm.

"Sylvie?" she called again, though it was clear she was alone in the room.

Rose padded out of the bedroom and down the hall to the bathroom. She pushed gently on the door, but when it swung open, she saw the bathroom was empty, the sink and toilet so bright white they almost glowed. Toothbrushes stood like little soldiers at attention in their holder. The sink faucet was dripping, each drop of water hitting the white porcelain bowl with an impossibly loud splash. Rose backed out of the bathroom

166

and went down the stairs and into the kitchen, to see if maybe Sylvie was getting a drink of water or milk. She eased her way down the carpeted steps, her hand on the smooth wooden rail.

When she got to the kitchen, there was still no sign of Sylvie.

Rose stood on the cold tile; moonlight streamed through the curtained windows, making the white squares on the linoleum floor glow. Her cold bare feet looked like dark paws against the white floor. The dinner dishes were neatly stacked in the wire drainer, and Mama's rubber gloves hung limply over the faucet. Behind the lemony scent of Mama's cleaning products, she caught the spicy, tangy scent of the chili they'd had for supper. "Chili con carne," Mama called it, which made it sound fancy, like something you'd order in a French restaurant, but really it was just ground chuck with canned tomatoes and beans.

Rose went to peer out the window that looked out on the driveway and the glowing *Tower Motel* sign. *Vacancy,* it promised. And there, down near the tower, a figure moved in the shadows, its blond hair gleaming in the moonlight as a white nightgown fluttered around its feet.

Sylvie.

And she was heading into the tower.

Rose hurried outside and carefully made her way across the driveway. The cold, damp gravel stabbed her bare feet, and the night air chilled her skin, giving her goose bumps beneath her flannel nightgown. She looked back at the house, checking the windows to see if a light had appeared in her parents' bedroom. But no one stirred. She could smell wood smoke, apples, rotting leaves—all the wonderful fall smells that she found so comforting during the day. At night, they smelled like something spoiled.

Rose reached the tower, which loomed like a giant in the moonlight. She was shivering now, her teeth chattering, and she could see her breath. She knew she should run back up to the house, crawl under her warm blankets, and forget the whole thing. But first she needed to see what on earth her sister was up to.

Maybe Sylvie was sleepwalking. She'd seen that in a movie once. You weren't supposed to wake up someone who was sleepwalking. Rose remembered hearing that somewhere. But how were you supposed to get them back to bed?

"Sylvie?" she called out as quietly as she could, peering through the doorway of the tower. It reminded her of a gaping mouth.

She listened. Silence.

"Sylvie?" she tried again. "What are you doing?" The inside of the tower was blacker than black. Anything could be inside. Anything at all. Teeth. A tongue. Ready to swallow her up. Crunch her bones. Turn her to vapor.

She stepped through the doorway, heart

pounding. It was foolish to be afraid. She'd been in the tower hundreds, maybe thousands of times. She knew the shape of each stone, the grain of the boards on the floor. But she'd never been there alone late at night, in the dark. The walls felt closer. She could smell the damp stone. She felt completely engulfed by the darkness, as if she really had been taken into the mouth of a giant.

But she wasn't alone, was she? Sylvie was inside somewhere.

"I know you're in here!" she called out, a little louder now. "I saw you!"

Footsteps creaked above her.

"Sylvie? Come down!" she called. "It's freezing out here."

And I'm scared. Scared of being eaten up.

She shuffled in the darkness, hands groping blindly before her, and found the ladder, which she began to climb, hands damp with sweat, mouth dry.

"Sylvie!" she hissed.

A soft rustle sounded from somewhere up above, but when she poked her head up and got a good look at the second floor, she found it empty. Moonlight streamed through the two windows, illuminating the rough-hewn floorboards.

This was silly. It was after midnight. What was she doing in here, playing hide-and-seek with her big sister? If Mama or Daddy caught them, they'd be grounded for a month, maybe worse.

Reluctantly, she began to ascend the second ladder, up to the top floor. When she emerged onto the roof, her nightgown glowed and drifted in the wind. Around her, the walls of the tower were a perfect circle of stone and mortar.

But, impossibly, she found herself alone.

Or almost alone.

There, against the far side, on one of the stone battlements, a large moth flexed its wings.

Rose moved closer.

It was a luna moth—a good four inches across, wings of the palest green with long tails and delicate, feathery antennas.

Rose knew it was far too cold out for a luna moth to appear—they usually made their appearance in early summer. She blinked, sure she was seeing things, but the moth remained.

Rose reached for it, and it took off, launching itself from the edge of the wall, flying drunkenly away from the tower, a fluttering ghost of a thing: there, and then gone.

An impossible thought came to Rose as she watched the moth disappear into the cold, dark night:

That luna moth was Sylvie.

Rose

"I saw you outside last night," Mama said, face stern.

Rose was doing her Saturday-morning chores—feeding Lucy and the chickens. She wore high rubber boots and last year's winter coat; it was too short at the sleeves now, but still warm.

"Me?" Rose finished filling Lucy's trough with grain and made sure she had enough water.

Taking care of Lucy was her favorite chore and had been her responsibility since she could remember. Though the cow had been born the same day as Sylvie, making them twins of a sort, it was Rose who truly loved Lucy best of all. When she looked into Lucy's large eyes, she believed the cow knew things, things that could never be spoken.

Rose loved all the animals. Once, when she was very little, they'd had a shaggy black farm dog named Ranger. Every night, he slept down in the kitchen, next to the stove. Some mornings, little Rose would wake up beside him, snuggled against his warm black fur.

"What are you doing out of your bed?" Mama would scold, and Rose would say that old Ranger must have come to pick her up and carry her down to sleep with him so he wouldn't be lonely.

"Rose thinks she's a puppy," Sylvie said. And Rose rather liked this, and went around barking instead of speaking until Daddy threatened to give her a good spanking.

"Please don't lie to me, Rose," Mama said now, coming into the pen. If she was up here, then that meant Sylvie or Daddy must be watching the office, dealing with checkouts. "It was after midnight. What reason could you possibly have to be wandering around outside after midnight?"

Rose gave the old Holstein a pat, right on her Vermont-shaped spot. "I was looking for Sylvie."

"Sweetheart," Mama said, lifting Rose's chin so that she would look up into her mother's eyes, "I asked you not to lie."

"I'm not lying!" Rose insisted—why was it she was always the bad girl, the liar, the one who got caught? "I woke up and she was gone. I came downstairs to look for her and saw her outside, going into the tower."

Mama gave her a disbelieving look.

"I went out and followed Sylvie into the tower," Rose explained. "And then she . . . disappeared."

But she hadn't just disappeared, had she? She'd climbed to the top of the tower and turned into a moth.

"People can't just *disappear*," Mama said.

"Well, Sylvie did."

But not really. She just . . . *changed*. Rose had

been thinking hard about it all night, puzzling over it, and again and again she came back to one startling conclusion: her sister was a mare! Just like in the stories Oma told her. Maybe Oma had even known; maybe that's why she told Rose so much about mares, to prepare her for the day she would realize that her own sister was one.

Rose wished, more than anything, that she could talk to Oma about all of this.

"Perhaps you only imagined you saw her," Mama suggested. "I'm sure she was right there in her bed the whole time."

Rose didn't answer. Arguing was useless.

The front door of the house banged open, and Sylvie emerged, wearing a bright-red cardigan and carrying a letter. When they got back from Barre last night, Sylvie had sat down at the type-writer and pecked away at the keys. Rose asked her what she was writing, but Sylvie wouldn't say. She claimed that Rose was being a pest and had better go to bed or else she'd go tell Mama.

"Are you going to tell Daddy I snuck out?" Rose asked.

"No, not this time. But if I catch you outside again, I will. Your father has enough to worry about these days; he doesn't need to hear about you sneaking around like an old alley cat."

Rose felt her muscles tighten. "What's Daddy worried about?"

She thought of the woman with the green coat.

Vivienne. He didn't look worried when he was with her.

Earlier this morning, when she first came downstairs, she'd heard Mama and Daddy arguing. She'd come in just as Mama said, "I'm not an idiot, Clarence." Then both her parents had seen her, and her father, flustered, said, "Don't you have chores to do, Rose?"

Now Mama looked at Rose a minute, considering whether or not to answer. She looked around to make sure Daddy wasn't close by. "He's worried about the highway they're planning to build. What it might do to business. He went to a meeting with men from town the other day; they believe that, once the interstate is complete, people won't have much reason to take Route 6 anymore."

"That won't happen," Rose said. "People won't forget us. Right here at the motel we've got things no one on the highway has. We've got the tower, the chicken circus, Lucy the cow." Rose gave Lucy a pat on her lucky spot. "People will still come."

Rose stopped talking when she saw that Sylvie had reached the mailbox. She opened it, slid her letter inside, and pulled up the red flag to let the postman know they had a pickup. Who had Sylvie written to? It made Rose feel twitchy all over, not knowing.

Mama smiled at Rose. "I hope so, Rose, I really do."

Rose slipped out of Lucy's pen, and Mama followed, latching the gate behind them, as Sylvie came up the driveway with a contented smile.

"So we have an understanding, then," Mama said. "No more wandering around outside after bedtime?"

Rose nodded, her eyes on Sylvie, who was going into the house.

"Promise me," Mama said, lifting Rose's chin again.

"I promise," Rose said.

Mama nodded. "Good girl. Now, finish up your chores, and then come in and have breakfast."

"Yes, Mama."

Rose waited until her mother was back in the house, busy in the kitchen. Looking through the windows, she didn't see anyone watching; she imagined they were all around the table, spooning out oatmeal, sprinkling cinnamon, brown sugar, and raisins on top.

Rose turned and ran down the driveway to the mailbox. She opened it, pulled out the letter. It was addressed to Alfred Hitchcock in Hollywood, California.

Without thinking any more about it, Rose slipped the letter into her coat pocket. Then she ran back up the driveway to join her family for breakfast.

Mr. Alfred Hitchcock
Paramount Studios
Hollywood, California

October 8, 1955

Dear Mr. Hitchcock,
My uncle Fenton took me to see *The Trouble with Harry* at the Paramount in Barre—the same place I saw you just over a week ago. We found the place where you signed the wall. I actually let myself touch your signature—what a thrill! I just loved the movie! Miss MacLaine was absolutely brilliant. I understand it was her first movie role. I'm wondering how you came to cast her? How does someone get a part in one of your movies if they're not already a star?

I have enclosed a picture of my sister Rose and I performing in our World Famous London Chicken Circus. It's something we do for the motel guests. We've trained the chickens to do all kinds of tricks, and at the end, I hypnotize them. It's really quite a show. Rose and I were in the newspaper for the circus last summer—a man came and interviewed us and took our picture.

If you are ever in Vermont again, I would love for you to come to the motel and see the circus.

I'm the older girl in the picture, with blond hair. Rose doesn't care for cameras, so she's making a face.

Rose is just as strange as usual. Well, maybe more so. Lately she's always watching me, spying. She hides in the closet, under my bed. She thinks I don't see her, and I pretend not to, just to see how long she can stay hidden, which actually turns out to be a rather long time. She even watches me when I sleep! Sometimes I wake up in the middle of the night, and there's Rose, standing over me with a flashlight, shining it down onto my face. Mama says not to pay Rose any mind, that she's just jealous. She's got a funny way of being jealous, if you ask me.

Well, that's all I can think of for now. I hope you are busy making your next picture—I can't wait to see it! If you ever have time, I'd love to get a letter back. Or an autographed picture even. That would make me feel like the luckiest girl in all of Vermont!

Sincerely yours,
Miss Sylvia A. Slater
The Tower Motel
328 Route 6
London, Vermont

2013

Piper

Piper stared at Amy's daughter, unable to shake the sense that she'd traveled back in time and was sitting with Amy again. The girl was a dead ringer for her mother; paler, certainly, and looking shell-shocked, but it felt eerily as if Amy had been cloned.

The girl was staying in a run-down trailer with her aunt Crystal—Mark's sister. Crystal had set them up at a kitchen table with a scratched-up Formica top, with warm cans of Coke and a plate of saltine crackers and squares of plastic-looking orange American cheese.

"My name is Louisa, but no one calls me that— only teachers on the first day of school, and the lady who works at the doctor's office."

"What do people call you, then?" Piper asked.

"Everybody calls me Lou. Just Lou."

She looked like a kid who never saw sunlight, a sickly kid; even her freckles were faded. Her eyes were a murky blue; her hair was fine blond wisps. There were shadowy blue-black circles under her eyes. Her lips were chapped.

The trailer was a dump, and Piper hated seeing any kid forced to stay here. The kitchen floor was sticky with God-knew-what; there were piles of dishes in the sink; the curtains, once white, were yellowed from the cigarette smoke that permeated every surface. Being in the trailer was like crawling into a giant ashtray.

Amy's sister-in-law, Crystal, had led Piper right inside. Crystal was tall and thin with frizzy brown hair that she kept pulled back in a dirty Scrunchie. Her nails were painted a green that reminded Piper of baby puke, and the polish was chipped and peeling. She had a canker sore in the corner of her mouth. "Can you keep an eye on her for an hour or so?" she'd asked. "I've gotta go to the store."

"Um, sure. Why not?" Piper had said casually, thinking, *Who leaves a traumatized child alone with the first person who walks through the door?*

Crystal lived in the trailer with her boyfriend, Ray. Ray was a bartender at a place in Barre where they had topless dancers (Piper had learned this from Margot). He was at work when Piper got there, but she saw evidence of him: a pair of large black motorcycle boots, a chipped coffee mug that said RAY on the kitchen counter, a photo of Crystal and a heavyset man with greasy black hair on the fridge.

Piper watched as Lou sipped at her can of Coke. She started to explain that she was an old friend of Lou's mother's, and that they had played together back when they were girls only a little older than she. That had made Lou smile, the idea that her own mother had been young once—as young as her, even.

"We used to roller-skate at the bottom of that old pool at the motel," Piper told her.

The girl suddenly smiled. "I've skated there, too!" she said. "I got bit by a spider down there once."

"Ouch," Piper said.

Lou nodded. "They live in the drain. It was a bad bite; it turned into this big old open sore that took forever to heal, and Mama wouldn't let me go in the pool anymore."

Piper gave a little shiver.

"I have to skate in the driveway now, but it's all pebbles. Sometimes Mama takes me to the bike path and then we—" She cut herself off. Her face looked so serious, and Piper felt all the breath leave her as she again realized how like Amy this girl was—the pouting lips, blue eyes with extra-long lashes, a smattering of freckles across her nose and cheeks.

Without thinking, Piper reached out a hand to stroke her straggly hair. She longed to brush it, to put little bows in it—something bright and cheerful. She thought of how Amy used to dye her bangs bright colors with Jell-O.

The girl flinched, and Piper pulled her hand away.

"I bet that was nice, riding on the bike path," Piper said.

Lou's eyes got stormy (again, just like Amy's) before she took a deep breath and closed them. "Aunt Crystal, she says it's okay to still love Mama, no matter what she's done. She says we've got to remember the good things about Mama."

Piper nodded.

"I got a friend who collects butterflies," Lou said suddenly. "Kendra. She's not very nice. Sometimes she rips the wings right off while they're still alive."

"That doesn't sound very nice at all," Piper agreed.

Lou nodded. "Sometimes she's mean to me, too."

"What does she do?"

Lou squeezed her Coke can, denting the sides. "Calls me stupid because I'm not so good with math and spelling. I get bad grades on quizzes and stuff. Mama always says there are different kinds of smart."

Piper nodded. "She's absolutely right."

The girl smiled at Piper, but then the smile faded. She started to pick at the skin around her thumbnail.

"Why did you come to see me?" Lou asked.

"Because I wanted to meet you."

Lou nodded and gave the Coke can another hard squeeze. "Do you want me to tell it like it happened?"

"What's that, love?"

"Every grown-up who's come says"—Lou puffed up her chest and put on a deep, authoritative voice—*"In your own words, tell us what happened."*

It reminded Piper of something Amy would have done.

"You don't have to tell me anything," Piper said, heart thudding. This was why she was here—wasn't it?—but suddenly she didn't want the girl to tell her what happened. She just wanted to sit here, sipping Cokes, and ask her more about school, about her friends. She wanted to find some little way to make Lou's life better, a tiny bit normal, not be just another adult ready to drag her through the horror of what had happened that night.

Lou shrugged. "I don't mind, I guess. The more I tell it, the more it becomes like a story. A real bad story that happened to some other girl."

Piper wanted to take her away from here, out of this shitty trailer, out of the town of London, where she'd never be allowed to forget the tragedy. She wanted to put Lou on a plane and bring her back to L.A., back to her tidy home. She could turn the office into a nice bedroom, with a canopy bed covered in stuffed animals. She could give Lou a good life. She could keep her safe.

Piper had never longed for a child. Her life seemed full without one. She had a successful business, lots of friends, the occasional (though rarely serious) romance. Yet this girl was awakening some deep, primal mothering instinct inside her.

"Only if you want to," Piper said.

"It was late," Lou began. "After midnight. I heard Mama downstairs in the kitchen, banging around. She did that when she was drinking sometimes . . . fell into things, opened and closed the cupboards real hard."

"Did your mom drink a lot?" Piper asked, swallowing hard. She hated the thought of Amy's becoming a drunk. Amy seemed bigger than that somehow, above addiction. But alcoholism, she knew, ran in families.

Lou squinted. "Sometimes. Daddy, he quit years ago, but Mama, she always kept a big bottle of white wine in the back of the fridge. So I heard her banging around in the kitchen first, then in the hall closet. That's when she must have been getting the gun. Daddy kept it there the way Mama kept wine in the fridge—just in case."

Sweat began to form on Piper's forehead and the backs of her hands. She loosened the scarf she was wearing, undid the buttons on her sweater. There was a rank odor in the room that seemed to be getting stronger. Something moldering: damp earth, fungus.

"She started up the stairs. She was saying a rhyme:

" 'When Death comes knocking on your door
you'll think you've seen his face before.
When he comes creeping up your stairs,
you'll know him from your dark nightmares.
If you hold up a mirror, you shall see
that he is you and you are he.' "

Piper shivered. She remembered Grandma
Charlotte reciting that same little rhyme to them
years ago, not long before everything changed.

Lou's singsong voice sent chills through Piper.
She wanted to beg her to stop, not to go any
further. Lou closed her eyes tight, and began to
rock slowly as she spoke.

"First, she went into her bedroom, where Daddy
was sleeping. She crept right in, quiet as a mouse.
But he must have woke up, because they started
arguing."

"Could you hear what they were saying?" Piper
asked.

"No, but there was a lot of noise, yelling and
stuff breaking, and Mama screaming. Then:
bang!"

Piper jolted.

"All I could think was that I had to hide. I
jumped out of bed and stuffed the pillows under
the quilt so she'd think I was in there, sleeping. I
saw that once. In a movie."

Piper nodded. "Then what did you do?"

"I opened the window that leads to the roof.

Levi and I used to do it all the time. We'd go out there sometimes to watch the stars."

Piper nodded. She remembered going out that same window when she slept over at Amy's—how they'd sit out on the roof and puff at cigarettes Amy had stolen from her grandma, take sips of the salty cooking sherry they'd found down in the kitchen. Amy would pretend she could name all the constellations, but Piper knew she was making it up. Amy's sky held nightmarish images: a toad swallowing a little girl, the queen of the spiders, a hand wielding an ax.

"Mama came back down the hall. I stood right by the window, listening. I heard Mama go into Levi's room."

" 'Mama?' Levi called. 'What are you doing?'

" 'Saving you.'

" 'From what?'

" 'Nightmares.'

"Bang! Bang! Bang!"

Piper leaned back, as if the shots had been fired into her own chest.

"Then she came for me. I saw the light when she opened the door. I was right beside the window, crouched down low. She walked up to my bed, and without pulling back the covers, she fired the gun again. Then she went back out into the hall, and there was one more shot. It was quiet after that."

Lou's eyes looked as glassy as a doll's.

"I stayed out on the roof even after everything got quiet. I didn't want to see inside."

Lou was silent for a moment, perhaps imagining what she might have seen if she'd gone inside. Piper struggled to keep herself from picturing it.

When she spoke again, her voice was shaking. "Finally, Jay Jay came out and found me, and he carried me back inside. My face was pressed against his chest. He told me to keep my eyes closed, not to open them until he told me to."

"Jay Jay?" Piper asked. She'd forgotten that Amy used to call Jason that. But how did Lou know?

"Mama's friend. He's a police officer. He came to the house to visit Mama last week. He must have said something that made her sad, 'cause when I walked in that afternoon, she was crying. Jay Jay was holding her hand."

Piper let out a little gasp, then faked a cough to try to cover it up.

"But that night," Lou continued, "when he carried me through the house and told me not to open my eyes, he was the one crying. And I knew that whatever had happened was real, real bad, to make a police officer cry."

Piper thought of a hundred things she could say, maybe should say—words of comfort or empathy, reassurance—but everything seemed grossly, insultingly inadequate. The refrigerator hummed. The clock on the stove ticked. Soda bubbled and ticked in their cans. A radio played off in another room, the music so faint Piper wondered if she might be imagining it. She thought of the little transistor radio Amy used to carry around tuned to the top-forty station.

"One time," Lou said suddenly, "Mama took me to the city and I saw a little stone man with wings carved into the top of a building."

"A gargoyle?" Piper asked.

"Yeah," she said, smiling. "That's what I imagined I was up there on that roof, holding still, trying not to breathe. A gargoyle."

Crystal returned from the store an hour later with a carton of cigarettes and an enormous bottle of generic diet soda. She soon made it clear that Piper's babysitting services were no longer needed. As Piper drove back to Margot's house, she replayed Lou's simple, terrible story over and over in her head, sorting through all the details one by one.

What had Jason been doing at Amy's last week? Surely, if Margot had known about this visit, she would have mentioned it to Piper. Which meant he'd kept it a secret, but why? Each possibility she let herself imagine was worse than the last.

But something else felt wrong about Lou's story, too.

The realization was gradual, the way night falls in the summer—the light fading slowly, so slowly it's barely perceptible—and then you see fire-flies, stars. There all the time, but only now visible.

Jason had clearly said that Lou had blood on her feet when he found her on the roof. If she'd crept out the window when she heard the first shot, stayed there perched like a statue while the nightmare inside went on, where did the blood come from?

1989

Piper

The condos where Piper and Margot lived with their mother were only a short walk from the motel, on the back side of the hill. Sometimes, when Piper walked down the path that led to the field that surrounded Amy's swimming pool, she thought of Narnia. Of how going to the motel was almost like stepping through the wardrobe and into another world. Amy and her grandmother were about as exciting and exotic and other-worldly as you could get. Especially now that they'd found Sylvie's suitcase and had a real live mystery to try to solve.

Piper knocked on Amy's front door now, with Margot beside her. Her shin stung and throbbed from yesterday. When she'd pulled back the gauze this morning, it was red and puffy. Piper had smeared on some bacitracin and covered it in Band-Aids. She'd managed to hide the injury from her mom, quickly throwing on a pair of sweatpants before her mom got home from work. If Mom saw it, she'd freak and might forbid Piper and Margot to go to the motel. She already didn't really approve of Amy and her family and worried that the old motel might be dangerous. Piper didn't need to give her proof.

"I really don't like you girls spending all your

time over there," Mom had told them. "There are other kids your age around, you know. What about that boy who lives in C Building? He seems nice. Maybe you should spend some time with him."

"Jason Hawke?" Piper snorted. "Mom, please. He's a dweeb."

"He is not," Margot argued. "He's got this cool telescope, and star maps that glow in the dark."

Piper rolled her eyes dramatically. "I rest my case. Total dweeb."

Piper knocked on Amy's front door again, louder this time. Grandma Charlotte had a hard time hearing. And if Amy had the music on upstairs, she wouldn't hear, either.

"Are we going to start searching all the rooms today? Or that old trailer?" Margot chirped.

"Don't know," Piper said. "We'll see what Amy's got planned."

"I've got all kinds of awesome stuff *planned,* but it would help if you two would get your butts over here a little earlier!"

Amy had sneaked up behind them. She was rocking back on her heels, practically dancing. She had on a Joan Jett T-shirt and the same ripped cut-offs she'd worn yesterday.

"I've been waiting for you for *hours!*" she said.

"Sorry," Piper said. "Mom went into work late, and she wanted to do this family-breakfast thing, and then we had to call our dad."

Last year, their dad moved to Texas with his new wife, Trish. Piper and Margot only saw him for one week in the summer and one week in the winter. Piper didn't mind. She really hated Trish, who had been the family's dental hygienist. It made her want to gag, thinking about how this woman had once had her gloved hands inside her mouth; had scraped and polished and forced floss between Piper's teeth. She'd had Piper chew the red tablets that showed, like bloodstains, the places she'd missed when she brushed.

"Yeah, yeah, whatever," Amy said. She had very little patience for anything that wasn't directly connected to her. "Come on, let's go to my room. I want to show you something."

Amy slipped between Piper and Margot and yanked open the front door.

"Who's there?" Amy's grandma called out from the kitchen.

"Just me, Grandma."

"Oh, Sylvie! You startled me."

"It's *Amy,* Gram," Amy called back. "Still just Amy."

The staircase was opposite the front door. Amy started up the wide, carpeted steps, the other girls right behind her. She took a right at the top of the stairs and went to her bedroom, at the end of the hall. "Come on, come on—wait till you see what I found! You guys are gonna flip!"

Amy's room had belonged to her mother and

Sylvie once upon a time, and still held some relics from those days—the twin bed and dark headboard with hazy old shellac, two banged-up wooden dressers her mom and Sylvie had used, and a matching bedside table. But there were differences: the boom box dominating the bedside table; the posters of Guns N' Roses and Annie Lennox; the vivid purple that Amy had painted the walls and ceiling. There were plastic beaded curtains hanging in the window, and when the sun hit them, prisms of color shot out and danced around the room.

Piper loved being in Amy's room. It was like being let into a magician's secret chamber—you never knew what you'd find, what Amy might do next.

"Look at this," Amy said. She was over at her desk. Piper saw that the old typewriter from the attic was sitting on top of it, a piece of paper fed into the machine. She moved closer and saw the words Amy had been typing:

Sylvie, Sylvia Slater, Miss Sylvia Slater, Where did you go, Miss Sylvia Slater?????

The hypnosis book was there, too, on a pad of paper, with a bookmark stuck inside. Amy had started reading it and taking notes.

Amy was waving an envelope around. "So,

when I took the typewriter out of its box, I found this stuffed at the bottom."

Piper read the address on the envelope out loud: "Mr. Alfred Hitchcock, Universal Studios, Hollywood, California." There was a four-cent postage stamp on the upper right corner. She saw that the return address was Sylvia Slater, Tower Motel, London, Vermont. "Wait, like Alfred Hitchcock the movie director?"

"Who's Alfred Hitchcock?" Margot asked.

"He made all these freaky old movies, like *The Birds* and *Psycho*," Amy said. "You've seen that one, right, Piper? That crazy shower scene?" She mimed stabbing the air with an invisible knife, making high-pitched sound effects with each thrust: *"Eee-eee-eee!"*

Piper shook her head. "Uh-uh." She wasn't allowed to see anything scary, anything that was rated R.

"Oh my God! We totally have to rent the video! I can't believe you haven't seen it! You know the best part? It's at a motel! Just like this one. It's even a motel no one ever comes to because of the highway—he could have taken the idea from right here."

Piper shrugged. "Sure, sounds cool. But what does the letter say?"

Amy pulled it out of the envelope with a flourish, handed it over. It was neatly typed on Tower Motel stationery.

October 3, 1961

Dear Mr. Hitchcock,
I have a new twist on my old movie idea for you. There is a motel. It has 28 rooms. Every-thing seems normal and nice and almost perfect there. But that's not the way it really is. Because this motel has a 29th room. A place where the darkest secrets you can imagine are kept.

Here is my plan: I am going to discover all the secrets of the 29th room, then I will come to Hollywood and tell them to you in person. I think that if you hear my story, you will agree it would make a wonderful, dark, twisted movie. The kind of movie only you can make.

I will be in touch soon, I promise.

Sincerely yours,
Sylvia Slater

"Bizarre," Piper said. "What's she even talking about?"

"It's obvious, isn't it? She's saying this motel has a secret room somewhere, a twenty-ninth

200

room, and she went looking for it. And check out when this letter was written: October 3, 1961. It's the day before she disappeared! I checked with my grandma this morning—Sylvie was gone on the morning of October 4."

"But how could there be a whole other room in the motel that you don't know about?" Margot said.

"Maybe it's not a real room," Piper guessed. "Maybe it's like a . . . a—whaddaya call it?—a metaphor or something. Or maybe she just made it up to get his attention?"

Amy shook her head. Her face was flushed and feverish-looking. "No. I think it's a real place, a secret room somewhere in this motel. And if we really want to find out what happened to Sylvie, we've gotta find it."

"So where are we supposed to start?" Piper asked.

"I think we have to look through that suitcase again. Maybe there's a clue in there. Then I think we need to search the motel, room by room."

"And that old trailer, too!" Margot said, caught up in the excitement.

"Every inch of this property," Amy agreed, nodding. "Come on, let's start with the suitcase."

Jason

Jason was hiding out in Room 4, watching and waiting to catch Amy alone. He had a second pack of cigarettes, taken from his brother's stash. He knew it was risky—surely Brian would notice that the carton was down by two. But his older brother was busy with his summer job at Joe's Pizza, and whenever he wasn't working the oven, he was out with his girlfriend, spending what little money he made. Jason counted on Brian's being too distracted to count his smokes.

Jason was bored. Tired of waiting. He peeled the cellophane off the pack, opened it up, and took one out. Holding it between his index and middle finger, he stuck the filter between his lips. He'd never smoked before, never even thought about it, but Amy smoked. Or at least she said she did.

He went to the nightstand to get the ancient pack of Tower Motel matches and chipped glass ashtray, stopping to admire himself in the mirror. In his brother's black Pink Floyd T-shirt, with a cigarette between his lips, he looked like a boy Amy might talk to. He messed up his hair a little, trying to give himself a disheveled, rock-star kind of look.

He carried the ashtray and matches over and sat back down by the window so he could keep watch for Amy. He struck one match. The head crumbled. Match two sputtered a bit, then died. Three, four, and five fell apart. He pulled a match from the back row and struck it, watched with surprise as it snapped to life. Just as he brought the lit match up to the end of the cigarette and began puffing, he caught movement out the window, through a crack in the blinds.

Someone was in the tower. Coughing, eyes watering, he stubbed the cigarette out in the ashtray, keeping his gaze on the old stone building.

A shadowy form moved up toward the open doorway, then shuffled back and was lost in the darkness. He'd seen a pale face, a long blue shirt—or a dress, maybe.

He jumped up, threw open the door of Room 4, and sprinted across the driveway toward the tower. He stopped when he got to the doorway and looked around. Empty.

He stepped inside, smelled dust and cement.

Then he heard it: a sound from up above, a scuttling sound, like a giant crab moving sideways across the floor, claws scraping wood.

"Amy?" he called in a croaking whisper. "That you?"

With his heart feeling like it was creeping up into his throat, he went to the ladder and climbed. When his head got to the top, there was nothing. Only an empty room. And a hole in the wooden floor. Not surprising—the boards all looked half rotten. And hadn't Amy said something about Piper's falling through?

"Amy?" he called again, voice hopeful but small, lost in the dark gloom of the room. Filtered sunlight came through the narrow slit windows. In real castles, he knew, windows like this were used to shoot arrows through in battle.

Very carefully, he pulled himself up and walked to the next ladder, testing each footstep, his eyes glued to the place where the floorboards had collapsed.

At the second ladder, he climbed again, rising to the top floor. There was nothing there, either. Only the wide-open sky up above, clouds so low they cast shadows over the tower and motel. A blue jay scolded him from a nearby tree.

He tried to tell himself that he'd been seeing things. That he'd imagined the figure in the doorway.

But, try as he might to convince himself, he knew it wasn't true. There *had* been someone there, and now they were gone. Impossible, but true. People, real flesh-and-blood people, couldn't just disappear.

So maybe it was a ghost, a little voice told him.

But Jason had never believed in ghosts. And he wasn't about to start now.

Piper

Piper, Amy, and Margot arrived at the tower just in time to catch Jason scuttling out.

"What are *you* doing here?" Amy barked.

Jason's hair was all messed up, and he was wearing a T-shirt that was about ten sizes too big. He looked like a scarecrow. More than that, he looked just plain scared—eyes wide and frantic, face pale and sweaty.

"Nothing, I was—"

"You were trespassing! That's what you were doing. There are laws against that, you know."

"There was . . . someone," Jason said lamely.

"Where?" Amy demanded.

"In the tower. I saw someone go into the tower. Someone wearing blue."

Amy pushed past him and shouted, "Anybody here?"

Her voice echoed, sounded far off. Of course there was no reply.

"No one here now, Jay Jay."

"Well, there was. I saw someone," he said, but his voice faltered a little.

Piper thought he was probably lying—trying to come up with a good excuse to be in here. Probably he'd just been lurking around, spying,

205

trying to catch Amy and Piper kissing again. Her face burned.

Margot, on the other hand, believed him. She peered at the ground around the tower. "Maybe they left a clue—footprints or something?"

Amy rolled her eyes and jabbed a finger at Jason. "Didn't I warn you about hanging around in here?"

"Uh, yeah."

"Soooo?" Amy drawled, hands on her hips, eyebrows raised.

"So what?" Jason asked.

"So get out of here. Go home. Now!"

He took off like a frightened rabbit, zigzagging his way up the driveway and past the pool, into the field behind it.

Margot bit her lip. "Don't you think that was kinda mean?"

"Mean?" Amy said, eyes dramatically wide as her voice got louder, angrier. "You have to be freaking kidding me!"

Margot shrugged. She was never afraid of Amy's moods, and because of this, she never knew when to back down, when just to let things be.

"I think he's lonely. I feel bad for him. Don't you, Piper?" She looked at her big sister, her eyes saying, *Back me up here.*

Piper was silent. She honestly didn't give a crap how lonely Jason Hawke was.

"Look," Amy said, clearly straining to be patient, "we've got something big happening here. Something secret. All of this—finding the suitcase, the letter, the search for the twenty-ninth room—we can't tell anyone about it, not until we know more. And we can't have some stupid kid nosing around, spying on us. He could wreck everything!"

You're the one who kissed him, Piper thought, but when Margot protested that she didn't see how Jason would wreck things, Piper turned on her sister.

"Don't be an idiot, Margot. What if he'd found the suitcase? What if he told people about it?" she asked.

Margot shook her head, her face set with its most stubborn look. "He wouldn't. He doesn't care about any of that."

"Oh, so now you're an expert on what Jason Hawke *cares* about?" Piper said, her voice dripping with disgust.

Margot looked down at her worn flip-flops. Each had a ragged plastic flower fastened to the strap between her toes. She said nothing.

"Come on," Amy said, tugging on Piper's arm, "let's go check out that suitcase again."

Piper followed Amy into the tower; Margot came behind them, dragging her feet, looking over her shoulder toward the hillside where Jason had disappeared.

1961

Mr. Alfred Hitchcock
Universal Studios
Hollywood, California

September 12, 1961

Dear Mr. Hitchcock,
Sometimes I worry that I might be going mad. Do you ever feel that way? I believe you have. That maybe it's part of having a creative soul.

Oh, the things I dream about and long for—impossible, maddening things.

The world looks at me and sees a happy girl. A girl bubbling with hope and optimism. So sweet. So innocent. Oh, the things they don't know! Could never guess at!

It's all an act; I am the greatest actress of all!

In this house of long faces and quiet arguments, I am the only bright spot. And I shine. Oh, how I shine and glimmer. Sometimes I catch them all looking at me with dazed half-smiles. A beautiful creature. That's what they see. Someone who can do no wrong. Only Rose suspects the truth. And so I do all I can to avoid her, to never look my sister in the eye.

It's not that difficult, really. She makes it easy. She's become such an odd girl. Always in trouble for one thing or another, no friends of her own, preferring the company of that sad old cow to any human.

Mama says Rose is jealous of me, but I don't think that's the case. I think she genuinely loathes me. But, then again, maybe I'm not so special —Rose seems to loathe everything and everyone. No one blames me for avoiding her.

The highway has come through, as promised, and ruined everything. It's just like what happened to the Bates Motel in your last picture, *Psycho*, only this is real life. My uncle Fenton took me to see that picture three times. It was your most brilliant (not to mention shocking!) yet. I liked it even better than *Vertigo*, which had been my absolute favorite film of yours. Fenton managed to talk the man at the theater into giving him the *Psycho* poster after the engagement was over, and I put it up on my wall, above my bed. Daddy made me take it down, though. He didn't want to have to see Janet Leigh in her underclothes every time he came into our bedroom. Fenton's got it up in his trailer now.

Sometimes I wonder if my letters might have inspired part of your story about the Bates Motel. Did they?

Just like the Bates Motel, no one comes to the Tower Motel anymore. The town of London, my family, the motel—they're all mere ghosts of what they used to be.

I hope you don't mind that I keep sending you letters. I understand you are very busy, and cannot write back, but I do wish I had some way of knowing that you were at least reading my girlish ramblings.

I need to know someone is listening.

Sincerely yours,
Miss Sylvia A. Slater
The Tower Motel
328 Route 6
London, Vermont

Rose

Rose sat in the living room, scowling at the balloons and streamers hanging above her head. Uncle Fenton had painted a banner that said *Happy 18th Birthday Sylvie* and hung it on the wall behind the couch. Fenton and Daddy had moved the coffee table, television, and chairs into the dining room, and Mama had set up snacks on the buffet table: meatballs and cocktail frank-furters on toothpicks, deviled eggs, a cheese ball encrusted with pecans. There were bottles of Coca-Cola in a bucket of ice.

Sylvie wore a sleeveless pale-green dress with a matching headband that she'd sewn herself from the same shimmering fabric. She had on the emerald earrings Mama had given her at Christmas, passed down from Oma. Mama had only two pieces of jewelry of her mother's: the emerald earrings and a pearl necklace sent over from England after Oma's death. Mama had never worn either of them—"not really my style," she would always say with a wry smile, but Rose knew she was saving the jewelry, that it was too special to wear for cleaning motel rooms and mending other people's clothes. That the jewels were to be part of the girls' heritage. Once Sylvie got the earrings, Rose knew the pearls would be hers. Maybe when she turned sixteen, or perhaps even before.

Mama had let Sylvie borrow her red lipstick, and she looked all grown up, hardly recognizable as the young girl who'd once run the chicken circus. Sylvie had invited three of her friends: Marnie, Kate, and Dot. The other girls oohed and aahed over Sylvie's dress and how beautiful and sophisticated she looked. They took dainty bites of the snacks as they chatted about work (Sylvie and Dot both worked at Woolworth's) and a big football game the London Raiders were playing that weekend. Marnie, who was a year younger and still in high school, was going steady with the quarterback. Sylvie didn't have a boyfriend, didn't seem to have any interest in one. When Davy Palmer invited her to the dance last weekend at the Elks Club, she'd told him she had other plans, then just stayed home. Since graduating that summer, Sylvie had helped out at the motel (on the rare occasions when there were guests), worked part-time at Woolworth's, and done some typing for a friend of Daddy's who ran an insurance agency. Every Saturday, she'd go out to the movies with Fenton and Rose. Other than that, she hung around the house, reading magazines and listening to records.

Chubby Checker was on the stereo, and Sylvie begged her guests to do the twist. Daddy and Fenton stood together, smoking, and talking quietly. Mama hovered over the food, flitting back and forth with fresh plates from the kitchen.

Things between her and Daddy had been funny lately. Funny in a bad way that made Rose's stomach hurt when she thought too much about it. Rose could hear them fighting sometimes. About money, about the motel, about lots of things. Sometimes Daddy would stomp off and be gone all night. He'd show up the next morning in his rumpled clothes, and Mama would serve him breakfast, pour coffee into his cup, as if everything were perfectly normal.

Rose stood up and went to stand against the wall, a bottle of Coca-Cola growing warm in her hands. She'd turned fourteen back in May, and though she was younger, she was taller than her sister and outweighed her by a good thirty pounds. She'd chosen an old dress for the party, not one of her best, but one she liked well enough, because the red plaid made her think of Daddy's hunting jacket. And she felt like a hunter. Watching and waiting. Rose had been doing this for years now, desperate to catch her sister in the act. In the act of *what*—of transforming into some sort of beast or insect, as mares will do? Did Rose really believe that? Even now, at fourteen?

Yes.

She would never admit it to a living soul, because surely they would think she was mad. No one would believe that beautiful, perfect Sylvie, with her glowing smile and movie-star looks, the girl who had graduated at the top of her class, could be a monster. And, of course, monsters weren't real, were they? Only in the movies, and then they were blobs or giant insects or were-wolves or aliens from outer space. Fenton took Rose and Sylvie to the movies every Saturday, and she'd seen them all. And yet she'd seen nothing that explained what her sister might be.

All she had to rely on was her memories of the stories Oma had told.

"A mare, once transformed, will still have some of its human traits and memories," Oma explained. "They can recognize people they know, places they've been. But even if they wouldn't hurt a fly in human form, once they've changed, they become very dangerous indeed."

Rose imagined her sister, waking up in the night in some other form—not a beautiful luna moth, but something far more dangerous, something that showed her true nature—a monstrous moth creature with compound orbs that sparkled with hints of Sylvie's own bright-blue eyes, great leathery wings, and a sharp proboscis meant for tearing into flesh and sipping blood.

Sylvie still disappeared from their room at least once a week—lately, more. But Rose was never able to catch her in the act. Rose was the only one who got caught, time after time, while Sylvie always managed to find her way back to bed. Rose knew that if she wanted to expose Sylvie she'd have to be trickier. She'd have to think like a hunter.

"Come on, Rose, dance with us," Sylvie called out. She and her friends were still doing the twist to that Chubby Checker song, and even Mama and Daddy and Fenton had joined in. Mama danced stiffly, but Daddy smiled at her the whole time as they twisted, arms swinging, hips gyrating, feet pivoting on the hardwood floor.

"Yeah, you should see my little sis," sang Chubby Checker, and then, as if on cue (wasn't everything Sylvie did carefully choreographed to look perfect somehow?), Sylvie danced over and took Rose's hand. Everyone was watching, waiting to see. Would the awkward, ugly sister who couldn't dance join the radiant one? Or would she shake her head, pout, and refuse to budge, like a grotesque plaid ladybug? That was what people expected.

I'll surprise them all, Rose thought, smiling widely, setting her soda down, and moving out into the middle of the room with her sister. Rose didn't follow Sylvie's movements the way everyone else did (or tried to); instead, she invented her own, faster and more frantic, a version that involved flinging her hair back and forth and swinging her whole body. It felt good to move like this. Like she didn't give a damn. Like she

218

was the girl who was full of surprises. Everything was a blur of light and color: the balloons Scotch-taped to the ceiling, the pink and white streamers, even the three girls who were tittering as they danced in a loose circle with Uncle Fenton. Her parents seemed to move in slow motion, their eyes on her for once; and Sylvie, who was fluttering in her green dress, looked less like a girl and more like the luna moth Rose had found once out in the tower.

"Rose, dear," Mama said, stepping forward and placing her hand on Rose's arm, "I'm afraid you're going to hurt yourself."

And the room erupted with laughter. Rose stopped dancing; when she pushed the hair away from her eyes, she saw that everyone was watching her and laughing.

Damn them all to hell and back again, she thought.

"That was some dancing, sis," Sylvie said, laughing, covering her mouth with her hand.

And damn you most of all, Rose thought, backing away, to her corner and her warm bottle of soda.

Sylvie went over to choose another record— Elvis this time, "Stuck on You." She asked Fenton if he'd dance with her, and the two of them moved into the center of the room, both glancing Rose's way. Sylvie said something to him, and he doubled over laughing; when he stood back up, his face and ears were bright red. He collapsed on the couch, still chuckling, watching Sylvie and her friends dance.

Rose went to the window and looked down the driveway at the motel sign. They hardly ever had guests nowadays. Not since the highway came through last year, ruining everything. The truck drivers took the interstate now, as did the families on vacation, the tourists coming in droves. They'd even lost many of their regulars: Bill Novak, who'd come from Maine with a truck full of lobsters and fish; Joseph the shoe salesman; the families who had come each summer, eager to see the circus and look at the tower again.

It wasn't that Daddy didn't try. He sent out more flyers, paid for advertisements in every newspaper and magazine he could find. He even tried to put a motel sign along the highway, at the London exit, but the highway department tore it down. No matter what he did, the cars buzzed by.

Rose was no idiot. She knew that they were going broke. That they'd long ago eaten through whatever meager savings they'd had. Mama had taken on seamstress work, and Sylvie was always looking for more hours at Woolworth's and the insurance agency.

Fenton now worked at a garage in town, repairing cars and driving the tow truck. And Daddy dreamed up new schemes, new ways to bring people back. But nothing he tried worked.

No one came to see the chicken circus, the Tower of London, or Lucy the state cow. And Lucy wasn't doing well—she'd been losing weight, sleeping all the time. This morning, Rose couldn't even coax her to eat her breakfast.

Earlier today, Mama had been at work on the latest edition of *The London Town Crier*. It would be a thin issue, and the big news was the closing of Libby's Market; people would now have to drive all the way into Barre to buy groceries. Mama tried to balance the bad news with one of her best recipes—this one for lemon-chiffon pie, which promised to be as light as a cloud.

The dancing was over now, and they all milled around the snacks.

"Presents," ordered Daddy, thrusting a small, rectangular wrapped gift into Sylvie's hand. Sylvie removed the bow and tugged gently at the shiny blue paper. It was a pen-and-pencil set in its own velvet-lined case.

"For writing down all your fancy thoughts," Daddy said.

"Oh, Daddy, it's perfect," Sylvie exclaimed, throwing her arms around Daddy's neck and kissing his cheek.

"This one's from me," Fenton said, pulling a large, flat package from behind the couch. Sylvie tore at the paper. It was a framed poster for *North by Northwest*—Cary Grant, an intense, determined look on his handsome face, running from the biplane bearing down on him from behind.

"Oh, Fenton," Sylvie said. "Thank you!"

He smiled sheepishly. "My buddy at the Paramount saved it for me."

"Mine next," said Mama, and she came forward and handed Sylvie a much smaller box.

Rose had a sick feeling in her stomach as Sylvie opened the gift, all eyes fixed on her.

"Oh, Mother!" Sylvie gasped as she pulled out a string of pearls—Oma's pearls.

Rose felt a scream building inside her, but her throat was too tight to let it escape. Her face burned; her whole body surged with furious heat.

It couldn't be! Sylvie had the earrings. The pearls were Rose's. But now Sylvie had both.

"It isn't fair," Rose choked out.

"What's that, Rosie?" Daddy asked.

"That necklace was meant to be mine," she said. "Oma would have wanted me to have it. Sylvie didn't even like her."

She loved me best.

The room was silent, everyone looking her way. Sylvie's three friends looked uncomfortable, Fenton chewed his lip, and Mama was staring at Rose as if she were a stray dog soiling her living room. Sylvie looked down at the pearls. And Rose was sure that, just for an instant, she could see through her sister's disguise: there, holding the pearls, stood a terrible insect with bulging round eyes, shimmering green wings, and mouth parts that clicked as they rubbed together.

"I hate you," Rose spat at her sister. "I see what you are, even if no one else does!"

She stormed out of the room and back toward the kitchen, choking back sobs. There, in the center of the kitchen table, was the three-layer devil's-food cake with white icing that Mama had made. *Happy 18th Sylvie* was written across it in careful cursive.

Rose heaved out a sob. The music came back on in the living room. The Marcels singing "Blue Moon."

> . . . you saw me standing alone
> Without a dream in my heart

It was no good and Rose knew it. No one was ever going to see Sylvie for what she really was. Not until Rose showed them. It was all up to her.

And she knew just what to do.

"There's only one way to catch a mare," Oma had said. Now she was glad that she'd paid such careful attention as a little girl.

Rose raised her arm and drove her fist into the cake so hard that she heard the plate beneath it crack. Then she lifted her fingers to her mouth, coated with cake and icing. She licked off her hand as she moved to the kitchen door and outside, her teeth aching from the sweetness.

Mr. Alfred Hitchcock
Universal Studios
Hollywood, California

September 16, 1961

Dear Mr. Hitchcock,
I am eighteen today.
   And I am a wicked, wicked girl.

Yours, as always,
Miss Sylvia A. Slater
The Tower Motel
328 Route 6
London, Vermont

Rose

Later that night, Rose found herself back down in the living room, watching Sylvie dance; her sister was doing the twist, pivoting like a screw that couldn't decide which way to turn, the top half of her body going one way, the bottom the other. Then, as Rose watched, Sylvie's head turned completely around, so that the back of it faced forward. She reached up and parted her hair to show that her skull had split, forming a second mouth. A grotesque mouth with red lipstick.

"Come dance with me," the new mouth said, the hair around it writhing like tentacles. Around Sylvie's neck—twisted like horrid, flesh-colored licorice—was the pearl necklace.

Sylvie took a step toward her, the mouth smiling now, laughing even, the red lips stretched back. It looked obscene, like a lady's private parts.

Rose screamed. She screamed and screamed, but could not move as Sylvie moved closer, her hair dancing like snakes around Rose's face. Sylvie put a hand over Rose's mouth and nose, covering them so tightly, so completely, that Rose could not get any air.

She woke up gasping for breath, again overwhelmed by that now familiar feeling of being paralyzed. She struggled to move, to bring her body back to life. When she was finally able to lift her head and sit up, she found that she was alone in the room and it was morning. The clock said nearly eight. She'd slept in. She took a few gulps of air, tried to still her panic.

A dream. Only a dream.

Downstairs, she heard voices: her father, mother, and Sylvie sitting down to breakfast.

Sylvie's bed, across the room, was neatly made.

Rose got up and began to make her own: pulling back the covers, smoothing the sheet, and folding the top edge over neatly. As she straightened her pillow, she discovered two short, thick strands of black fur stuck to the cheerful yellow pillowcase. Rose frowned at them curiously for a moment; they hadn't had a cat or dog since old Ranger had died. She brushed them off, then picked up the pillow. That's when she found them: Oma's emerald earrings, left there like a secret gift just waiting to be found.

Rose's mind raced, all thoughts of the strange black hairs driven away.

Sylvie must have done it. Sylvie must have realized how unfair it was that she got both the necklace and the earrings. Maybe Mama had spoken to her, told her to do what was best: "Give your poor sister one of them. It's only fair."

Or maybe she'd done it on her own, to show she was bigger than all of this pettiness, to be the hero in some new shiny, Sylvie way.

Rose imagined it now. She'd go downstairs in the earrings, and her mother and father would be so proud of Sylvie for being so kind, thoughtful, and generous. They'd be so focused on Sylvie that they wouldn't notice how the cut green stones brought out the flecks of green in Rose's hazel eyes, how they made her beautiful. And surely, Rose thought as she carefully carried the teardrop-shaped earrings over to her dressing table with the mirror, surely they would make her beautiful. She clipped them onto her earlobes, tucked back her tangled hair, and admired the way they caught the light. Exquisite. That's what they were. The loveliest thing she'd ever owned.

She took her time brushing out her hair and put it in a careful braid. She chose a maroon dress, one of her best, with lace at the sleeves. It was a dress Sylvie had helped her pick out, saying it was perfect for her milky complexion and dark hair.

When they saw her come down the stairs, they'd forget all about that other girl—the one who'd ruined the cake and said she'd hated her sister ("The cruelest possible words one could utter at a birthday party," Mama had said last night). Maybe they'd even forget that they'd grounded Rose, given her all of Sylvie's chores in addition to her own for the next month. They'd see that this new Rose was clearly some other girl, a nicer girl, a beautiful girl who would never do anything so naughty. As if the old Rose had been under a spell she'd woken from. And all it took was the magic earrings to do it.

Rose finished making her bed, checked herself one more time in the mirror (now who's the movie star?), and headed down the hall to the stairs, beckoned by the scent of bacon and coffee, the familiar clank and clatter of breakfast being served, her family's voices.

She entered the kitchen as elegantly as she knew how, back straight, head held high, feet light on the linoleum floor. When Sylvie looked up at her, she dropped her fork.

"My earrings! I couldn't find them after the party, but I was sure they'd turn up. You've had them the whole time, haven't you?"

Rose took a step back. There was some mistake. There had to be.

"You . . . you left them for me."

The room felt smaller. Rose took a gulp of air—suddenly she understood. Sylvie had left the earrings for Rose, not as a gift, but to make it look as if Rose had stolen them. And Rose had walked right into the trap, like a fool. The certainty of it hit her hard in the solar plexus, forcing out what little air was in there.

Sylvie stood up and stepped toward Rose, shaking her head. "If you'd wanted to borrow them, you could have asked. You didn't need to steal them."

"But I . . . I found them, under my pillow." Rose

took a step back, nearly tripping over the leg of a kitchen chair.

"Rose," Mama said, voice stern, "take off the earrings. Now."

Rose did as she was told, fingers shaking. She saw how foolish they looked—the dainty, glimmering green stones in her hand with dirt under the nails and deep in the creases of her skin. It was all wrong. As she handed them over to Sylvie, she looked up at her sister's face, half expecting her to turn her head completely around, to start speaking from an ugly gash of a mouth on the back of her head. But Sylvie only smiled sweetly, a look of pity in her eyes.

Rose felt dizzy. Sick to her stomach. She needed to sit down, but couldn't make her legs move in the direction of a chair.

"You need to leave your sister's things alone," Daddy said flatly, still clutching the newspaper, not even looking up from the stories of the day. The Russians were testing more nuclear bombs, but President Kennedy had tests of his own going on. Only a matter of time until the whole world blew up. Sometimes, like now, Rose found herself wishing for it, willing the bombs to start falling from the sky, beautiful and strange.

He stood up and snapped the paper closed. "Coming to help me with the books, Sylvie?"

"Yes, Daddy," she said, clearing both her plate and his. "I'll be right there." Then she turned to

Rose again. "Honestly, Rose, the next time you want to borrow something, just ask."

Mama smiled at her older daughter—so kind, so forgiving. But it was all an act, and Rose knew it. Rose gave her sister the most sinister look she could muster—a look that said, *You're not fooling me.*

After Sylvie followed Daddy out of the kitchen, Mama started collecting dishes and putting them in the sink. She picked up Rose's plate, too, even though she hadn't eaten.

"Mama, I'm telling you: Sylvie gave me those earrings. She left them for me this morning under my pillow."

She's the monster. Not me.

Mama turned and stared at Rose wordlessly for a moment. The look on her face made Rose's blood run cold. It was an expression that said, *I don't know you at all; you are a stranger to me.*

"You must stop these lies, Rose," Mama said at last. "And if you ever, ever steal anything from your sister again, there will be very serious consequences."

Rose

The next night, Rose woke up with a start. She glanced over to Sylvie's bed and saw that her sister was gone. Rose threw off the sheets and got out of bed, holding her breath, listening. Where was her sister—her wretched, cruel sister, who'd planted the earrings to make her look like a thief? What could she be up to next?

Rose felt it then: the thrum of certain danger. Something bad was going to happen. She just knew it. The air felt the way it did just before a thunderstorm: all charged up, heavy, and waiting.

Rose went to the window, pulled back the lace curtains, and peered down at the yard, bathed in silver moonlight. Pebbles on the driveway glinted like jewels, and down at the office, moths flocked to the light out front, hovering, banging uselessly into it. The motel sign was all lit up, but Route 6 was empty this time of night.

Tower Motel, 28 Rooms, Pool, Vacancy.

Rose didn't understand why Daddy even bothered with the sign: it was a waste of electricity. The only cars passing through were local.

Rose could hear the distant rumble of trucks passing by on the interstate. It was like a living thing, the highway. Always awake, always buzzing with traffic.

And then, there, by the tower, a shadow. Sylvie, slipping through the doorway of the tower in her nightgown.

Pulling on a robe, Rose crept out of the room and down the hall, only pausing as she passed her parents' room. She could wake them, tell them, "Sylvie's out of bed again. She's down at the tower right this minute." But they'd never believe her; Rose knew that. They wouldn't even get out of bed to check her story. And even if they did check, if they did catch Sylvie sneaking around outside, that would be a disaster of a different sort. She could only imagine what lengths Sylvie might go to, to try to pay her back.

But maybe, she told herself, if she followed Sylvie, caught her in the act, she'd have evidence, proof. And then Rose might, for once in her life, have the upper hand.

She moved on, past her parents' room, down the carpeted stairs, and crept out the front door. The night was strangely warm for so late in September. The air was sticky, and moist like breath. They hadn't had a hard frost yet; summer was still hanging on. Crickets chirped. Cicadas buzzed. In the driveway, a praying mantis rested, spiked arms bent in a way that looked like prayer, but that was really an efficient pose for snaring prey.

Sylvie told her once that the female praying mantis always cuts off the head of her mate. "A cannibal of the worst sort," Sylvie explained.

She'd said it during dinner, and Mama had flashed both girls a warning look.

Rose continued down the driveway, the pebbles rough and warm beneath her bare feet. The lights in all the motel units were off, with no cars parked out front.

"Clarence, you need to face facts," she'd heard her mother say to her father just last week. "We need to close down."

"Not yet," he said. "There's still a chance things may pick up. We've got foliage season coming. No one wants to look at the leaves while speeding through on the interstate."

Rose heard something (a small, strangled cry?) coming from the tower up ahead. She stopped and held her breath, listening hard. She was only fifteen feet away now, standing right at the edge of the shadow it cast with the moon behind it.

She was sure then that she heard her name in a hushed voice. *Rose—hurry—*

Did Sylvie know she'd been followed? Worse still, did she want Rose to follow her? Was Rose walking right into a trap?

Rose took several steps forward, careful to stay in the shadows. She kept her eyes trained on the open doorway.

She thought she heard a low hum, then a rustling.

Suddenly she wanted to turn around, to run back to the house and wake up Mama and Daddy:

Sylvie's in the tower. She's turning into something terrible.

But she needed to see. That need pulled her along, some invisible wire growing tighter and tighter, the tug fierce and impossible to resist. As she took another step forward, she heard what sounded like the rustle of large wings.

A shadow passed in front of the open doorway, from left to right. It moved quickly, a blur in the darkness. And were those wings? Extra arms flailing?

Rose gasped—then, realizing too late that she'd made a sound, clapped her hand over her mouth.

"Rose!" a voice shouted. It was Sylvie's and not Sylvie's. Familiar, yet with a strange rasp and hum. And it was angry.

Rose turned and took off, running, running as fast as her legs would take her, up the driveway, her bare feet pounding on the pebbles, her eyes fixed on the house. She did not dare look back. Behind her, she heard the rush of wings coming closer. Closer still.

Heart hammering, she reached the front door at last. She pulled it open and slammed it closed, locking it quickly.

"Rose," her mother called from upstairs. "Is that you?"

"Yes," Rose said, so happy to be back, happy to be alive, she didn't care if her mother caught her.

"What are you doing out of bed?" Mama had

appeared at the top of the stairs, and was tying her robe.

Should she tell? How could she? There was no way Mama would believe what Rose had just seen; she scarcely believed it herself.

"Nothing," Rose said, working hard to slow her ragged breath. "I couldn't sleep. I came down for a drink."

"Okay. Just get yourself back up to bed soon. It's after midnight."

"Yes, Mama."

Rose went into the kitchen, flipped on the lights, opened a drawer, and pulled out the largest kitchen knife she could find. Knife in hand, she poured herself a glass of juice and sat at the table. Ten minutes later, she heard Sylvie rattle at the locked front door. Then she must have taken the key from under the mat, because the door opened. Rose steeled herself, knife clenched in her hand. She tried to prepare herself for the sight of the monster Sylvie entering the kitchen, winged and lashing out at Rose with her extra arms and snapping mandibles. Rose would aim her knife right at the creature's chest—go for the heart. But what if the thing had no heart? Yellow blood, that's what insects had.

Instead, she heard Sylvie's footsteps padding softly up the stairs and going down the hall to their room.

Safe. She was safe. For now.

Rose sat at the kitchen table all night, thinking, planning. Her mind raced, but there were two facts she clung to: Her sister was a monster. And Sylvie now knew that Rose had seen her, which put her in more danger than ever before.

2013

Jason

Jason could smell trouble as soon as he walked into the bedroom. He was exhausted. All he wanted in the whole world was to peel off his uniform, hit the shower, then make his way down to the kitchen, open up a beer, and mindlessly devour whatever the spicy thing was that Piper had stewing on the back of the stove.

Piper was sitting in the rocking chair in the corner of the bedroom, flipping through a magazine. As soon as he walked in, she closed it and stood up.

"I'll leave you two," she said, and hurried out of the room without even meeting his eye.

Margot was propped up in bed, covers pulled tight to her neck. Her face was blotchy and puffy: she'd been crying.

He reached for her, his stomach twisting with worry. Had something happened with the baby? But why hadn't they called him?

"Margot? You okay?"

She flinched slightly and he pulled back his hand.

"What was going on between you and Amy?" Margot asked.

Jason drew a sharp breath. "Me and Amy? Nothing. What are you talking about?"

"You were there, in her house, last week. You went to see her."

Shit. She knew. How could she know?

"What were you doing there, Jason?"

"I . . ." He fumbled for something to say, some way out of this. "Where did you hear that?"

"Piper visited Lou today. She said she came home from school last week and you were there with Amy. And I want to know what you were doing there, Jason."

The girl. Of course.

But what the hell was Piper doing, talking to her? He took a deep breath to calm himself. He looked at Margot and recalled the feeling of her flinching at his touch. He could still feel her recoiling from him, moving farther away as the seconds ticked by. She inched her way over in the bed, putting as much space as she possibly could between the two of them.

He had to find a way to make this right.

Tell the truth, his conscience told him. *Tell her everything.*

Well, maybe not everything.

"Margot, it's not a big deal, really. Amy called me at the station. She was upset. She asked if I could stop by; she wanted to talk about something."

"About what?" Margot asked.

"Her mom, mostly," Jason said. "You know she put Rose in the nursing home? She was just really shaken up about some of the things Rose said when she started to get confused."

Margot looked at him for a long time. "So *she* called *you?*"

"It seemed strange to me, too, believe me. Kind of random. But she said she remembered me as being objective. She wanted to talk to someone who wasn't involved."

"Did she ever do this before?" Margot asked. "Call you and ask you to come over to *talk?* To be *objective?*"

Jason shook his head. "No. It was the first time, I promise."

"Why, then? Why did she call *you?* Why now?"

"I don't know," Jason admitted. He rubbed his face with the palm of his hand.

"And she just talked about her mother?"

"Pretty much."

"What about? What was she so upset about?"

"Like I said," Jason explained, "her mom had gotten pretty delusional. She was saying some whacked-out stuff."

Margot was watching him carefully.

"What kind of whacked-out stuff?" she asked, twisting the covers.

No point lying now. God only knew how much the kid had told Piper, or how much of the conversation she might have actually heard in the kitchen that day. "Apparently, Rose believed that there were monsters at the motel." He

241

chuckled nervously. "She was trying to convince Amy."

"Monsters?" Margot repeated.

"I know, crazy. Poor old Rose is a little off in the head," Jason said. "I guess the years of hard drinking kind of took their toll."

He shifted from one foot to the other and looked at his wife, who was now all the way over at the edge of the bed. Neither of them spoke.

"Why didn't you tell me?" Margot asked.

"I didn't want to upset you."

Margot snorted out a disgusted laugh. "Upset me? Going to see an old friend, an old girlfriend even, wouldn't have upset me. Not if you'd come home and told me about it. But the fact that you lied about it, hid it from me—what am I supposed to do with that, Jason?"

"I never lied, I—"

She shook her head. "Sometimes a lie isn't what's said, but what's unsaid. An omission."

"And what about the things you hide from me?" Jason snapped. He felt his temper rising, though he tried to rein it in. "Your *omissions?*"

"I have *never* hidden anything from you, and you know it!" Margot snapped back.

Jason took a breath, tried to keep his voice calm.

"You told me you didn't know what '29 Rooms' meant."

Margot's face shifted from angry to guilty. She looked away.

"You *do* keep things from me," he went on quietly. "Important things. You always have. I'm not an idiot, Margot. I know you, Piper, and Amy were up to something that summer, and that whatever it was ended your friendship. I was the outsider then, and I guess I'm still the outsider now."

He watched her, waiting to see if she might finally tell him, finally let him in. But she remained silent, her lips tightly pursed.

1989

Piper

"I swear," Amy said as she fitted the master key into the lock on Room 3 and turned it. "It was an actual, for-real ghost."

Their plan was to search each motel room for clues about what might have happened to Sylvie. Piper doubted they'd find anything, but, then again, she'd never have guessed they'd find long-lost Aunt Sylvie's suitcase hidden under the floorboards of the tower.

"Ghosts aren't real," Margot said matter-of-factly as they entered the dusty, long-abandoned motel room. Just as with Rooms 1 and 2, there was nothing unusual in this one. A bed with the same ugly paisley bedspread, chewed through in spots by mice. The ceiling was crumbling, and the dim turquoise carpet was stained from water damage. There was a big scorch mark on the floor near the desk, in the exact shape of an iron.

Piper checked under the bed, and only found the foul smell of moldering carpet. Margot peeked into the bathroom, rattling the rings to the disintegrating shower curtain as she pulled it back.

Since Piper and Margot had arrived this morning, Amy had been insisting that some ethereal creature had visited her in the night.

"I swear," Amy said. "I wasn't dreaming. I woke up and it was just like . . . there . . . at the foot of my bed."

"And what'd it look like again?" Margot asked. "A dog with a human face, or a human with a dog face?"

Amy banged a drawer open, pulled out a mildewed Gideon's Bible. "You've gotta believe me! It was real! You believe me, don't you, Piper?"

Piper nodded. "Sure. I believe you saw *something*. Or thought you did."

Amy shook her head and dropped the old Bible back in the drawer. "There's no *thought* involved. I opened my eyes and it was there, just kind of hovering, watching me sleep in the dark. I got a glimpse of a pale face, but it turned away, and then it was, like, all covered in fur, or like it had a fur suit on or something. And then it was like it had this dog face. With a snout and stuff. But then it was gone! Poof."

"Maybe you just thought you were awake but you were still dreaming?" Piper suggested. "That happened to me once, I—"

"I was totally awake. This was not a dream!"

"Maybe it was Bigfoot," Margot suggested.

Amy blew out an exasperated breath, making the pink bangs fly out. "Would you get serious? It was *not* freaking Bigfoot!"

"Okay," Margot said. "So it was a pale-faced,

furry ghost who just disappeared when you turned on the light?"

"Ugh, you guys are hopeless. Just forget it. If it comes back again, I'll get proof. I'll sleep with a camera next to my bed," Amy said, and then sighed. "Let's get out of here. There's nothing in this room."

"Three down, twenty-five to go," Piper said. They left Room 3, locking the door behind them, and moved to Room 4.

"Lock on this one's broken," Amy said, sticking the master key back in her pocket as she pushed the door open. She stepped into the room, then froze. "You smell that?"

"Cigarette smoke," Piper said. The other rooms had smelled faintly of it, but this was much stronger.

And there was something else different, too. This room felt . . . *lived in.*

Amy nodded and walked over to the window; an ashtray sat on the sill, with a barely smoked cigarette crushed in it.

"Someone's been here. This is no twenty-year-old cigarette butt."

"Your grandma, maybe?" Margot said, sounding unconvinced.

Amy shook her head. "Nah. Why would she come all the way down here to smoke? Besides, she only smokes Virginia Slims. This isn't one of hers."

Piper got down and looked under the bed. "Um—guys?—there's stuff under here. A bunch of stuff, it looks like."

Amy pushed her aside and reached under to pull out a heavy pair of binoculars, then a red plastic flashlight. She switched it on. It worked. She dragged out a plastic two-liter Coke bottle full of water. Then a small paper bag, like what some kids carried lunch to school in.

"What the . . ." Amy said as she opened the bag and peered inside. She dumped the contents onto the bed: a skeleton key on a heavy ring, sunglasses, a silver earring, a few pieces of Tower Motel stationery, an old glass soda bottle, and a book of matches.

"What is all this stuff?" Margot asked, leaning in.

Amy picked up the earring. "This is mine. So are the sunglasses."

"Creepy," Margot said.

"Yeah," Piper agreed, "maybe you've got your very own stalker. I mean, why would you have binoculars in here unless you were using them to watch the house? There's nothing else around."

"Maybe it's the Bigfoot guy!" Margot said. "Mr. Man-Dog. Maybe he's been living here, watching you!"

"You should tell your grandma," Piper said.

"No way! She'd probably call the cops, and they'd come and start poking around."

Piper didn't think that was such a bad idea and almost said so, but she didn't want to sound like a baby.

"I say we put everything back," Amy said. "Then we just keep an eye on it. We check the room several times every day. Maybe we'll catch our smoker."

Piper agreed, but didn't like it.

She wasn't so sure she really wanted to catch the smoker, and even less sure that the smoker would respond very kindly to being caught by a bunch of girls.

And what if Amy's ghost was real—what if whoever had been staying here had sneaked up to the house and into Amy's room to watch her sleep?

Jason

Jason knew there was no going back to Room 4. They'd be watching it now. Maybe they'd even set some sort of trap. He watched from the edge of the woods as they went into one room after another, until all twenty-eight had been visited.

What were they looking for?

When they came out of the last one, they were tired, arguing. It was nearly dinnertime.

Margot said something about Bigfoot.

Amy said something about a ghost. Then she said words Jason caught clearly: "If it comes back tonight, I'll take a picture."

He watched Margot and Piper head back to the condos through the path in the woods. After waiting five minutes, just to be sure, he started toward the path himself, staying just at the edge of the woods that bordered the Slaters' meadow.

"That you, Jay Jay?" Amy's voice called out from far away, back down at the motel.

He turned. Amy was down by the pool, holding the binoculars from Room 4. *His* binoculars. She had them pointed right at him.

He stopped, gave a nervous wave.

"What are you doing?" she asked.

"Walking."

"Duh!"

"I've gotta get home. I'm late for supper."

"Come back tomorrow, then. First thing. There's something I want to ask you."

He nodded. "Tomorrow morning," he called down.

The next day, he was up early. He gulped down some orange juice and a bowl of raisin bran, then ran back to the motel and waited for Amy by the pool. She came out of the house and crossed the cracked patio, with the binoculars hanging from her neck on their heavy leather strap. She was carrying a square piece of stiff paper in her hand.

"Okay, Mr. Scientist. What do you make of this?"

She thrust it at him. It was square photo with a white frame—a Polaroid. He squinted down at it.

"What do you see?" Amy asked.

He thought carefully as he looked at the photo. Was this some kind of Rorschach test?

"It's all blurry," he said at last.

"Don't you see it?" Amy asked.

Clearly, he was failing the test. "Um, what is it I'm supposed to see?" It was dark and grainy, and there, off to the left, was a blur of white.

"The ghost!" Amy said, snatching the photo from him; she jabbed her finger at the white blur. "I took this in my room last night. Our house is totally haunted. Maybe the whole motel is! That's what I wanted to ask you about. You said you saw someone go into the tower. Someone dressed in blue, right?"

"Right." He nodded.

"But when you went inside, whoever it was had vanished. I think there's a ghost, and *you've* seen it"—she jabbed a finger at him—"and *I've* seen it." She touched her chest with her thumb. "And I think I know who it is."

"Who?"

She groaned impatiently. "I can't tell you that! Not just yet, anyway. Piper and Margot, they don't believe me. But they haven't seen it yet, right? And we have."

"But I—"

"Please, tell me you believe me, Jay Jay. Please, please, please. Tell me that what you saw might have been a ghost."

Jason hesitated, thinking. He didn't believe in ghosts. And the figure in that blurry photo in Amy's hand could've been anything. Yet here was Amy, practically begging him.

"Sure," he said, "I guess it could have been a ghost."

"I knew it!" she exclaimed. "I knew you'd believe me, even if no one else did." She threw her arms around his neck, knocking him off balance a little. He started to sway backward, but Amy caught him, pulled him up, and then kept pulling him closer, until her lips were on his.

In that moment, Jason believed wholeheartedly in the ghost of the Tower Motel.

Piper

From Piper's vantage point on the little hillside between the woods and the empty pool, she could clearly see what was happening in there: Amy kissing Jason Hawke. Margot, just behind Piper, hadn't seen yet.

"Margot, run ahead and scope out the trailer," Piper ordered, her voice smooth but steely. "See if you can find a way in; just don't go in until we get there." Once her sister had skipped off, Piper approached the edge of the pool. Amy had a pair of binoculars around her neck. Piper realized with a rush of anger that they were probably the ones they'd found yesterday in Room 4—even though the plan had been to put everything back exactly the way they found it.

"Oh, hey, Piper," Amy said when she looked up and saw her standing there.

Her voice was light and cheerful, like everything was perfectly normal. Like being in the pool kissing Jason was exactly where she was supposed to be. Piper said nothing. She didn't dare open her mouth, worried a scream would come out. She shoved her trembling hands deep into the pockets of her jeans as Jason, bashful, smiled.

"What's *he* doing here?" Piper said at last.

"He came to talk to me about something," Amy

said. "But he's going home now. Right, Jay Jay?"

Jason looked confused and then wounded. "Huh? I . . ."

"I'll see you around. I've got plans with Piper and Margot today."

Amy was holding something in her hand. Something flat and square. A Polaroid picture.

Jason climbed the ladder out of the pool, but then he turned back to Amy. "Maybe I can stop by later?" he said. Amy looked at Piper and rolled her eyes in a dramatic, can-you-believe-him kind of way.

No, Piper couldn't believe him. But what she really couldn't believe was that Amy had kissed him again.

"I'm kinda busy all day," Amy told him. "But another time. Totally."

He nodded and sulked off.

"What was that about?" Piper asked, voice shaky.

"Nothing. It was nothing, Piper."

"It didn't look like nothing."

"Well, it was."

"Why'd you kiss him again?"

"God, what are you, my mother? The kissing police?"

"No, I . . ."

"Look at this," Amy said, holding the photo out for Piper to inspect. "What do you see?"

Piper couldn't see much. The picture looked all

messed up, like the chemicals hadn't developed right. "It kind of looks like a butterfly."

Amy shook her head. "The ghost came back last night. I got a picture. This is proof!"

Piper squinted down at the photograph. "It's hard to tell what it is."

"Jason could tell what it was. He believes me," Amy snapped.

Piper swallowed hard. So this was how it was going to be. "We should go catch up to Margot before she gets impatient and goes into that old trailer on her own," Piper said. "The place is probably a death trap."

The old trailer's tires were flat, and the tall grass of the field behind the house had grown up around its sides. It must have originally been painted blue and white, but the colors had faded, and in a few patches had been scraped away to reveal bare, rusty metal. The windows were cracked and filthy, and a heavy padlock hung on the front door.

"I couldn't see a way in," Margot said. They had found her sitting on the cinder-block steps leading up to the front door. "Where'd Jason go?"

"Home," Piper said, firmly. Then she turned to Amy. "So you've never been inside?" Piper asked, nodding at the trailer with the padlocked door.

"Nah. It's always been really trashed. And I never found the key. But I think that if we break that window over there we can climb in. It's pretty much broken already."

"Do you think that old key we found in Room 4 could be the right one?" Margot asked.

"Nope," Amy said. "That's an old skeleton key. It wouldn't work in this kind of lock."

Amy picked up a rock and used it to finish the job on the window, carefully pushing all the bits of jagged glass from the edges. Then she pulled an old rusty lawn chair over and climbed up, to hoist herself through.

"Careful," Piper called. "Don't cut yourself."

"Whoa!" Amy called, her voice echoing. "Holy time warp."

Piper climbed onto the chair and peered through the open window. There was a scattering of glass on the floor, and Amy was standing in a tiny kitchen, opening cabinets.

"I want to see, too," Margot protested.

Piper turned back to her little sister. "It's too dangerous. There's broken glass everywhere, and who knows how sturdy the floor is." She pointed down at her leg. "You don't want to end up like me, do you? Besides, someone needs to be lookout. If Amy's grandma catches us, we're in big trouble."

Grandma Charlotte had gone out to the grocery store. They should be all clear, but you never knew.

Piper pulled herself up and shimmied through

the window, crunching on broken glass once she got inside. Her shin was throbbing. The gash where the splinter had gone in was still red and puffy and hot to the touch when she got up this morning.

"That looks bad," Margot had said. "Maybe we should tell Mom."

"Don't even think about it," Piper had said in her most deadly-serious big-sister voice.

She'd slathered the wound in bacitracin, covered it with Band-Aids, and worn jeans in spite of the heat.

The air inside the trailer was musty. A thin plywood veneer covered the walls and ceiling. It was peeling and had come completely off in places. The turquoise cushions on the two benches at the table were full of holes, their stuffing pulled out by generations of mice and squirrels.

"Check it out," Amy said. "Everything's still here." She opened the cabinet doors, showing Piper the stacks of cups, plates, bowls, and pots and pans. There were even some ancient cans in the cupboard—string beans, creamed corn, Campbell's tomato soup—swollen, rusted, and surely festering with botulism.

A small bedroom sat at one end of the trailer. Above the bed was an old movie poster: *Psycho*, the Alfred Hitchcock movie Amy had been telling her about. Piper opened the tiny closet and found it stuffed full of shirts on hangers, coats, a pile of jeans stacked on the shelf, boots and shoes on the floor.

"So what's the story with this guy Fenton?" Piper asked.

"I asked Grandma Charlotte last night and she gave me the lowdown. Turns out he was my grandfather's, like, third cousin twice removed or something. His parents died when he was little, and he was kind of adopted by my grandpa's parents. He grew up on the farm, just like my grandpa, but he was way younger. When Grandpa went off to war, Fenton stayed behind and worked on the farm. Later, when they turned the farm into the motel, Fenton was kind of the handyman, helping build stuff, fix stuff, whatever. But after the highway got built, everything started to fall apart. Fenton left one day to go out west." Amy shrugged. "That's the story my grandma tells, anyway—but you know how full of holes her stories can be." She poked around in the closet. "You've gotta wonder, why would this guy leave all his clothes?"

"Maybe he left in a hurry?" Piper suggested. "Maybe he was in trouble or something and had to get away fast."

There were books and magazines stacked all over the place—on the kitchen counters, the floor beside the bed, along the windowsills— slim paperbacks with yellowed pages and old magazines with names like *Weird Tales, Fantastic Adventures, Astounding Science Fiction.*

"You'd think, if he was taking off for a new life out west, he'd pack a few things, maybe even straighten up." Amy went into the kitchen and looked in the sink. "Holy crap, there are two dirty cups in here. He didn't even do the dishes before he left."

Amy turned and picked up a book from the counter; on its cover, a scantily clad girl was standing in front of a spaceship. "Guess the dude liked his sci-fi."

Another book sat in the middle of the kitchen table: *The Stars My Destination.* Piper noticed there was a piece of paper being used as a bookmark. She flipped the book open and saw that the paper was Tower Motel stationery, folded in half. On it, neatly typed, were the words:

I know what you are and what you do. You have to stop. If you don't, I will find a way to stop you.

"Take a look at this," Piper said, handing the note over to Amy.

"Whoa," Amy breathed.

"Hey!" Margot called through the open window at the other end of the trailer. "I hear a car coming up the driveway—you better get outta there!"

Amy tucked the folded piece of paper back into the old paperback, shoved it in the waistband of her shorts, and pulled her T-shirt over it. She climbed through the trailer window, Piper right behind her.

"Your grandma's home, I think," Margot said, voice low.

"Come on," Amy said, "let's go back to my room."

Amy's grandma was unloading bags of groceries from the back of her Oldsmobile when they got to the driveway. "Give me a hand, will you, girls?" she called out.

They each took a load into the kitchen.

"Grandma, did Fenton go away before Sylvie ran away or after?"

"Right before. I always told your grandfather that Fenton running off like that might have put the idea in Sylvie's head. Made her think it was perfectly normal to go sneaking off for parts unknown in the middle of the night."

"Do you know what happened to Fenton? Did you ever hear from him?"

"Hmm? No, no, we never did," Grandma Charlotte said, stuffing a gallon of milk into the fridge. "Now, why don't you girls go on upstairs? I'll put these things away. Then we can make cookies. I got some of that dough in a tube—we just have to bake them."

"Sure, Grandma, sounds great," Amy said. "But one more thing . . ." She reached into her back pocket and pulled out the Polaroid.

Oh, no, Piper thought. *Not the freaking ghost-dog picture again.*

"What do you see, Gram?"

Grandma Charlotte stared down at the blurry picture for what felt like forever. At last, she recited:

"When Death comes knocking on your door,
you'll think you've seen his face before.
When he comes creeping up your stairs,
you'll know him from your dark nightmares.
If you hold up a mirror, you shall see
that he is you and you are he."

Amy took a step back. "Way creepy, Gram." Amy glanced at Piper and Margot and gave them a dramatic, my-kooky-old-grandma eye roll.

Grandma Charlotte smiled vaguely and went back to the groceries.

"Go on upstairs now, Sylvie. I'll call you down when it's time for cookies."

Amy nodded, muttered, "It's *Amy,* Gram," and headed out of the kitchen, Piper and Margot behind her.

"Well, *that* was weird," Margot said under her breath once they got to the stairs.

"Yeah, my grandma's full of freaky little poems and rhymes. Stuff her mom taught her when she was a kid. But don't you think that's a little suspicious?" Amy whispered.

"The poem?" Piper said.

"No, dummy, the thing with Fenton! Fenton leaves—in such a hurry that he left all his crap behind—and then Sylvie takes off right after, and neither of them is ever heard from again?"

"It's a little weird," Piper admitted.

"But what does it mean?" asked Margot.

"I don't know," said Amy. "But it's another piece of the puzzle."

They got to Amy's room and closed the door; Amy pushed the latch closed. She went to her desk, pulling the paperback sci-fi book out from under her shirt. Suddenly she froze, as her eyes fell on the typewriter.

"What the *hell?*" she whispered.

There was a piece of Tower Motel stationery rolled into the carriage of the old Royal De Luxe. A message had been neatly typed:

> You found the suitcase and typewriter, but there are bigger things to find.
> Keep looking.
> Maybe, just maybe, you'll find the truth.

"What is this?" Piper asked.

Amy's eyes were huge. "Don't you get it? It's a note from Sylvie. From Sylvie's ghost!"

"Wait, Sylvie's *dead?*" Margot asked.

"I'm sure of it," Amy said. "It's got to be her ghost that's been visiting me. Jason saw it, too, that day in the tower, remember? He saw someone in blue go in and never come out! And if she was still alive, if she really ran away, why would her suitcase be here?" Amy paused dramatically. "I think she *planned* on leaving that night, but someone stopped her!"

"Like who?" Piper asked.

"I don't know," Amy said. Her eyes were glittering with excitement. "But, obviously, she wants us to find out."

1961

Alfred Hitchcock
Universal Studios
Hollywood, California

September 18, 1961

Dear Mr. Hitchcock,
I feel like an actress already. Playing different roles for different people. Sometimes I almost forget who the real me is.

Does that make any sense?

Do any of your big stars ever feel that way when they're playing a role— that they get so caught up in pretending to be someone else they start to forget who they really are? I can't imagine Janet Leigh or James Stewart getting lost like that. But maybe I'm wrong. Maybe any one of us can get a little lost sometimes.

Sincerely yours,
Miss Sylvia A. Slater
The Tower Motel
328 Route 6
London, Vermont

Rose

Rose was awakened by a gunshot. Daddy's rifle. She knew the sound by heart. Daddy had taught her and Sylvie to shoot, practicing with old tin cans on the fence out behind Fenton's trailer.

She leapt out of bed, glancing at the clock; she'd overslept again. Sylvie's bed was already neatly made.

Mama and Sylvie were sitting at the kitchen table, steaming bowls of oatmeal in front of them. Sylvie looked up, saw Rose, then shot Mama a worried glance. Mama pursed her lips.

"I heard a shot," Rose said.

Mama nodded, eyes down on her oatmeal.

"What happened?" Rose asked, heart sinking into her stomach.

Mama sat up so that her back was as straight as the chair she sat in. "Honey, Lucy got worse. She wasn't able to stand at all this morning."

"No!" Rose said. Daddy wouldn't do it. He couldn't possibly shoot Lucy. Not without letting Rose say goodbye.

"She was in terrible pain," Mama said.

"No!" Rose cried again, running out of the kitchen, through the front door, down the steps, across the yard, her robe flying out behind her like a cape. Fenton and Daddy were coming back toward the house. Daddy was carrying his Winchester rifle.

"How could you?" Rose screamed.

"Rose, the animal was suffering," Daddy said.

"You could have called the vet! You could have woken me up!"

I could have fixed her. I could have gotten her to stand up and eat.

Daddy shook his head. "There was nothing either you or the best veterinarian in the world could have done for that old cow, Rose. Her time had come."

"It's not fair. You don't get to decide!"

"It was the kindest—" Daddy began.

"You're a murderer," Rose spat.

Daddy looked at her but didn't speak. His eyes looked hollow, sad. "I'm sorry," he said at last, and walked past her, into the house.

"I hate you," she called after him. "I hate everyone in this whole terrible family."

Daddy didn't so much as pause; he just kept right on walking, gun in his hands.

Rose started to head for Lucy's pen, but Fenton grabbed her. "No," he said. "It's best if you don't see her." She shook him off and ran across the yard and to the fence.

There was her beautiful cow, a small round bullet hole right in the center of her forehead. Rose opened the gate and lay down beside Lucy, buried her face in the cow's still-warm fur and cried.

She cried for what felt like hours, days. Flies came and landed on her and Lucy, and Rose flicked them away, used the sleeve of her robe to clean the blood from Lucy's forehead.

She had lost her only true friend.

"I'm sorry, girl," she cried. "I'm so, so sorry."

"She had a good life," Fenton said.

Rose turned around. Fenton was there behind her, leaning on the fence. Had he been there the whole time?

"If she'd been any other cow, she would have been made into hamburger years ago. Your daddy, he loved Lucy. You don't know how hard it was for him to shoot her today. And you know what he wants to do? He wants to bury her in the back field. Dig a big old hole and have a real funeral. Send her off right."

Rose kept her face buried in the cow's warm chest, ran her hands over her ribs, her shoulder blade, down her bumpy spine.

"I should have been here," Rose said. "I didn't even get to say goodbye."

"Now, Rose, your dad didn't want to upset you, that's all. I think he still sees you as a little kid, fragile. You're tougher than he knows, Rose."

She lifted her head, nodded.

"Smarter, too," Fenton said. "Your father—both your parents, really—they don't give you enough credit."

For a second, Rose was surprised. Then, she

thought, *Exactly.* For once, someone had it right. "Thank you," she said.

"In fact," he said, "I bet there's not a whole lot that goes on here that you don't know about. I bet the things you know would surprise everyone."

She nodded up at him. If only he knew the half of it. But then, feeling the need to prove herself, she said, "I know about Daddy."

"What about him?" Fenton said.

"That there's another lady he sees. Her name is Vivienne."

Fenton blew out a breath. "You know about that, huh? Well, do us all a favor and don't mention that one to either of your parents."

"Mama knows already," Rose said.

"Yeah, well, just 'cause she knows doesn't mean she needs to be reminded, right?"

Rose nodded. She felt strangely powerful. The keeper of grown-up secrets.

"Hey," Fenton said. "Seeing as how you've already missed the school bus, how about you come to the trailer for a cup of cocoa? Then I can give you a lift to school when you're good and ready. How does that sound?"

Rose wiped her face with the back of her hand. "Okay," she said, standing on rubbery legs. She followed Fenton past the swimming pool (closed down for the season), and across the grass to his blue-and-white trailer.

"Take a seat," he said once they were inside.

Rose sat at the little table while he moved around the small, efficient kitchen, heating milk, stirring in cocoa powder and sugar.

Clang, clang, clang, went the spoon in the saucepan. Maybe it was Rose's imagination, but there was something odd about Fenton today. He seemed out of sorts. Nervous. He wasn't quite looking her in the eye. She guessed he was just feeling bad about Lucy. Men had a hard time expressing emotion. She'd read that in an article in one of Sylvie's magazines and believed it was true.

They were quiet a minute while Fenton worked at the stove. Rose looked around. Fenton's trailer was always clean, but cluttered—paperback books, tools, and motorcycle parts covered every surface. In spite of the apparent chaos, Fenton always seemed to know where everything was.

"This what you're reading?" Rose asked, picking up the paperback in front of her. There was a napkin stuck in it, being used as a bookmark.

The Stars My Destination, the cover said.

"Uh-huh," Fenton said.

"Is it good?" Rose asked.

"Pretty good. People can teleport. It's actually pretty interesting."

"I wish I could teleport," Rose said.

Fenton grinned at her. "Where would you go?" he asked.

"Anywhere," she told him. "Anywhere but here."

"I know the feeling," Fenton said. He got two mugs down and carefully poured the cocoa into them. He put a cup right in front of her. She wrapped her hands around it, fingers soaking up the warmth.

"Do you?" Rose asked.

"Sure. I mean especially now, things being the way they are. The motel, the whole town, it's all in pretty bad shape, right? You've gotta wonder if we all wouldn't be better off someplace else."

Rose nodded and took a sip of her cocoa. It was perfect: sweet and chocolaty and just what she needed.

"Sylvie wants to go to Hollywood," Rose said. Her sister had covered her side of the bedroom with pictures of movie stars cut from magazines. Above her bed, she had a drawing Fenton had done for her of the Hollywood sign up in the hills.

Fenton nodded. "I know, and she will one day. I'm sure of it."

Fenton drummed his fingers on the table. He took a sip of his cocoa, then pushed the cup away and reached into his shirt pocket for his cigarettes. He shook one out and lit up, squinting at Rose through the smoke.

"Rose," he said, "there's something I want to talk to you about."

His voice was as serious as serious gets. Was it about Lucy? About how crazy Rose had been acting? Maybe he was going to give her hell for ruining Sylvie's birthday cake—everyone else already had. Maybe it was more about Daddy and Vivienne. About how her parents' marriage was in rough shape, just like everything else around here.

Whatever Fenton was going to say, she was sure she didn't want to hear it. She wanted to do the little-girl trick of sticking her fingers in her ears and singing loudly so she wouldn't hear. But she wasn't a little girl anymore.

"What?" Rose asked, setting down her mug. Suddenly the cocoa was so sweet it made her teeth ache.

Fenton took another drag of his cigarette. The smoke drifted out of his mouth like blue-gray fog.

"About what you saw last night."

The words hit Rose right in the stomach, knocking the wind out of her.

"What I . . . saw?" she stammered once she had her breath back.

Fenton nodded, looked her right in the eye. "Out in the tower. After you followed your sister there."

"I don't know what you mean," Rose said, pushing herself up and away from the table. She backed up on shaky legs.

"Don't play games," he said, rising, stepping toward her. "This is serious. Do you know what could happen if people find out?"

"Find out?" Rose croaked, backing farther, feeling for the door behind her, remembering her sister, how she hadn't been simply Sylvie anymore, but some sort of hideous monster— something with extra arms and wings.

What *would* happen if people found out?

And how was it that Fenton knew? Had he known all along, been in on her secret? Was he one of them, too? Another monster?

"Rose," he said, "I need you to promise me that you won't tell. If you did . . ." His eyes flashed with a strange rage Rose hadn't expected. They had a reddish glint in the dim light of the trailer.

"I have to go," she said. She turned and pushed the door open, jumped down the steps, and started heading across the field.

"Wait!" Fenton called. "Don't you want a ride to school?"

Rose didn't answer. She ran back to the house and up the stairs, past her mother doing dishes in the kitchen.

She got to her bedroom and locked the door.

Fenton knew. Fenton was Sylvie's protector. Had she turned him into a monster, too? Could mares do that? She couldn't recall Oma ever mentioning it—but, then, she hadn't known just how closely she should have been paying attention to Oma's stories.

How far would Fenton go to keep Sylvie's secret?

Rose flung herself down on her bed to think. She pulled the covers up over her head and shut her eyes as tight as she could, trying to bring on darkness.

At last, she knew what she had to do.

She rose from bed, went to Sylvie's desk, and sat down in front of the typewriter. She carefully loaded in a sheet of clean, white motel stationery and began to type.

I know what you are and what you do. You have to stop. If you don't, I will find a way to stop you.

Rose left the note there in Sylvie's typewriter. Then she got herself washed and dressed and asked her mother if she could please drive her to school.

Rose

Rose avoided both Sylvie and Fenton when she got home from school that afternoon, sticking close to Mama, offering to do one chore after another: folding laundry, starching Daddy's shirts, dusting the living room.

During dinner, Daddy asked Fenton to fix the lights in the motel sign down by the road. "One whole side is burned out. Can't see the sign when you're heading into town."

"Not that it matters," Mama mumbled in a voice so low Rose wondered if her father even heard it.

"We've got lightbulbs in the garage," Fenton said. "I'll fix it after dinner."

After dinner, Daddy went into town and Mama headed up to her sewing room. Sylvie offered to help Fenton fix the lights on the sign. Rose slipped up to their room and tried to concentrate on the book she was reading for school: *Little Women.* She was so tired, though—her eyelids grew heavy, the words blurred on the page. She finally fell asleep, still dressed, the bedside lamp burning.

She was awakened when Sylvie came in. Rose glanced at the clock: it was nearly midnight. Sylvie's eyes were red, and her hair was a mess.

"Where've you been?" Rose whispered, squinting up at her sister.

"Out walking."

"With Fenton?"

Sylvie didn't answer. She snapped off the light, changed into her nightgown in the dark, and crawled under her covers. Rose fell back asleep to the sound of her sister softly crying, face buried in her pillow.

"You haven't seen Fenton, have you, dear?" Mama asked when Rose got in after school the next day. Sylvie was at Woolworth's. Mama was in the kitchen, washing dishes.

Rose shook her head. "Not since dinner last night," she said, helping herself to a shiny red apple from the bowl on the counter.

Mama turned off the water, went to the cabinets, and pulled out a glass casserole dish.

"It's the strangest thing," she said. "He didn't show up for work at the garage today. His truck is there in front of the trailer. Your father had a list of things for him to do this afternoon, but it seems he's gone and vanished."

"Vanished," Rose repeated.

"I know he's been talking about leaving for ages. He even told your father he was saving for a bus ticket out west. But I can't believe he'd just leave all of us without even saying goodbye. The truth is, I'm worried. What do you think, Rose? Did he say anything to you? Or did Sylvie mention anything?"

Rose shook her head. "I don't think so. Maybe. Yesterday morning, when I had cocoa with him, he said he'd been thinking about leaving."

Disappearing.

You've gotta wonder if we all wouldn't be better off someplace else.

And he'd also wanted to talk to her about what she'd seen. About Sylvie.

Rose thought about Sylvie coming into their room last night, how disheveled she'd been. As if she'd been in some sort of struggle.

A terrible thought began to rise.

"Tuna casserole for supper," Mama announced. "Your favorite."

But it wasn't her favorite at all. It was Sylvie's.

Rose got up and left the kitchen.

"Where are you off to?" Mama called.

"Chores," she said.

"Good girl," Mama called after her.

Rose hurried to Fenton's trailer, tossing her uneaten apple into the field. The door was unlocked. She held her breath and let herself in. It was exactly the way it had been yesterday, when they sat drinking cocoa. Their cups were still in the sink, unwashed, the dregs of her cocoa at the bottom of one. She went into his tiny bedroom. The single bed was neatly made. On the table beside it was a teetering pile of paperback books. She rifled hastily through his closet. It felt strange to be in here, snooping like this, but it was necessary. Surely, if he'd bought a bus ticket out west, he'd have packed a bag, but it didn't look like anything was missing. Shirts hung on wire hangers. His big black motorcycle boots were on the floor—there was no way he'd go anywhere without those. She found his keys on the hook next to the front door, the lucky rabbit's foot Sylvie had given him dangling from them.

This was all wrong.

Rose's stomach was clenched tight; her head began to ache. The skin on the back of her neck prickled.

Stay calm. Look for clues.

She left the trailer, walked through the field, by the pool, and down the driveway to the sign. Both sides were lit up. It had been fixed.

She went back up the hill and stopped in front of the tower, peering in through the open doorway.

Don't go in, a little voice told her. The hair on her arms stood up. But she took a deep breath and walked inside. It was just the tower, after all. And it was daylight. What could possibly be hiding in there now?

You know.

You know what could be there, hiding. Waiting.

But Sylvie was at work, counting out change from the cash register at Woolworth's, smiling at the customers, and telling them to have a nice day. Rose was safe.

Except she didn't feel safe.

It was freezing inside the tower; the stones trapped the cold, and the walls never let sunlight inside. The air smelled damp and rotten.

Get out, the little voice told her. *Run while you still can.*

Her feet crunched on something; she was stepping on glass, grinding it to powder beneath the heavy soles of her dull leather oxfords. She bent down to look more closely: a broken lightbulb. She saw the tube of threaded metal from the bottom, the string of filament, and a thousand tiny pieces of shattered glass. Amid the fragments of glass were a few dark splotches of something. She reached down and touched it. Blood. Dried, but still slightly sticky. Rose's stomach turned, and her whole body felt unsteady.

The drops moved in a rough line to the center of the room, where a dinner-plate-sized puddle of blood had formed. It was dark, thick, and congealed, and it seemed to Rose that there was an awful lot of it. She could smell the sharp, ironlike tang of it, feel it on the back of her throat. She swallowed hard, willing herself not to be sick.

This was not a simple cut from a broken lightbulb.

Something horrible had happened here.

You know what this is.

You know what did this.

Rose felt a sharp, jabbing pain in her left temple as she tried to think, to decide what to do next.

Run! the voice in her head screamed. She should tell her mother. Tell her everything. That Sylvie was a mare, that she'd done something terrible, as Rose had always known she would. Together, they would have to find a way to stop Sylvie, to keep her from hurting anyone else. There was so much blood. Her mother would have to believe her.

Rose ran back to the house and burst into the kitchen, where her mother was chopping onions.

"Mama! You've got to come quick! The tower . . ."

Mama turned, impatient. "What are you on about, Rose?"

"Please, let's go—" Rose began, but Daddy walked into the kitchen, and the words died in her throat.

"Clarence," Mama said with a sigh, setting down the chopping knife, "you're getting mud all over my clean floor."

"I've got a job for Rose," he said. He looked terribly old to Rose, his face thinner, his hair sprinkled with gray. When had this happened? How had she not noticed it before?

Rose's heart was beating so hard she was sure he could hear it. She was sure she could still smell the blood, taste it in the back of her throat, all mixed together with the scent of damp stone and mortar. She thought of telling them both everything, of taking Mama's and Daddy's hands and leading them to the tower, showing them the glass and blood, saying, "Our Sylvie is not who you think she is."

But it had to be just Mama. Daddy would never believe her. Even now, he looked at her with annoyance, perhaps a strange apprehension. She was the daughter who told lies, who smashed birthday cakes. The girl who had told him yesterday morning she hated him.

Why, he might even think she was the one responsible for the blood in the tower.

Of course he would, the voice confirmed. *Don't be an idiot.*

"I have to talk to Mama," Rose said, her voice the quiet trickle of a stream running dry. "There's something I need to show her."

"It can wait," Daddy said, voice firm.

She thought, *No, no, it can't.*

"Go help your father now," Mama said. "Whatever it is can wait."

"But—"

"No arguments," Daddy said. He looked so serious. She followed him quietly out of the house, across the driveway, and to the little workshop he and Fenton used.

Maybe Fenton was inside. Maybe her father had found him, hurt, stabbed, and he needed her help.

Then her father would have to believe about Sylvie! When Fenton told his story, they'd know what they were up against.

But when she stepped into the workshop, she saw only the workbench, rows of tools, the stack of tires, and chains for the tractor.

There, on the workbench, was a large wooden cross, nailed together and painted white.

"I want you to make a marker for Lucy's grave. Paint her name and something about her. Something nice. I dug a place for her out back. A nice spot in the meadow. I've been working all day."

Her father left her, and Rose dipped the brush into the can of red paint.

Red paint like red blood.

She had to hurry. Hurry and tell Mama what had happened to Fenton. Do it before Sylvie got home.

She looked down at the cross. Lucy deserved more than a rushed job, though. She thought of her father digging a deep hole, working all day, even skipping lunch, probably.

She considered for a few minutes, then carefully painted the words:

Here Lies Lucy, Beloved State Cow
You will live on forever in our hearts
You were the cow that changed everything

Then, as a finishing touch, she got out the black paint and put splotches on the white cross, making it Holstein-colored. One of the spots, right near the top, was in the careful shape of the state of Vermont. Daddy would be pleased.

When she finished at last, she quickly washed out the brushes with paint thinner and raced back to the house to find her mother.

Sylvie was already home, setting the table for dinner. She wore a blue dress with matching hair ribbons that made her eyes look like a summer sky.

Only a monster could be so beautiful, Rose thought. *Only something trying to camouflage itself, to lull everyone into a sense of ease.*

"There's something I need to show you," Rose almost whispered the words to Mama. Sylvie looked up, glared at Rose. Was she worried? Did she know what Rose had found?

"Not now, dear. I've got to get this casserole in the oven." Rose looked at the counter. A glass dish was half full of noodles, tuna fish, and canned cream-of-mushroom soup. Mama was chopping celery and mushrooms.

"Please," Rose whimpered. "It can't wait."

"I'll be through in ten minutes," Mama promised. "Go up to your room. I'll call you when I'm finished."

As Rose climbed the stairs, she heard Sylvie say, "What do you think is the matter with Rose now?"

Mama mumbled something Rose couldn't make out. *Chop, chop,* went the knife on the wooden cutting board.

Half an hour ticked by. Rose tried to focus on her own homework. But the math problems on the paper just turned into blood splatters and broken glass against a wooden floor.

"Rose?" Mama called, coming up the stairs. "What is it you wanted to show me?"

"Outside," Rose said, jumping to her feet. "In the tower."

Mama's face got tight, with the corners of her mouth pulled down. She wiped her hands on her apron and nodded.

"All right," she said. "If you insist."

Rose practically ran to the tower, but Mama followed slowly. Mama never hurried for anything.

It was dusk now, the September sky a murky gray.

"Do you remember when Oma told me about mares?" Rose said, as she approached the doorway. "Well, I've found one."

Rose looked back at her mother, waiting for a response, but Mama said nothing. Her face twitched slightly.

"We have a mare here, at the motel. And it's done something terrible."

Rose felt almost giddy as she said the words. At last, her mother would have to believe her. She'd show her the blood, then tell her the truth about Sylvie. Mama would take Rose in her arms and whisper, "Oh, you poor dear, it's terrible, the things you've been through. Terrible that I've never believed you. I'm so sorry."

But when Rose reached the spot, she stared at the floor in dismay. There was nothing. The floor was clean and bare—no trace of blood or glass. Rose blinked down, her eyes filling with furious tears of disbelief. She half-wondered if she could have imagined it. She bent down and touched the floor; it was slightly damp, and she was sure she detected the faintest hint of lemon cleanser.

No! No, no, no!

"There was blood," Rose said breathlessly. "And broken glass! From a lightbulb."

Fenton must have been carrying the lightbulb—holding it in his hand when Sylvie attacked him. Sylvie in *mare* form, a terrible creature with wings, extra arms with hideously sharp claws, mandibles for a mouth.

"Rose, please. No more of your stories."

"It's not a story, Mama! It's Sylvie! She's not who you think she is. She goes out each night and she—"

"That is *enough*." Mama's eyes had lost any trace of patience. "There are no such thing as *mares!* Not another word about any of this—not to me, not to your father or anyone else. If you know what's good for you, you'll put it all out of your mind. You'll go inside, finish your homework, do your chores, and get yourself to bed early. Do you understand?"

Rose bit her tongue hard, teeth clamping down until tears came to her eyes. She nodded. Yes. She understood. She was entirely on her own. She'd get no help from Mama or anyone else.

Mama led the way back up the driveway to the house. When Rose looked up, she saw Sylvie standing in front of their bedroom window, watching her and Mama with a worried scowl.

Alfred Hitchcock
Universal Studios
Hollywood, California

September 19, 1961

Dear Mr. Hitchcock,
Father had to put down Lucy the cow. We were born on the same day, Lucy and I. Lucy was born with a black spot in the exact shape of the state of Vermont. People used to come from all over just to see her, to take her picture. My father always said that Lucy's birth was a sign, a lucky sign that good things were in store for our family. So what does her death mean? Even more bad luck, I suppose.

My uncle Fenton is gone and it's all my fault. I am a terrible person. A monster. You would be shocked if I confessed the things I have done.

I'm sorry to burden you with all of this, it's just that I have no one else to turn to. I feel I will burst inside if I don't tell someone the truth—

291

someone who might just understand that every one of us has evil inside them. Every one.

Sincerely yours,
Miss Sylvia A. Slater
The Tower Motel
328 Route 6
London, Vermont

Rose

It was now the first week of October; two weeks since Fenton had disappeared. Rose had been watching Sylvie and getting ready. She had strained to remember everything Oma had told her. The more she thought about it, the clearer it was that her grandmother had known about Sylvie, that she had been trying to prepare Rose.

"Is there a way to stop a mare, Oma?" Rose asked once when they were together in the woods.

Oma nodded. "Yes, but it is not easy. A mare is a dangerous creature, Rose, and very, very clever." She reached out and brushed away the bangs that had been covering Rose's eyes.

"But there's a way?"

"If you bind a mare in iron, whether it is in human or animal form, it will be unable to transform."

"Iron?" Rose asked. "You mean chains?"

"Chains, leg irons, a cage perhaps. There is a story I have heard about a bear kept by King Henry at the Tower of London."

"The real Tower of London?" Rose asked.

Oma smiled. "Yes. The *real* Tower of London. The story goes that the bear was actually the king's mare lover—only when he released her from her leg irons at night could she return to her human form."

"Do you think it's true?" Rose asked.

Oma considered a moment, and popped a horehound candy into her mouth before she answered. "I think it is a story. Like all stories, it has pieces which are true, and pieces which are fiction. Nothing is ever really what it seems. Remember that, Rose."

Rose had found her father's old canvas army backpack in the garage and filled it with the supplies she thought she might need: a length of iron chain, a rusted trap her daddy had used to trap foxes when he was a boy, her butterfly net, the biggest kitchen knife, and a silver Ray-O-Vac flashlight.

The bag was terrifically heavy, the contents rattling and jabbing into her back. She'd sneaked out of bed while Sylvie was still sleeping and gone to the workshop to find the packed bag just where she'd stashed it under the bench, behind a large can of gasoline. She'd put on her darkest clothes—a pair of navy dungarees, a black turtleneck—an outfit to help her blend into the night.

Now she stood in the open doorway and waited, watching the house. It didn't matter if Sylvie didn't come tonight. Rose would wait. She'd come back tomorrow night, the night after as well. She'd wait as long as she needed, hiding in the shadows, ready to do whatever it took.

It didn't take long.

Just an hour or so after Rose got outside, Sylvie slipped out the front door, with her robe wrapped around her and pink slippers on her feet. She looked right, toward the workshop and Rose, then left, down the driveway, toward the motel and tower. She seemed to hesitate in the doorway, then finally pushed off and hurried down the driveway at a near run as her robe flapped behind. She was headed straight for the tower.

Come get me, she seemed to say. *I dare you.*

"It's now or never," Rose said, hearing the Elvis song in her head.

Tomorrow will be too late. . . .

She moved slowly, carefully, sticking to the shadows, careful not to jostle the contents in the bag, because they would clang.

She didn't have much of a plan. Just get to the tower. Find Sylvie. Wait for her to transform. Capture her.

Somehow, she'd chain the Sylvie monster. Get Mama. Make her believe.

Rose stood with her back against the tower, the backpack weighing achingly on her shoulders. She listened at the doorway.

"Sylvie?" she called.

"What is it you want from me?" her sister asked, a voice from the shadows.

"Want from you?" Rose shrugged the backpack

off as carefully and quietly as she could. Her head began to ache, a slow and steady throb like a pulse in her forehead, spreading to her left eye.

"Why haven't you told?" Sylvie asked.

Rose squinted, trying to quiet the sudden, stabbing pain. She tried to concentrate on getting Sylvie to transform. What would it take? Perhaps if she felt threatened.

"No one would believe me if I did," Rose said. "You're the good girl. You always have been. No one would believe me if I told them what you really were."

Rose could hear her sister begin to cry, softly at first, then louder.

"What *am I?* What am I, Rose?"

"A monster." It felt so good to say it out loud. "And you've fooled everyone but me. I know what you did to Fenton."

"Fenton," Sylvie said, sobbing now.

Rose pulled the flashlight out of the bag but stayed where she was, just outside the tower door, waiting for her moment.

"It was his doing as much as mine," Sylvie said, sniffling. "It was wrong, I know, but he's gone now, so it won't happen again."

"No," Rose said, stepping forward, swinging her body around so that she stood in the open doorway. "It won't happen again. Because I'm going to stop you."

She flipped on the flashlight, steeling herself

against what she might see: her sister in hideous insect form with six legs, wings, a shiny exoskeleton. But there was just a girl in a robe with pink slippers on her feet. Her face was red and splotchy, her hair sticking up everywhere in a very non-Sylvie way.

Rose took a step into the tower, keeping the beam of her flashlight pointed at Sylvie's face. The determination on Rose's face must have scared Sylvie, because all of a sudden she grew wary.

"Rose, you just stay away from me," Sylvie warned, moving now, inching sideways toward the ladder. "If you don't, I'll tell Mama."

"I won't let you do it again," Rose said flatly. "I won't let you hurt anyone else."

Rose's head was throbbing now, the pain bright and blinding. The beam from the flashlight seemed to pulsate, making her sister's face waver, almost as if she weren't really there at all. Rose's skin prickled, felt hot and itchy.

Sylvie ran for the ladder and started to climb.

Rose ducked back outside, grabbed the backpack, and followed her sister up the ladder, the flashlight tucked in the back waistband of her pants, her sweaty hands sticking to the wooden rungs. The ladder felt like it was moving. But it wasn't just the ladder. It was the whole tower: each stone and board was pulsating, throbbing in time with the pain in her head.

When she surfaced on the second floor, Rose ran the beam of light in a circle. No Sylvie. Only the round walls, and moonlight streaming in through the slit-shaped windows.

She had to hurry now. She couldn't let Sylvie get away.

If Sylvie transformed, she might just fly away, wings beating, head with mandibles swiveling, free forever.

Heart and brain pounding, Rose labored up the second ladder, leading to the roof. Her arms and legs were heavy and stiff, like they didn't belong to her. The wind picked up, sending a chill through her. She reached the top and shone the flashlight around, the beam bouncing off the walls with their battlements.

There was her sister, still in human form, standing close to the low wall. The moonlight had turned everything a bright, sparkling blue. The scene before her pulsated along with the throbbing in her head.

"I'm going away," Sylvie said. She was no longer crying. She spoke defiantly and dramatically. "I'm going far away, and I'm never going to come back. I'm leaving tonight. Just go back to the house, Rose. Pretend you never saw me and I'll be gone by morning, and you'll never see me again."

"No," Rose said, stepping toward her sister. "I can't let you do that. I know how dangerous you are."

"You don't know anything! You're crazy." Sylvie laughed raggedly, though her eyes looked frightened. "Stay away," she said again.

She backed toward the wall. Rose ran for her, and was on her in an instant, seizing her arm.

"For God's sake, Rose! Let go!" Sylvie cried, frantically trying to snatch her arm away. But Rose held firm.

They spun, stumbling, scratching each other. Rose grabbed Sylvie's hair and jerked her head forward, half expecting to see a terrible mouth hidden on the back of her sister's head. Sylvie shrieked, dug her nails into Rose's arm, and raked them down, leaving trails of blood. They twirled together, stumbling like drunk dancers doing their own version of the twist. The stars above them blurred. Everything took on a sickening yellowish tinge. Rose staggered, her legs suddenly not working right. Sylvie's nails felt as if they were clawing their way down to the bone. Rose dipped forward and sank her teeth into her sister's forearm until she tasted blood. Sylvie cried out and released her grip. The terrible dance slowed. Sylvie looked, unbelieving, from the wound on her arm to Rose's face.

"My God," Sylvie breathed. Her face was white; her lips were colorless; her eyes seemed to bulge from their sockets. "What's *happening* to you?" She pulled back from Rose with all her strength.

Sylvie slipped from Rose's grasp. Rose fell to

the floor. Sylvie, suddenly free, stumbled back two steps and hit the wall hard. It caught her at the waist, and she was gone, over the edge, flipping over backward in a clumsy dive.

"Sylvie!" Rose screamed, only it came out as a strangled-sounding growl. She tried to get up, but found her body was frozen, her muscles unable to respond to her mind's command to move, her head swimming, the pain in her head pulsing. She lay there for what felt like ages, while strength returned to her limbs and her vision cleared a little.

At last, in slow motion, she was able to stagger over to the edge. She willed herself to look down, to search the pool of darkness at the bottom for her sister's crumpled body. But there was nothing—only the cold shadow of the tower.

"Sylvie!" Rose called, her voice hoarse and strained, searching the darkness. Surely her sister couldn't have walked away from the fall—it was a good thirty feet down.

But where was she?

Gone. Sylvie was gone.

"No," Rose moaned. She sank down to her knees, head hurting so bad she was sure that something inside was going to explode.

Then, at the edge of her vision, she caught movement: a quick fluttering, the slight glow of nearly iridescent wings.

And there she was: Sylvie, in luna-moth form,

rising from the darkness below, coming to rest on top of the stone wall. With her pale-green wings spread wide, she was beautiful, luminous, glittering, as though made of stardust.

Slowly, Rose felt for the pack, which had fallen off during their struggle, reached inside, and pulled out the butterfly net. She stood up and crept forward slowly, net behind her back.

"Got you!" she cried, slamming the net down on top of her sister.

She held the butterfly net closed carefully as she climbed back down to the base of the tower. In the kitchen, she used her flashlight to find the large glass jar that her mother sometimes made sauerkraut in. She put the moth inside and screwed the lid on tight. Then she took the jar out to the shed, found a roll of baling wire, and wrapped it over and over around the jar, making a metal cage, so that it would be impossible for her to transform back into a human.

Once she was back in her bedroom, Rose placed the wire-wrapped jar on the floor beside her bed.

"I've got you," she said again to the moth in the jar. It was clinging to the inside of the glass and seemed to make no move to find a means of escape. The moth was perfectly still, as if she knew she'd been caught at last. Maybe she even wanted to be. Maybe it was time to surrender.

Rose

Rose woke up in the morning with a tinny taste in her mouth, her body spent and exhausted. She'd dreamed of knives and claws, and razor teeth. She lay there for a minute, breathing a little too hard, eyes closed, listening for her sister.

Then she remembered.

Rose turned and reached for the jar beside her bed.

The luna moth was not moving. It lay on its side, lifeless.

Rose began to scream.

"What is it?" her mother asked, hurrying into the room, still in her nightgown.

"Sylvie!" Rose said, holding up the jar wrapped in wire. "It's Sylvie! I've killed her."

"Rose," Mama said, voice shaky as she took a step back, looking stunned.

"This is Sylvie! Here in the jar! Look!"

Mama's confused eyes locked on the jar in Rose's hand. "Don't be ridiculous," she said at last.

Rose sobbed. "She was a mare. I wanted to show you. To prove it. I didn't mean to kill her."

Mama shook her head. "You listen to me, Rose. That moth is not your sister."

Mama's eyes moved from the jar to Sylvie's

302

empty bed and the open closet door, where many of the hangers hung empty.

Rose blinked, trying to understand what she was seeing, where Sylvie's things could have gone. She remembered last night, how Sylvie said she was going away. Had she packed everything up to leave before she headed out to the tower? Was she really planning to run away, worried she'd be caught for killing Fenton?

Mama then moved to the desk, where a piece of paper was loaded into the Royal typewriter.

Mama pulled the paper out, read it out loud:

I can't stay here any longer.
    I'm sorry. I love you all and know you'll understand.
    I'll write once I've settled.
All my love,
Sylvie

"What's all the commotion?" Daddy called from the doorway, where he stood, shoulders slumped, wearing his old rumpled pajamas.

"It's Sylvie," Mama said, voice shaking, as she stepped forward to hand him the typed note. "She's run away."

A door closed in Rose's chest. She knew Mama was wrong.

She'd killed Sylvie.

Yes, Sylvie may have been a monster, but

Rose hadn't meant to hurt her. She just wanted to catch her. To prove to the world what Sylvie really was. Now no one would ever believe. They'd all think that Sylvie had run away, gone off to some bright new future. And Rose alone would bear the burden of the truth.

She clung desperately to the glass jar, looked at the beautiful broken creature inside, and began to sob.

2013

Piper

"It's for you," Margot said, holding the phone out to Piper. They were sitting together, having a luxurious breakfast in bed. Piper had made crêpes with apple butter, turkey bacon, sliced melon, and fresh-squeezed orange juice.

Jason had gone to work early without so much as a glance at Piper. Piper had heard him and Margot talking late into the night, Jason's voice desperate and at times angry. At one point, she heard him snarl, "You and Piper and Amy." Apparently, they hadn't resolved things: when Piper got up to use the bathroom in the night, she saw Jason snoring on the couch, four empty beer cans on the coffee table, and the sports channel playing on the muted TV.

Margot hadn't said a word about Jason so far this morning, choosing instead to talk about everything Piper should accomplish today. Not only was there a crib that needed to be assembled, there were curtains with little elephants to hang, and bags of tiny onesies and footie pajamas to put in drawers. Up until this point, Margot and Jason had left everything unpacked or stored away. If the worst happened (It couldn't possibly, could it? Life couldn't be that unfair . . .), the last thing they wanted was an adorable elephant mobile hanging over an empty crib, or drawers full of tiny clothes that would never be worn. But now the baby's arrival seemed imminent, and Margot was feeling completely unprepared. She also seemed to desperately need something to keep her busy, something to focus on that wasn't Jason or Amy. She showed Piper checklists from books and Web sites, and made frantic lists of things they didn't have and would need to get: diaper-rash cream, a rectal thermometer, tiny nail clippers.

Piper was loving it.

"For me?" Piper said, reaching to take the phone from Margot. Margot shrugged, looking equally puzzled. Who on earth would be calling Margot's home phone looking for Piper at 10:00 a.m. on a Monday?

"Hello?" Piper said.

"Piper? Hey, this is Crystal. Lou's aunt?"

"Oh, sure, hi." Piper's pulse quickened a bit. Had something happened to the little girl?

"So . . . Lou hasn't stopped talking about you since yesterday. Guess you made quite an impression. She keeps asking when she can see you again."

"Oh, that's nice. I could come by and visit again sometime."

"Yeah, well, here's the thing. I've gotta work this afternoon, and I don't have anyone to watch her. Would you mind?"

"This afternoon?"

"Just for a couple hours. Until Ray gets home at three. Lou's really not all that comfortable with most adults, especially now. It would be a real favor."

"Uh, sure. I guess I can do that."

"Cool. Oh, and maybe you could go by her house first? She needs some things. Clothes and toys and stuff? When they brought her over, all she had was the stuff she was wearing. She doesn't want to go back there—can't say I blame her."

"But isn't it all sealed off? Will the police let me in?"

Margot's eyes got huge as she watched Piper. "The motel?" she mouthed. Piper nodded.

"It's all clear. I talked to the cops this morning. They're done up there and said we could come anytime. Ray won't go, and, me, I can't stand the thought of going anywhere near the place. I mean, Mark is"—her voice faltered—"*was* my *brother.*"

Piper didn't know what to say, so she said nothing.

"So would you mind?" Crystal went on. "Picking up a bag of stuff for Lou and bringing it by later? I can't tell you what a help it would be. I leave for work at one."

Piper didn't want to go to the motel, no way, no how. Didn't want to see where Amy and her family had died so horribly. But then she thought of Lou—her pale face, her smile that reminded Piper so much of a young Amy. The poor kid had been through so much; didn't she deserve the slim comfort of her own clothes, a few favorite stuffed animals to provide some sense of normality, to remind her of the time before this nightmare? It seemed like the least Piper could do.

"Sure," Piper said at last. "No problem. I'll see you at one."

She hung up and told Margot what was going on.

"Holy crap! You've gotta go check out the motel! Take a good look around."

Piper groaned. "You're kidding, right? The thought of even setting foot near that place makes me sick, and you want me to play Nancy Drew? What am I even looking for?"

"Evidence that we're right. That Amy didn't kill her family."

"Don't you think the police would have found that if it existed?"

Margot shook her head fiercely. "It's a cut-and-dried case to them. Besides, no one knows that motel like we do, right?"

"Jason will kill me if he finds out I went anywhere near the motel."

"Please. You'll be back in no time. He'll never know! You can stop at Rite Aid on your way back and get the stuff on our list. If he calls or stops by, I'll tell him you're out shopping. Then you come back here for lunch—and to tell me *everything*—and head over to Crystal's to baby-sit Lou. No problem."

"I don't know. . . ."

"For Christ's sake, Piper. You already told Crystal you'd pick up clothes for Lou, right? I mean, you don't expect Crystal to go out there, where her brother was killed? And so, while you're there, just . . . look around. See what you can figure out."

Piper was silent, trying to come up with a way to make Margot understand that it was impossible, that she couldn't bear it. Then Margot said, quietly:

"You know Amy would do it for you."

So that was that.

Piper gripped the steering wheel of her sister's Subaru tightly as she came up to the Tower Motel sign.

28 Rooms, Pool, No Vacancy.

Piper flipped down her turn signal, her eyes on the tower. She recalled Lou's description of the sound of the gun, the footsteps.

Could Amy possibly have shot her husband and son?

Or had there been someone else there?

Something else?

She remembered the notes left for Amy in the typewriter all those years ago, and Amy's insistence that Sylvie's ghost had come back and was visiting her in her bedroom at night. The fuzzy Polaroid photo she waved around as proof.

The old gravel driveway was nearly washed out. Piper moved slowly; the car bumped as she passed the leaning stone tower and the long shadow it cast. She shivered.

Just a building, she told herself.

But it wasn't just a building, was it?

She knew the truth.

There was no way she was going in the tower, not today, not ever, in spite of her sister's guilt trip. She'd just tell Margot the tower was too dangerous, the wood floors rotted through. *I was thinking about my own safety,* she'd say, *about how I didn't want your baby to grow up without her kooky aunt Piper.*

Kooky. That was something Amy might have called her. Back then.

Suddenly she was twelve again. Gangly and awkward, all legs, feathered hair.

Naïve. Just so young.

There was so much we didn't know.

But there were also the things she *had* known. She'd known that she loved Amy; known it, but never admitted it to anyone, even herself. And somehow or other, in spite all the affairs that came after, both men and women, nothing compared to that wild adolescent longing she felt for Amy. It was Amy she went back to in her mind.

Amy. Always Amy.

Piper passed the first building of units, Rooms 1 through 14. Some of the windows were broken, and the roof had collapsed in three places. She remembered searching through Room 4 and finding binoculars, Amy's sunglasses, the heavy old key ring and key. Was the lock still broken? If anyone could get inside, they might even be sitting there now, peering between the slits of the ruined plastic blinds.

She pulled the car up to the main house, shut off the engine, and sat for a minute, listening to the car tick as it cooled.

Crystal was right—the police were gone. There was no sign of crime-scene tape, no clue that anything horrible had happened here. It looked like any other badly neglected house in rural New England: shutters hanging unevenly, paint peeling, the yard and once-upon-a-time gardens overrun with weeds. It really didn't look all that different from the way Piper remembered it when she was a kid. A little smaller, maybe (didn't everything look smaller once you grew up?), a little more . . . dark. Was that the right word?

Piper half-expected to look up at the dormer window on the right and see Amy looking down, waving. *Come up. I have something to show you. Something exciting. Sylvie's left another message. She came back last night, stood at the foot of my bed. Here, I've got a picture. . . .*

Piper got out of the car, blinking up at Amy's old bedroom window. There was no movement there or at any other window. No one home.

It's because they're all dead, a little voice reminded Piper, but she shook off the thought, made herself walk to the front steps, climb the crumbling concrete and stone, and push open the heavy front door.

1989

Piper

"Oh my God, I'm so happy to see you!" Amy threw her arms around Piper, buried her face against Piper's neck. Piper could feel her hot breath, and then (did Piper imagine it?) Amy gave her the tiniest little nibble, her teeth grazing the tender skin just to the left of her windpipe.

"She's left us another note," Amy said now, voice rising like bubbles in a cold glass of ginger ale, going up, up, up, then bursting, tickling someone's nose.

"In the typewriter?" Margot asked, coming through the front door behind Piper.

"Yeah, just like the last."

"Mmm," Margot said, playing the skeptic, looking quite grown up with her doubtful eyes and wrinkled nose. Last night, at home, Margot had said she was pretty sure that Amy had written the first note herself.

"But why would she do that?" Piper asked. Sometimes she thought Margot acted like a little old lady, serious and thinking too hard about stuff, which sucked the fun out of everything.

Margot thought for a second. "Because Amy always likes things to be more exciting than they really are."

Piper had thrown a pillow at her, furious

because she knew that, on some level, Margot had it right. Wasn't that probably why Amy had kissed her? Just to make things more exciting? Because Amy hated anything dull and boring.

"I was even thinking that maybe she put the suitcase there herself, set the whole thing up, so we'd have this fun mystery, this game to play," Margot said.

"Right," Piper said. "And planned how I'd fall through the floor right where I did, too, I guess?"

Margot shrugged her shoulders. "Maybe."

"Well, I think that's total crap," Piper had said.

But did she? Did she really? Wasn't there a chance Amy had written the note from supposedly dead Sylvie herself?

Right now, still feeling the chills that came from having Amy's mouth on her neck, Piper felt sure that she would believe anything Amy told her.

"Show me the letter!" she asked Amy now.

Amy's face brightened. She turned and darted down the hall. Piper followed. Her right leg was killing her, but she managed not to limp. The redness and puffiness seemed to be spreading; her skin felt like it was on fire. She knew she should tell her mom, would *have* to tell her mom if it didn't get better soon, but she didn't want to get in trouble, or, worse, to be banned from the motel. She'd have to make up a lie—maybe that she'd hurt herself playing in the woods.

"Hello, girls!" Amy's grandma called from her usual spot in the kitchen.

"Hello, Grandma Charlotte," Piper said.

"Sylvie, what are you girls up to?"

"*Amy,* Gram. My name is Amy. Sylvie's gone."

She's not gone, though, thought Piper. *She's up in Amy's room, tapping out notes on the typewriter—that's where she is.*

An odd thought occurred to her then: that Sylvie had never really left. She'd been in hiding this whole time, sneaking around the house, tower, and motel. Living in abandoned rooms, hiding in closets, stealing food from the kitchen at night, making friends with the mice in the walls, visiting Amy late at night, when no one else could see. It wasn't a ghost Amy had seen, but an actual person living the life of a phantom.

"Come on," Amy urged, taking Piper by the hand and leading her up the steps; Margot followed right behind, taking two steps at a time. Amy's hand felt cool. Or maybe it was Piper's hand that was hot. She didn't feel like herself; her head seemed to be floating up above her body like a balloon.

Amy had hung an old *Please Do Not Disturb* sign from one of the motel rooms on the door to her room.

"Check this out," she said, standing over by the typewriter. There was an old sheet of Tower Motel stationery tucked into it:

Find the 29th Room.

Remember, no room is built without a plan. Find the plans, you find the room.

Then you'll understand.

"Whatever happened to Sylvie, the key is the twenty-ninth room! Like she talked about in that letter to Alfred Hitchcock."

"But we've searched the whole motel!" Piper said, exasperated. "We've been in every room. There's nowhere else to look."

Amy thumped her fingers down on the typed note. "Find the plans, you find the room. You know, my grandfather designed this whole motel. He must've drawn up plans for it, right?"

Maybe Margot was right. Maybe Amy was setting all this up somehow, leaving little clues like bread crumbs. It was all some crazy game to make the last few days of summer vacation a little less boring.

"So let's go find them! My grandfather's old office is full of papers and junk. Let's go check it out!"

2013

Piper

Piper could almost hear the vague echoes of footsteps as she stood in the front hall now: her own, Amy's, Margot's, as they trotted down the stairs and ran into the office to search for evidence of the twenty-ninth room. She followed the ghost steps down the hallway and peered into the office, which looked nearly the same as she remembered: peeling wallpaper, teetering stacks of papers, boxes and books everywhere.

The air in the old house smelled musty, used up. She longed to open a window, but knew it wasn't her place. Besides, she wouldn't be here long. She was getting Lou a bag of clothes, and then she was getting the hell out.

Off to her left, she heard a slight shuffling sound coming from the kitchen. Mice? Or old Grandma Charlotte pushing back her chair?

> When Death comes knocking on your door,
> you'll think you've seen his face before.

Piper jumped as her phone rang, chirping "Like a Prayer" too loud in this quiet place. She fumbled through her bag, trying to answer it as quickly as she could.

"Hey," she said, voice library-quiet.

"Did you find anything?" Margot asked.

"Not yet. I just got here, for God's sake," Piper said.

"Sorry. Where are you right now?"

"The front hall." Glancing furtively around, she saw no sign of movement.

But was there another noise from the kitchen? The shuffle of feet?

If you hold up a mirror, you shall see
that he is you and you are he.

"Piper?"

"Yeah?"

"I've changed my mind. I have a really bad feeling about this. I think you should get out of there."

"I'm glad you feel that way, 'cause that's exactly my plan. I'm just gonna run upstairs and grab a few things for Lou; then I'm gone."

"Call me when you're done."

"Will do."

"And—Piper?—hurry."

As if she needed encouragement.

Piper hung up and hustled up the stairs. She was stopped short by the bloodstains. They were everywhere—the carpet was saturated in places, covered in thick smears, smudges, and grotesque footprints of dark coagulated blood. There were even some reddish-brown splatters on the faded wallpaper.

Down the hall to the left was the master bedroom. That was where Amy's husband had been found, the first to be shot. In the middle of the hall was the bathroom, then the second bedroom, which used to be Grandma Charlotte's. Piper gave the door a tentative push, and it opened to reveal posters of football players, a huge spaceport built from Legos on the dresser.

Levi's room. Eight years old, and the second to die. The bed frame was bare, the mattress taken away.

Piper backed up, head swimming, stomach queasy.

She moved along the edge of the wall, doing her best to avoid the stains on the floor (was this all Amy's blood?) as she lurched down the hall on rubbery legs.

Just do what you need to do and get out, she told herself, heading for what must be Lou's room, down at the end of the hall.

The room that had once been Amy's.

She remembered the little motel sign that had hung from the doorknob back then: *Please Do Not Disturb.*

She put her hand on the knob now, the knob that Amy had touched countless times, that had once been warm from the heat of her hand.

Now it was as cold as ice.

Go away, it seemed to say. *You don't belong.*

She held her breath and pushed the door open.

The sight of the room hit her square in the chest. There were bloodstains on this floor, too, though not nearly as much as in the hall. Its floor had been covered in the same ugly carpet that was in the hall back when Amy lived there, but at some point they'd torn it up and painted the wide pine boards white to make the room feel bigger and brighter. Lou had Amy's old twin bed, with its battered oak headboard. Were those even the remnants of Amy's Scratch 'N Sniff stickers and glow-in-the-dark stars? Piper looked at the dresser and nightstand, all in the same place, as if bolted down. And were those faint traces of purple paint at the edges of the wall that had been covered over with rose-petal pink?

The room was neat. No clothes strewn on the floor, no toys and books and candy wrappers scattered everywhere. There was a shaggy bright-pink rug by the bed, and a glass of water on the nightstand. The mattress was bare except for a pile of stuffed animals mounded in its center.

And there, on the desk, an old typewriter.

Could it be?

Piper stepped forward to it and ran her fingers over the machine: a Royal Quiet De Luxe.

Beside it sat a stack of plain white paper.

Without even thinking, Piper reached for a piece, rolled it into the machine, and put her fingers over the keys. It amazed her, how effortless it was, how satisfying to give each key a hard tap and hear the gentle thwap of the letter striking the ribbon and paper. The typewriter had been kept cleaned and oiled, and the ribbon was fresh. Her fingers found the sturdy round keys: punch, punch, punch, bang, bang, bang.

Amy, Amy, Amy, she typed, thinking that perhaps the old Royal might act as a sort of Ouija Board and Amy could type out a message to her, as they'd once believed Sylvie had done.

Are you there, Amy?

Nothing. This was pure foolishness. She wasn't a twelve-year-old girl anymore.

Still, she typed one more line:

I'm sorry

And she *was* sorry. Sorry for what had happened to Amy and her family. Sorry that she hadn't made more of an effort. Amy had pushed her away at the end of that summer, and Piper hadn't put up a fight; she'd just let her go and tried to pretend it didn't matter at all. She was sorry that she had moved away and done her best to forget Amy and the tower and everything that had happened that long-ago summer; to put it all in a box at the back of her mind, like packing away outgrown childhood toys. Yet somehow the very act of trying to forget had made all the memories stronger, had turned Amy into an archetype that she compared everyone else with. And, somehow, no one ever measured up.

Wasn't it true that, after Amy cut her out of her life that summer, Piper had always kept herself at a distance from people, never let herself believe any friend or lover would stick around? Sitting at the desk in Amy's old bedroom, Piper understood suddenly that somewhere tucked deep inside her was a broken twelve-year-old girl reeling and pissed off because her best friend had dumped her. Piper took in a ragged breath. If she let herself think of all the ways this had held her back over the years, of all the relationships she'd ended because she was sure it was only a matter of time until she was abandoned, she didn't know if she'd be able to bear it.

Yanking the paper out of the typewriter, she crumpled it up and shoved it into her purse, which she left on the desk as she went to work. She found a flowered duffel bag in Lou's closet and quickly loaded it with underwear, socks, T-shirts, shorts, and jeans. Everything was pink and purple and covered with hearts, peace signs, glittering sequins, or a mix of all three. She threw in a pair of sparkly silver sneakers and some leopard-print flip-flops.

Behind her, she heard something out in the hall. Scrabbling, quick steps.

"Hello?" she called. Had the police come back, realizing there was one more thing they forgot to take with them? Or maybe they'd seen her car and wondered who was trespassing on the crime scene? Piper went out to the hallway and stood at the top of the stairs.

"Anyone there?" she called.

From somewhere, a soft, Amy-like giggle. Surely Piper had imagined it. Still: time to go.

She hurried back to the bedroom, went to Lou's bed, and selected a floppy pink rabbit and a dingy rag doll with yellow yarn for hair that looked like it had been loved nearly to death.

Good enough.

She hefted the bag, grabbed her purse, and hurried out of the room and down the hall. When she paused at the top of the stairs, she was sure she heard something behind her, coming from Lou's room. Short, trotting footsteps. The sound of nails (or was it claws?) on the painted pine-board floor.

Piper raced down the stairs and headed toward the front door, but then forced herself to stop in the entryway and turn back. She was waiting for a dark, terrifying shape to fill the stairway. She listened. There was nothing. Just the sound of her own frantic breath. She'd imagined it. Of course.

Her phone rang—Margot again. Piper dug around in her bag, and the crumpled piece of typing paper fell out by accident. She watched it fall to the floor as she answered.

"Piper?" Margot said anxiously. "Where are you?"

"On my way out. Just at the front door now. I got together a bag for Lou. I'll make a quick stop at the drugstore for the baby stuff and then come right back. Half an hour, forty-five minutes tops."

"Okay," Margot said, clearly relieved.

"You want me to pick up anything special for lunch?" Piper asked.

"Lunch? Even eating for two, I couldn't possibly have room for lunch after that huge breakfast you made."

Piper smiled. "I'll fix us a salad or something. See you soon."

She hung up, put the phone back in her bag, and reached down for the crumpled paper, not wanting to leave her weird litter behind for anyone to wonder at, especially not a cop returning to check on one last thing at the crime scene.

She opened the paper, trying to imagine what they might think if they found it, this bizarre message typed to a dead woman.

But that's not what was on the sheet. The words she'd typed were gone.

She let out a strangled cry.

(And was there another, distant, mocking cry that echoed hers from somewhere upstairs?)

Over and over, one line after another filled the page, from top to bottom:

```
29 rooms
29 rooms
29 rooms
29 rooms
29 rooms
```

1989

Piper

29 rooms.

Up until now, it had seemed like something made up; something from a Trixie Belden book, maybe: *The Mystery of the 29th Room.*

Piper pictured Trixie and Honey creeping around with a flashlight, tapping on walls, looking for a secret door to a secret room.

But now, as they searched through old papers and drawings that had belonged to Amy's grandfather, Piper began to wonder, what if it was real?

What if there really was a twenty-ninth room?

"Look at this," Amy said. She was sitting on the floor next to a couple of banged-up cardboard boxes labeled *Daddy's Paperwork* that she'd dragged out of the closet. She'd been emptying them haphazardly, crazed, glancing at each bit of paper for a split second before tossing it carelessly off to the side.

Now she held a stack of photos in her hand, each showing the motel in a different stage of completion. First it was only a foundation, then a roughly framed outline of two buildings that slowly added a roof, doors, and, finally, windows. In each photo was Amy's grandfather, dressed in khaki work clothes, holding a hammer, saw, or trowel.

"Maybe he didn't have any plans or blueprints or anything," Margot suggested. "Maybe he just made it up as he went along?"

Piper shook her head. "You can't put up a whole building that way. Especially not if you're not a carpenter or architect or anything. I'm sure he had plans."

"Well, they're not in this box," Amy said, pulling the last photos and yellowed papers out of the first box, letting old bills and ledger pages drift to the floor.

She opened the next box. This turned out to be full of photos and papers from her grandfather's days as a pilot in the army. There were lots of letters from his parents on the farm back at home; Amy skimmed through some of them and read bits aloud. They told about how much milk the cows were producing, what a good helper Clarence's young cousin Fenton was turning out to be, the scrap-metal drives being held all over Vermont; they were peppered with gossip from town—Violet Stafford finally got a marriage proposal from Hank Ritter, Mr. Erickson had to close the local branch of the bank, little Richie Welks won the fishing derby last Saturday.

"I'm surprised he didn't get *bored* to death by these letters," Amy complained, tossing them back into the box.

"Nah," Piper said. "I bet it was kind of comforting to get all that news from home. To see things back there were just as dull as ever. If I was up in an airplane getting shot at by the Germans, I'd want to know that back at home things were quiet and calm, and there were cows still waiting to be milked, and a plain girl waiting for a marriage proposal."

"I guess." Amy shrugged.

Margot dragged a metal file box out of the closet and popped open the clasp.

"What have you got there?" Piper asked.

Margot started flipping through the papers. "Looks like your mom's stuff, Amy. Birth certificate, high-school diploma . . . Wait a sec, there's something down at the bottom." She pulled out a stack of letters in worn envelopes held together with disintegrating elastic bands.

"Check it out," Margot said, handing them to Amy. "It's more letters to that movie-director guy from Sylvie!"

Amy took them and thumbed through. "You're right. They're all addressed to Alfred Hitchcock, and they've got stamps, but it looks like they were never mailed. See, no postmark."

"Weird," Piper said. "Why go to the trouble of writing the letters, putting stamps on them and everything, if you're not going to send them? And what's your mom doing with them?"

"Beats me," Amy said, tossing the letters back into the metal box. "But they're not helping us with the plans for the motel."

She rummaged around in the closet again and pulled out a brown leather folder with a clasp. "Bingo!" she cried, as she opened it up and peered inside. "Sketches for the motel!"

Piper moved close against Amy and looked at the papers Amy was eagerly pulling out of the folder. Clarence's careful renderings of the motel he imagined were drawn in pencil on yellowing paper. There were structural drawings that showed the framing with measurements and elevation drawings from every angle.

The girls studied them, searching for some sign of a secret passageway or hidden door, perhaps a room between rooms.

"There's not a damn thing in either building," Amy said at last. "There are the twenty-eight motel rooms, the office, the laundry area and boiler room underneath the office. That's it." She blew out an exasperated breath, making her pink bangs puff out.

A framed drawing of the tower was propped against the side of the desk. Piper picked it up. Also done in pencil, it showed the outside of the tower: the door, the windows, and the battlements. She looked at it carefully, noticing the attention to detail—each rock a different shape and shade, the shadows in the open doorway seeming almost alive somehow. Amy's grandfather was a talented artist.

Then she noticed it: there, in those shadows, was

something else. Faint writing; ghostly unfamiliar letters she could barely make out. She pulled the picture closer and squinted down at it, finally understanding what the problem was.

The writing was backward.

"There's something written on the other side of this drawing," she said. Amy snatched it from her, immediately flipped the frame over, and went to work bending the wire brads that held the cardboard back on. Soon she'd pried one edge out; then the whole piece of thin black cardboard was in her hand, the drawing on top of it. She carefully pulled them apart and turned the tower drawing over.

On the other side was the original sketch for the tower. There were dimensions for its diameter and height, and the plan for the floor joists and rafters. In the right-hand margin were calculations for the amount of cement, lime, and sand that would be needed.

The drawing showed the three floors the girls had all explored: ground floor, second floor, and the rooftop surrounded by the ring of battlements.

But there was something else: a fourth floor, a basement room that looked as if it was accessed by a trapdoor in the floor above. This room was labeled with Amy grandfather's careful lettering: "oubliette."

"What's 'oubliette' mean?" Amy asked.

Piper jumped up, went to the desk, and got the

heavy dictionary she'd seen there when they first entered the office. She thumbed through the alphabet until she got to "O." Otter. Ottoman. Ouabain (Piper's eye caught on this a moment—a poison).

"Here it is," Piper said. With her finger on the word, she blinked down at the definition; her voice shook as she read it out loud: " 'A concealed dungeon with a trapdoor in the ceiling as the only means of entrance or exit.' "

"Holy crap!" Amy exclaimed. "A dungeon? There's a hidden dungeon at the bottom of the tower?"

"We don't know that," Piper said. "I mean, it's here in the drawing, but—"

"Come on," Amy said, already on her way out of the office, "we've gotta go find it!"

2013

Piper

Piper dumped the flowered duffel bag in her car, her hands trembling.

She knew what she'd typed.

How, then, did the page get filled with *29 rooms* over and over and over?

She started the engine, yanked the shifter into reverse, and hit the gas; gravel spat out from under her tires as she backed up, spun around, and headed down the steep driveway.

Was she going crazy? Had she typed the words herself in a sort of fugue state?

She remembered Amy's obsession with hypnosis—with that damn book she'd found that had belonged to Sylvie. Amy would say that it was possible to do just about anything in a trance state. Even to receive messages from the dead.

"Damn it," Piper said, hitting the steering wheel with the palm of her hand. Just then she was passing the tower, and she glanced inside, through the doorway blocked by two boards forming an X. *Danger,* warned the dripping red spray paint above.

A shadow moved across the floor inside.

There was someone in there!

Piper slammed on the brakes, heart hammering, palms sweating.

Maybe there had been someone in the house with her after all. Someone who had replaced her paper with another. (But how? When?) Improbable as it seemed, Piper clung to this new idea. It felt far better than believing that either a ghost or Piper herself had typed the message.

She jumped out of the car, went around to the rear, opened the hatchback, pulled up the carpeted panel, and grabbed a tire iron. She wasn't going in there unarmed.

She stood, looking at the great crooked tower before her, the metal tire iron clenched in her hands. This was a stupid idea and she knew it. She should get right back in the car, lock the door, and call Jason at the police station to tell him someone was sneaking around at the motel. But that would mean having to admit to him that she was at the motel. He'd probably ask her to pack her bags and get on the next plane back to Los Angeles. And what if whoever was in there got away—sneaked out through some opening in the wall of the disintegrating tower—while she hid quaking in the car, awaiting rescue like a fairy-tale damsel?

She stepped toward the doorway, eyes searching inside the decrepit tower for any sign of movement. Outside, the cement was crumbling, and the whole structure leaned a good ten degrees toward the house.

It looked like an accident waiting to happen.

She peeked in over the X of boards nailed over the doorway. The floorboards looked rotten, and the ladder that led up to the second floor was missing several rungs. Above her, the word *Danger* seemed to glow like the once-upon-a-time motel sign must have.

Tower Motel, 28 Rooms, Pool, Vacancy.

She took a breath. Heard Amy's voice in her ear:

"Don't be a chickenshit."

1989

Piper

"I am not a chickenshit," Piper said, her whole body rigid as she stood before the open door to the tower.

"So—let's go," Amy said, sweeping her arm grandly toward the entrance in a you-first gesture. "We've got a dungeon to find."

Piper's shin throbbed out a warning, a Morse-code message of pain, as she remembered falling through the floorboards. She didn't want to go in there. Didn't want to go prying at the edges of floorboards, shining the flashlight Amy had taken from the kitchen drawer into the shadows, like some wannabe teen sleuth. If there really was a dungeon down there (Surely there couldn't be? Why on earth would Amy's grandfather have built a dungeon?), she sure as hell didn't want to see it. She didn't think Margot should, either.

"Maybe you should go home," she said to her sister, who was marching along with purpose, looking more like a little adult than a ten-year-old kid walking into a death trap.

"I'm not scared."

Maybe you should be. Maybe we should all be.

"Yeah, come *on*, Piper," Amy groaned. "Take a hint from Little Sis here. Let's go."

Piper followed Amy into the tower. She walked

slowly, testing the boards beneath her feet with each careful step. They felt springy, flimsy. How had she not noticed this the other day?

Margot stood in the doorway, eyes wide as she watched.

Amy was walking without care, stomping down on the boards, trying to pry up the edges of them with her fingernails. "I don't see anything that looks like a trapdoor," she said.

"Remember upstairs," Margot said. "There were two layers. The actual floor, and then the boards below for the ceiling."

"Right," Amy said. "So maybe the door isn't right here. Maybe it's just a couple of loose boards. Come on, Piper. You start at that side; I'll start over here. Check every board to see if it's loose. We'll keep going until we meet in the middle."

Piper nodded. "Margot, you stay outside and watch. If we fall through or anything happens, you run up to the house and get Amy's grandma, okay?"

Amy laughed. "If you go get Gram, you better make sure we're dead first. Because we totally will be if she finds out we've been in the tower."

"Just be careful," Margot said, hovering in the doorway.

Piper thought it was way too late for that.

She got down on her hands and knees on the wide knotty-pine planks that made up the floor.

She imagined Clarence Slater, a young man then, having the boards milled, laying them down himself, pounding nails, building his wife her own Tower of London.

A tower with a secret dungeon.

"Doesn't the real Tower of London—you know, in England?—have a dungeon and a torture chamber and stuff?" Piper asked.

"I think so. I dunno," Amy said, thumping and prying at the floorboards.

"So maybe he just added one to this tower to make it more like a real replica, you know? To be authentic."

"Maybe," Amy said. "But why keep it a secret, then?"

Piper had begun at the door, following that board to its end on either side, checking the boards that butted up against it. Row by row, she studied the floorboards, working her fingers into cracks, trying to pry them up, but the old rusty nails held fast. Across the tower, Amy did the same on her side, scuttling crouched-over, pinching at the boards like a crab in flip-flops.

They moved closer to the middle. Amy groaned in frustration. "It's got to be here," she said.

"Maybe there is no trapdoor, no oboe—whatever," Piper said, trying not to sound too hopeful.

"You guys sure about this?" Margot called from the doorway.

Amy was staring at the ladder in the center of

the room. "Of course!" she said, leaping to her feet so hard and fast that Piper could see the boards sinking beneath her.

"Watch it!" Piper warned.

You'll fall straight through the floor and end up in hell.

"The ladder," Amy said. "It's not attached, right? It's just kind of held in place by little stoppers at the bottom."

Amy grabbed both sides of the ladder and lifted; the whole thing moved. It wasn't all that sturdy: only a couple of two-by-fours making up the side rails, with short pieces of the same lumber cut for rungs. It rested on the floorboards, held in place by two sets of cleats made from strips of wood. Amy heaved the ladder up and clear of the cleats.

"I could use a little help here," she grunted. Piper stepped forward and grabbed the right side. Together, they lifted it up, then angled it sideways, brought it down awkwardly, and laid it on the floor.

"Be careful," Margot warned.

Amy crouched down, fit her fingers along the edge of the board the ladder had been resting on, and gave it a yank; it wiggled like a loose tooth.

"Come give me a hand," she called to Piper. They both began to pry up the board that had been under the ladder, and soon discovered that it was attached to the board just behind it—these came up together in one solid piece.

"They're nailed together," Amy said, as they flipped the piece over, setting it to the side. On the underside, four strips of wood were nailed cross-wise, holding the boards together. "They acted like one big piece. And with the ladder on top, none of it moved. No one would know they were even loose unless you got the ladder out of the way!"

Piper was only half listening. She was looking down into the hole left in the floor. There, between two heavy floor joists, was a trapdoor on rusted metal hinges. A large, sliding metal bolt was latched on the other side.

"Hand me the flashlight," Amy said, scooting forward on her belly so that she could reach the latch.

"Wait!" Piper said suddenly. It was clear that the heavy metal bolt had one purpose: to keep whatever was down there from getting out. "Maybe you shouldn't. Maybe we should get your grandma or something?"

"Just get me the damn light, will you?" Amy said, then wiggled the bolt. It slid open with the sickly scraping sound of metal against metal. Piper brought the red flashlight to Amy just as Amy heaved the trapdoor open.

The first thing that hit them was the smell: cavelike, damp, and dusty. It was the smell of lost things, of decay. Amy shone the flashlight down into the hole. The batteries were low, and it cast a dull, orangey glow.

"What's down there?" Margot called from her post outside. She really was a good sister, Piper thought with a pang of something like regret.

"Hard to tell," Amy said. "I think there's furniture. A bed, maybe?" She leapt up, shaking the floorboards again. "Let's get the ladder. We can use it to go down."

"Amy," Piper said, "I *really* don't think—"

"You don't have to come. You can stay up here and hold the ladder." Amy's words were taunting. *Chickenshit,* they seemed to say.

"Of course I'll come," Piper said, thinking, *I go where you go.*

Together, they got the ladder and carefully lowered it down into the darkness, leaning it against one side of the trapdoor.

"I'll go first," Amy said. "Hold the ladder."

She climbed carefully down, testing each step before she put her weight on it.

"Crap," she called once she was down all the way. "I forgot the light. It's pitch-black down here. Bring it, okay?"

"Okay." Piper tucked the plastic flashlight into the waistband of her shorts and positioned herself to start climbing.

"Don't go," Margot said from the doorway.

"It'll be okay," Piper said, meeting her sister's eyes. "I'll be careful. And I'll be right back. I promise."

No way was she staying down there long.

Amy held the ladder for her, and, slowly, she made her way down, shin throbbing with each step, until her feet touched the hard cement floor. Amy put her hand on Piper's back, and Piper jumped.

"Got the light?"

"Yeah." Piper handed it over, without turning it on. Amy would do the honors.

"Ready?" Amy asked.

Piper swallowed.

"Sure."

The light came on suddenly, illuminating the room with a dim orange-white glow.

"Oh my God," Amy stammered.

Piper couldn't speak. Couldn't make a sound, even though she felt a silent scream building somewhere deep inside her, coming out through her open mouth in just a sad, moist puff of air.

"What is this place?" Amy's voice was squeaky and strange, totally unfamiliar to Piper. Then she realized: it was the first time Piper had ever seen Amy truly frightened.

"Everything okay?" Margot called from up above. "What's down there?"

Piper looked around, scanning the small circular room from right to left. Just to her right was a pair of heavy chains, their ends embedded in the cement wall. Each chain ended in a rusty shackle.

And Amy was right—there was a bed. It was wooden and covered with leather straps and buckles. A mildewed blanket was balled up at the head of the bed.

It's a torture chamber. Piper wanted to say the words out loud, but couldn't speak, couldn't even think clearly. *Your grandfather built a torture chamber.*

She thought of the serious-faced man she'd seen in all the photos—the army pilot with the Purple Heart medal, father and husband, a man of vision, who had built a motel with a tower.

But the tower had a secret room in the basement.

A secret room for doing terrible things.

Had he taken motel guests down here—salesmen far from home, who would never see home again? She knew there were men who did stuff like that, people like John Wayne Gacy or Ted Bundy. But they were just bogeymen she'd heard about on television, not much more real to her than werewolves or zombies.

Amy gasped sharply, breathed, "Oh, no. Oh, shit."

Piper wanted to close her eyes and feel her way back to the ladder, up the rungs, and into daylight, to forget all about what she had seen. She certainly did not want to see whatever it was Amy was looking at.

"Look," Amy said, putting her hand on Piper's arm, tugging, pointing. Piper reluctantly turned and saw what the flashlight's dim beam was illuminating.

On the opposite side of the room lay what looked like a pile of clothes. Then she saw the yellow-white gleam of a skull, dried strands of wispy hair, empty black eye sockets.

"It's Sylvie," Amy said, voice shaking. "We've found her."

2013

Piper

Piper thought of that hideous skeleton face as she stepped into the tower: its jaws yawning open beneath the two empty eye sockets that had looked up at them and seemed to say, *You've found me at last.*

Those eyes had stayed with her all these years, had followed her everywhere she'd gone. They were a part of her, something she would never forget.

After they saw that skeleton, with its awful death-grin, nothing had ever been the same again. It was the last afternoon the girls would ever spend with Amy, the last time they'd ever go to the tower or even the motel. Everything changed when they climbed down that ladder into the twenty-ninth room.

And here she was again.

What might she find this time? Another body? Not likely, she thought grimly. The police had found all the bodies up in the house.

She thought of the blood-soaked carpet in the upstairs hall. What if whatever had gone up to the house had started here, at the tower?

What if it was here still?

She stood as still as she possibly could, listening, the tire iron heavy in her hands. Slowly, she moved forward, testing the floor with each step for places that were rotted through. She knew that if she stayed right on top of the joists she'd be okay. Like a tightrope walker, she followed the line of nails that marked a sturdy joist underneath (at least, she hoped it was sturdy).

The ladder leading to the second floor was gone now. She looked up at the inaccessible opening in the ceiling. Daylight from the upstairs windows was streaming down through it, and Piper suddenly remembered the feel of Amy's lips on hers . . . and the pain that followed her long-ago fall through the floorboards.

She still bore a scar, a jagged white line that ran along her left shin. The wound had become terribly infected, turning her whole lower leg a hot, red, swollen mess. In the end, when she'd finally shown her mother, she'd been rushed to the ER, where she was admitted and put on IV antibiotics. By the time she was out of the hospital, school had begun, and her mother had forbidden her two daughters to go to the motel ever again—it was "a death trap."

If only she knew how accurate her description had been.

Hadn't Grandma Charlotte used the exact same words to warn them away from the tower? If only they'd listened.

Of course, it turned out to be easy to avoid the motel: Amy didn't want anything to do with

Margot and Piper. While Piper was in the hospital, Margot said she had sneaked in a few phone calls to Amy, but Grandma Charlotte made vague excuses, claimed Amy couldn't come to the phone but she'd be happy to take a message.

Now here Piper was again, back in the tower, one word loud and clear in her head: *Run.*

Chickenshit.

"Am not."

There on the floor, where the base of the ladder once stood, was the wide board bearing the familiar cleats that marked the entrance to the secret dungeon below. She took in a breath, got down on her knees, and began to pry up the board with her fingers. It moved easily, and was still attached to the adjacent floorboard—although the whole unit felt lighter than she remembered. She easily lifted the boards up and out of the way, revealing the trapdoor, its rusted hinges, and the heavy bolt that was meant to keep all of its secrets locked up tight.

She put her hand on the deadbolt, hesitating. The metal was cold, covered in a thin crust of orange-brown rust.

Before she could think any more about it, she slid it open. Keeping her right hand on the heavy tire iron, she eased open the trapdoor with her left.

The smell of damp cement came wafting up—no stink of rot or ruin, only the smell of a wet basement. And there, just below the opening, was a folding metal stepladder. That wasn't there in 1989. Someone had been in the basement since.

"Okay," she said out loud, finding comfort in hearing her own voice. "What now?"

Go down, Amy whispered in her ear. *Or are you . . . ?*

"I am *not* chickenshit," Piper said aloud, and, to prove her point, she swung her legs over, down into the opening, feet finding the rungs of the metal ladder, while she kept the tire iron clenched in her right hand. Slowly, she descended—all alone, not even a flashlight to guide her.

At last, her feet found the floor.

And something touched her.

An insectlike buzzing, the rapid flutter of wings against her backside.

And there was music.

Madonna.

Her phone! Only her phone vibrating in the back pocket of her jeans. She grabbed it and answered.

"Can you pick up some saline nasal drops?" Margot asked.

"What?" Piper said, trying to steady her breathing.

"And a bulb syringe. I don't think I put them on your list. It's in case the baby catches a cold or is too stuffed up to nurse. Are you finding everything okay?"

"Yeah, fine," Piper lied, swallowing hard. She

was sure that she felt eyes on her—that she wasn't alone down here. "No problem." She peered anxiously into the darkness, tried to make out shapes, any sign of movement. The room didn't feel long abandoned to her. The air smelled damp and musty, but there was something else mixed in with it—something sweet and fruity that reminded her of the smell of Amy's lip gloss.

Piper's stomach tightened, as did her grip on the tire iron.

Was the skeleton still there, lying where they'd left it?

Amy had ordered Margot and Piper, made them promise, never to discuss what they'd found in the oubliette that day in 1989. "If you ever breathe a word of this to anyone, I'll kill you," Amy said. "I swear it." And, what with Piper's hospitalization, her mother's banning the girls from the motel, Amy's telling them to stay away, and the start of school, it was easy to keep the secret, even convince herself that maybe it had never happened. Through the years since, Piper would sometimes catch Margot looking at her funny, and she imagined her sister was thinking about Amy and the motel and everything that had happened. A few times, usually when she was drunk, Piper herself almost brought it up, but could never quite find the words. The sisters kept their promise.

"Piper?" Margot said now, voice suspicious. "You *are* at the drugstore, right?"

Damn. Margot knew her too well. But if Margot even suspected Piper had gone into the tower, she'd freak, probably call Jason and the whole London Police Department to come escort her out safely.

"Of course," Piper said, smiling, concentrating as hard as she could on sounding like she was actually in a brightly lit drugstore, perusing the aisles for new baby paraphernalia. She closed her eyes and imagined she was there, visualized herself standing in front of a display of thermometers. "Working my way down the list. It's taking a while, though—I didn't realize I'd have so many decisions to make. Do you have any idea how many kinds of rectal thermometers there are?"

"Piper—"

"Gotta go. It's crazy in here, and I can hardly hear you. I'll get the nose drops—can't have Junior being all stuffed up. See you soon." She hung up before Margot could say anything more.

Then she turned her phone around so that she could use the faint firefly glow it gave off to see what she could. She held it out and waved it around, scanning the dark landscape of the twenty-ninth room.

To her great relief, there was no skeleton curled against the wall.

The bed with the straps was still there. On top of it, Piper made out a sleeping bag and a flashlight. She moved toward it slowly and reached for the flashlight. When she flicked it on, she expected that the batteries would be dead. The sudden brightness hurt her eyes.

So the light hadn't been sitting down here for twenty-odd years. She did a quick sweep of the room to reassure herself that she was alone. The heavy chains still hung from the wall. But there at the ends, where the shackles were, she saw that each cuff had a new addition: a small brass padlock that was run through the ends. Piper moved closer for a better look. The brass shone in the light, not even slightly tarnished.

Someone had added these locks recently.

She pointed the beam of the flashlight back at the bed and saw that the sleeping bag looked nearly new, the quilted nylon covering not the least bit frayed or dingy. But it had a strange lump in the center, like a boa constrictor that had just had a large meal. She patted down the outside and felt something definitely hidden inside. Slowly, she unzipped the bag; the pull-tab moving down the metal teeth was incredibly loud in the silent room.

Once the bag was unzipped, she shone her light on the objects that had been tucked away inside.

Piper recognized the old book on top right

away: *Mastering the Art and Science of Hypnotism.* And she knew without looking that there would be an inscription on the first page, *"To Sylvie, the world's greatest chicken hypnotist, with love from Uncle Fenton, Christmas 1954."* And in the margins she'd find Sylvie's careful notes recording her experiments with hypnosis.

Below the hypnosis manual was the battered old leather-bound scrapbook they'd found in Sylvie's suitcase, full of pictures of movie stars from the fifties and sixties. Sylvie's scrapbook, her book of dreams and wishes. Beside all this were three packs of Juicy Fruit gum, one of them opened, the wrappers crumpled up and tossed in the sleeping bag. This was the source of the sweet, fruity smell that seemed to fill the room.

And tucked under everything, a typed note, neatly folded.

Dear Sylvie,
I'm sorry, so sorry for every-thing that has happened.
    Some things, as you know, simply cannot be helped.
    Please forgive me.
Your sister forever and ever, no matter what,
Rose

Piper pulled out her cell phone and called Margot.

"Still having trouble with the thermometers?" Margot asked.

"This baby-preparation business is harder than I thought it would be," Piper said in what she hoped was a light, rueful tone. "Hey, listen. I was thinking I'd like to pay Amy's mom a visit. Do you know what nursing home she's in?"

"Sure," Margot said. "She's up at Foxcroft. But according to Jason, poor Rose is in rough shape. Hardly knows her own name."

"I think I'll give it a try anyway. Maybe I'll head over—if there's time, before I see Lou; if not, I'll stop by after," Piper said. "Who knows what she might be able to tell me?"

Like who (or what) was being kept down in this room.

1989

Piper

"Grandma," Amy panted. "Gram! You have to come quick! Call the police. We found her! We know what happened!"

They came tearing into the kitchen, Amy in the lead. Piper's hands were shaking; her legs felt rubbery and strange, and her cut throbbed in time with her heartbeat. Amy's grandma was standing at the stove, browning a pan of ground beef and onions. She kept cooking, as though she had not heard Amy.

"Gram, you need to come with us *right now,*" Amy said, voice desperate, pulling on her grandmother's sleeve like an impatient little girl.

"What are you on about?" Grandma Charlotte asked, turning from the sizzling meat to look at the girls. "Come where?" She looked more tired than ever, dark circles resting like bruises under her eyes. She hadn't put any powder on today, and Piper could see blue veins running under her skin, like lines on a map. Rivers and highways.

"To the tower. Please. You'll see."

"You aren't supposed to play in the tower," Grandma Charlotte said calmly. "It's dangerous there."

It sure turned out to be dangerous for Sylvie, Piper thought.

"Gram, I'm telling you—*we found Sylvie!* She never left. We found her suitcase! It's been hidden in the floor of the tower all this time. And there's a secret room in the basement of the tower—like a *dungeon!* And there's a skeleton down there. It's got to be Sylvie."

Amy's grandma looked at Amy, then the other two girls. Her eyes were pale and watery. She turned the burner off on the stove. The cooked-meat smell was nauseating.

"I think it's time for your friends to go home," she said.

"No," Amy said. "They were there when we found her suitcase, and they've been searching for clues right along with me. I wouldn't have found Sylvie without them, and they want to know what happened as bad as I do. And the police will want to talk to them, right? To all of us."

Grandma Charlotte shook her head. "No police. And your friends need to leave now."

"But, Gram, we—"

"No police."

"Okay," Amy said. "You let Margot and Piper stay and we won't call the police."

Grandma Charlotte gave a reluctant nod. "Come sit," she said, voice firm. They followed her to the kitchen table. She picked up her pack of Virginia Slims and adjusted the big glass ashtray.

"Come sit"? She was being awfully calm for someone who'd just been told there was a dungeon on the property holding the skeleton of her long-lost daughter.

She knows, Piper thought. Somehow, she knew about the room and what was down there. What if she was part of it? Some sick husband-and-wife torture team. That's why she didn't want them to call the police. Piper should grab Amy and Margot, get them out of the house, run to their safe condo, tell her mother everything. She knew this, and yet she stayed.

Grandma Charlotte lit up a cigarette and blew the smoke up in the air. "There's something I need to tell you. Something I hoped I'd never have to talk about again, but now I see there's no choice."

"Oh my God," Amy said, leaning back in her chair so that it tottered precariously on its two back legs. "Don't tell me you knew? You knew Sylvie was down there, dead, this whole time? Jesus, Gram, she was your *daughter!*"

Amy's grandma shook her head. "That's not Sylvie down there."

"But it's got to be; we found her suitcase, we—"

"It's not her."

"Well, who is it, then?"

Grandma Charlotte drew in a long breath, then let it out. "It's Fenton. The girls' uncle."

"Fenton? No." Amy shook her head. "It can't be Fenton. It's Sylvie. I know it is. *I saw her ghost.* She's been leaving me notes in the typewriter."

That gave Grandma Charlotte pause. "You saw Sylvie's ghost?"

Amy nodded. "She comes to me in my room when I'm sleeping. She leaves me messages on the typewriter. She's the one who told us how to find the twenty-ninth room."

Grandma Charlotte looked down at the cigarette in her hand. She shook her head, but said nothing.

"Grandma, how do you know that skeleton is Fenton?"

Grandma Charlotte looked up to stare at Amy through the haze of cigarette smoke. "Because I'm the one who put him down there."

"*You* killed Fenton?" Amy asked.

"No. I just hid the body."

"So what happened to him?" Amy demanded.

Grandma Charlotte looked at Piper and Margot.

"Tell me," Amy insisted.

"If we go down this path, if I tell you the truth . . ." Grandma Charlotte's voice trailed off.

Amy pushed her chair back from the table, the metal legs scraping the linoleum floor. "If you don't tell me what's going on, I swear I'll call the police and show them the suitcase and the body in the tower. I'll let them figure it out."

"You can't do that, dear," Grandma Charlotte said kindly.

"Why not?"

"Because, if anyone were to find out what really happened to Fenton, no one would ever leave our family alone."

"Jesus, Gram! What happened to him? Tell me now or I'll call the cops. I swear it."

Grandma Charlotte sat up straight, looked right at Amy. "Our family is cursed," she said at last.

"Cursed how?" Amy said.

Amy's grandmother crushed out her cigarette. "Wait here," she said, heading out of the kitchen.

"So, if that skeleton is Fenton, what happened to Sylvie?" Piper whispered, once Grandma Charlotte was out of earshot.

"And what does she mean, 'cursed'?" Margot asked, voice trembling.

Amy said nothing, just watched as her grandmother came back into the kitchen holding a large glass jar. She carried it carefully and placed it gently on the table.

Inside was a large, pale-green moth with dull, tattered wings, long dead.

"What is this supposed to be?" Amy asked.

"It's a luna moth," Margot said, leaning closer to peer at the creature, which lay on a bed of dried-up leaves. One of its tissue-paper-thin wings had broken off and lay beside it. The legs were bent, the antennas thick with soft fuzz.

"The night Sylvie disappeared, Rose, Amy's mother, followed her sister out to the tower and caught this moth. She believed it was Sylvie she caught. The next day, Sylvie was gone."

"Wait," Piper said. "She actually thought her sister was a *moth?*"

"Actually," Grandma Charlotte said, "she believed Sylvie was a monster: a creature who could change form from human to animal, a creature capable of great harm. She thought she caught her sister that night. But she was wrong."

Amy stood up fast, knocking her chair backward. "I've heard enough," she said.

"Your mother—" Grandma Charlotte began.

"I know, you're going to tell me my mother is *nuts,* but I'm sick of hearing it. Maybe you're the crazy one—maybe my mom can't stand being here because of *you!*"

"Amy!" Piper said.

"What? You think I'm being mean? She's known all along that there's some secret torture chamber underneath the tower with a body in it! Now she's saying my mom thinks her sister turned into a bug?"

"You came to me for answers," Grandma Charlotte said weakly.

"And your answers are *bullshit!*" Amy yelled.

"Amy," Piper said, "I think—"

"Leave," Amy said, her chin quivering, eyes glassy. "I want you both to leave. Leave and don't come back. Go back to your clean little condo, your normal little life. Your mom, who's probably got dinner waiting."

Grandma Charlotte was crying—holding the jar with the luna moth and staring at it, her tears falling down onto the glass.

"Let's just—" Piper tried again, standing.

"And if you ever, *ever* tell anyone about what's in the tower, about any of this, I swear to God, I'll kill you dead." Amy glared at them with such venom that Piper felt her legs nearly give out beneath her.

"Of *course* we'd never tell," Margot said, tears now spilling down her cheeks.

"Swear on your life," Amy said.

"We swear, we swear, Amy, we're you're *friends,*" Margot said desperately.

"Amy," Piper said again, taking a step toward her, but Amy turned away, wouldn't meet her eye. Amy's shoulders were trembling, and Piper wanted more than anything to go to her, to tell her that everything was going to be okay.

But nothing was going to be okay.

She'd known it the moment they found that suitcase, but it was like a chain of dominoes that there was no way to stop, and now the last one had fallen. There was no going back.

2013

Piper

"Lou?" Piper called, stepping into the trailer, carrying the duffel bag stuffed full of pink and purple clothes. She'd knocked, but when no one answered, she'd let herself in. She found the girl sitting at the kitchen table, squeezing thick ribbons of chocolate syrup onto bread.

Piper had run to the drugstore (spending no time at all on rectal-thermometer selection), then back to Margot's, where she found her sister sound asleep. She'd deposited the plastic Rite Aid bags on the floor near Margot's bed, and left her a note: "Going to watch Lou for a couple of hours, then off to Foxcroft. Back by dinner."

"That your lunch?" Piper asked the little girl. Lou was wearing the same clothes she'd been in the last time Piper had visited her. Her hair was in tangles.

Lou stuck two pieces of chocolate-covered bread together to make a sandwich and smiled up at her. "Want one?" she asked.

"No, thanks," Piper said, looking around the kitchen. "Where's your aunt Crystal?"

Lou frowned slightly, then took a big bite of her sandwich. "Don't know," she said, mouth full. Chocolate sauce dribbled down her chin.

"Did she leave already?"

"Mmm-hmm."

"Really? When?" Piper asked.

"This morning. She got mad at me. Said she was going to call Social Services and find some other place for me to go."

"What? Why on earth would she say that?"

Lou shrugged. "Because of Ray, I guess."

"Ray?"

Lou nodded her head. "They got in a fight. About me. He doesn't think I should be here. Not enough room, he said, for three people, so he went out last night to go stay with a friend."

Piper cringed at the thought of their fighting like that in front of Lou. And how could Crystal even think of getting rid of Lou, much less say it to her face? Didn't she realize she was all Lou had?

"Let me just see if I can reach Crystal," Piper said, smiling and pulling out her cell phone.

She dialed Crystal's cell, got voice mail, and left a terse message. "I'm at the trailer. Maybe I misunderstood, but I didn't think you had to leave for work until one. Lou says she's been by herself since this morning. Call me when you get this."

"Is Crystal in trouble now?" Lou asked.

"No, sweetie. I just wish she hadn't left you on your own like this."

Lou nodded. "I don't like it here," she said. "I want to go home. I want my mama." Her eyes filled with tears.

Piper took Lou in her arms and held her, stroking her tangled hair. "I know. I'm sorry."

They stayed like that a few minutes, Lou snuffling into Piper's shoulder, and Piper wondering what she could possibly do to help this girl.

"Well," she said at last, when Lou pulled away, rubbing at her red eyes, "let's see if I can find something to fix for a proper lunch." She began opening cabinets and found very little: canned string beans, boxed macaroni and cheese, microwave popcorn, a dusty box of chocolate-cake mix. "Do you like macaroni and cheese?" she asked brightly.

"Mmm-hmm," Lou said, stuffing more of her sweet sandwich into her mouth.

Piper made lunch, chattering brightly about the most neutral topics she could think of—Piper's love of macaroni and cheese when she was a kid, the beautiful weather this time of year, how different Vermont was from Los Angeles, which is where Piper lived, did Lou know that? She cleaned up the tiny kitchen while Lou wolfed down the gooey orange noodles and soft green beans like it was her first meal in a week.

"How about we pour you a bath and get you into some clean clothes?" Piper asked. "I brought you lots of choices. You had a lot of nice things in your closet."

The girl nodded gratefully.

It took Piper fifteen minutes to scrub out the tub well enough that she'd feel comfortable putting Lou in it. With Lou hovering in the hallway, Piper continued to make cheerful chitchat while she worked, doing her best to mask her disgust. Finally, she poured a hot bath, got out the soap and shampoo (she even found some peaches-and-cream bubble bath under the sink and added it to the tub). She consulted with Lou, and they picked out a clean outfit of Lou's very own clothes. "Call me if you need anything," she said, closing the bathroom door.

She tried Crystal's cell phone again—no answer. She didn't bother leaving another message, but used her phone to get online and look up the number for the Mountainview Lodge, where Crystal worked. The woman at the front desk told her Crystal hadn't shown up for work. "When you do find her," the woman said, "tell her not to bother coming back to work. Our manager's pretty pissed. He's putting an ad in the paper for another girl to come clean."

Great. Just great.

"You doing okay in there?" Piper called to the closed bathroom door.

"Can you help me wash my hair?" the girl asked.

"Sure." Piper opened the door and stepped into the warm bathroom, which smelled powerfully of artificial peaches. Lou was lying back under a blanket of bubbles. Her hair was wet, and she smiled up at Piper, reminding her of some sweet water creature—an otter, maybe.

Piper got down on her knees and poured some shampoo into her hands, then began to massage it into Lou's hair. "Okay, rinse," she said, and down the girl went, submerging her whole head and face under the water. "Conditioner now," Piper said when she'd popped back up. "It'll help us get those tangles out."

She worked the thick conditioner in. "Let it sit a minute," Piper said, rinsing her hands in the murky water of the tub, then standing to dry them on a towel. Lou reached up to touch her hair, frothy with milky-white conditioner. Piper noticed purple bruises on the girl's arm and wrist.

"Lou," she said, keeping her voice calm, "what happened to your arm?"

"Nothing," Lou said, plunging it back into the bubble-topped water.

"Sweetie," Piper said, crouching down at the edge of the tub, "can you show me?"

Lou shook her head hard and fast.

"Did someone do that to you? Did someone hurt you?" Piper suddenly thought about the outfit Lou had been wearing—long pants and a long-sleeved shirt, whereas most kids her age were running around in T-shirts and shorts, thrilled to be out of winter clothes at last. Winters in Vermont were long and hard, and the minute the weather changed, people embraced it and didn't look back.

"Did . . . did Crystal do that to you?"

Lou shook her head again.

"Are you sure?"

"It wasn't her," Lou said, looking down into her fading bubbles.

"Who, then? Ray?"

Lou's lower lip started to tremble. She sank down low into the water until her ears were under the surface, her face just breaking it. "Mama," she said. "It was Mama."

Then she submerged herself completely and held her breath for so long that Piper was sure the child was trying to drown herself.

At last, she popped back up and began to scoop handfuls of bubbles and sing. Piper stood up on rubbery legs and left the bathroom, closing the door quietly behind her. Her hands were shaking, and her mouth had gone completely dry.

Maybe Amy had been a monster after all, a woman capable of child abuse. Murder, even.

After the bath, Piper and Lou unpacked Lou's things, and Lou seemed to delight in telling her the story of where she had gotten each article of clothing and stuffed animal. Piper made them microwave popcorn, and they watched cartoons on the living-room couch. When it was almost five, Piper sneaked out of the room to call her sister.

"Shit, Margot, I'm not sure what to do here.

Crystal's completely AWOL. No sign of this Ray guy—I don't even know his last name. I can't just leave Lou here like this."

Piper kept her voice low. She was in the kitchen, with her cell phone pressed against her ear, and Lou was in the living room, with the TV blaring some horrible cartoon in which characters shaped like sushi were pummeling each other.

"Just bring her here," Margot said. "She can keep me company while you run up to the nursing home. When Jason comes home, we'll figure out what to do. I think he's got some contacts at child protective services."

"They'll put her in foster care!" Piper protested.

"Which might mean she'd go into a clean, stable home where she'd be taken care of, right?"

"It just seems so awful," Piper said.

"More awful than leaving her alone in that trailer?"

Piper didn't respond.

"If you have a better idea, I'm open to hearing it," Margot said.

I keep her, Piper thought. *I bundle her up and bring her home to California with me. I could keep her safe. Get her some grief-and-trauma counseling. Give her the life she deserves.*

"Look, just bring her to our house, and we'll sort it out. Get her out of that shithole."

"Okay," Piper said. "We're on our way."

One hour later, Lou was sitting cross-legged on Margot's bed and teaching her new rules for Crazy Eights, cards fanned out expertly in her hands.

"Fours are a skip card," she explained, eyes lit up, clearly delighted to be teaching an adult. "I play one, and the next player's turn gets skipped. Queens make the game reverse directions. If you play a jack, the next player has to pick up four cards. Get it?"

"I think so," Margot said. "Why don't we just start playing, and you can help me out as we go along?"

Lou nodded enthusiastically.

"Are you sure you two will be okay for an hour or so?" Piper asked. Jason had called to say he'd be working late. There had been a bad accident out on River Road—a tractor trailer had overturned. Margot hadn't told him about Lou. She said he'd probably be pissed off about it on the phone, but once he came home and was with her, saw how adorable she was, it would be impossible to blame Margot and Piper for deciding to take her in. What else were they supposed to do?

Piper had left a note for Crystal on the kitchen table: "Took Lou to my sister Margot's. 185 Hillstead Rd." She'd added Margot and Jason's home number and her own cell-phone number. "CALL ME!" she wrote in all caps, underlined.

"We'll be fine," Margot said. "Won't we, Lou?"

The little girl nodded. Her hair was combed and pulled back in a French braid Piper had done. She still smelled faintly of peaches. She wore jeans and a long-sleeved pink shirt with a sparkly peace sign on the chest. Margot seemed to be loving the company, and Lou had taken to Margot right away. She had squealed with delight when Margot let her feel the baby kicking.

"How about if I stop and pick up a pizza on the way home?" Piper suggested.

"Pepperoni!" Lou chirped.

"Pepperoni it is," Piper promised.

"Maybe just a salad for me," Margot said. "Believe it or not, I'm still not all that hungry."

"Okay," Piper said, "I'm off. I'll be back in an hour or so."

"Where are you going, anyway?" Lou asked, looking at Piper over her hand of cards.

"Out to visit an old friend," Piper said. She thought it was best not to mention that it was Lou's grandmother she was going to see. She'd heard Rose and Lou had been close, but didn't know the details of what had happened to their relationship when Rose became ill. The last thing the little girl needed was to be reminded of another lost family member.

Lou smiled sweetly. "Tell her I said hello," she said, and in that uncomfortable instant, Piper was sure Lou knew exactly who she was going to see and why.

Piper

Foxcroft Health and Rehab smelled like sour milk and boiled meat. Grim-looking women and a few equally grim-looking men in scrubs walked the halls, pushing carts full of medications, snacks, and clean linens. Somewhere off in the distance, an out-of-tune piano was being played inexpertly.

Piper followed Marge S., the aide she'd met at the front desk, through a warren of corridors. They passed a nursing station where an overwrought-looking woman in Tweety Bird scrubs was on the phone saying, "I understand your position, but *you* need to understand that is simply not an option for her right now." Piper followed Marge S. down a hallway with residents' rooms on both sides. Each door had a bright sign announcing the names of the residents. Some were decorated with stickers and posters of puppies and kittens. One door had a wreath of artificial flowers. There were a few doors with bright-red stop signs bearing further instructions. They stepped around medicine carts and people napping in wheelchairs. An ancient-looking man in a colorless cardigan shuffled by, but stopped short when he saw Piper.

"*There* you are!" he cried with delight. Piper smiled nervously and kept going.

"Here we go," Marge S. said at last.

Rose Slater, said the sign. There was no second name, and when they entered the room, Piper saw the other bed was empty, stripped down to the bare mattress.

"Rose, honey, you have a visitor," Marge S. announced.

The woman in bed looked up, fixing her dark eyes on Piper. Her skin was thin and white, but taut and remarkably free of wrinkles. She wore a hospital nightgown and robe. She looked younger than Piper had imagined, and though Piper had never met her before, she would have recognized her as Amy's mother. From pictures, Piper had always thought Amy looked more like her aunt Sylvie, but now she saw that Amy had her mother's delicate nose, her brow, and her cheekbones.

Rose stared up at Piper with unblinking, cool eyes.

There was a TV across from the bed, dark and silent. A rolling table held a hairbrush, a water cup, and a plastic pitcher. Beside the bed, a small bureau. On it was a wind-up clock, ticking loudly, and a large glass jar, which Piper recognized at once. At the bottom of the jar lay the ruined luna moth.

"You're not her," Rose said, voice faded, but clear.

Piper couldn't tell if she was disappointed or relieved that Piper wasn't who she'd been expecting.

"Ms. Slater," Piper began, "my name is Piper. I was a good friend of Amy's back when we were kids."

Rose nodded. "I remember."

Piper nodded, too, though Rose couldn't possibly remember her—they'd never met. Maybe Amy had talked about her?

"I'll leave you two alone, then," Marge S. said. "If you need anything, just push the call button. And remember, Rose, if you want to get out of bed for any reason, you need to *call* first; otherwise, that pesky bed alarm will go off." Marge S. turned to Piper and said cheerfully, "Our Rose likes to go on walkabout!"

"Thank you," Piper said, watching the woman hurry out of the room and into the chaos of the corridor. An alarm was beeping shrilly as a resident hollered for someone to call her a taxi.

"I wonder," Rose said, "if you know anything about my granddaughter, Lou."

Piper smiled. "She's fine, Ms. Slater. She's an amazing kid. I was with her all afternoon. She's someplace safe, I promise."

"Safe?" Rose said. "Really? When Jason was here, he wouldn't tell me a thing."

"Jason? Jason Hawke?"

Rose nodded.

"He came to visit you here? When?"

"Yesterday morning," she said. "He thinks I'm senile, you know. Psychotic, even. That's what he wants to believe. What Amy wanted to believe, too. But the truth is, I'm the only one who knows what's really happening. I'm the only one who sees things for what they are."

"Can I ask you a few questions?" Piper said, moving closer to the bed.

"Isn't that why you've come? To hear about Sylvie?"

"And Amy and her family," Piper said.

Rose nodded. "Yes. Amy. I tried to warn her. She didn't listen. She locked me up in here instead."

"Warn her about what?"

Rose looked out the window into the growing darkness.

"They'll be coming with my medicine soon," she said, her dark eyes flicking back to the door. "We don't have much time."

Jason

Jason regarded the scene before him and wished like hell that there had been a tractor-trailer accident on River Road, like he'd told Margot. As much as he'd hated lying to her yet again, especially after last night, he knew he couldn't tell her the truth. If he told her about it, she'd want details, and a crime like this was the last thing any parent or parent-to-be wanted to hear about.

He remembered what Margot had told him last night: "Sometimes a lie isn't what's said, but what's unsaid. An omission."

Later, when he went to get into bed, she'd told him icily that she'd prefer it if he'd sleep on the couch.

"What?" he'd asked, stunned.

"I think we both need some space," she told him flatly. "And time to think things over."

He'd spent the night tossing and turning on the lumpy couch, replaying every decision that had led to this. Surely it would blow over, was just a matter of Margot's hormones making her overly sensitive—he'd never seen her so cold before. But, then, he'd never really lied to her before, had he? And he shouldn't have pushed her about her own omissions, not now. Not when being upset could put both her and the baby at risk.

He pushed the thought away and went back to scanning the crime scene, every horrific inch of it.

The girl had been found by two fifth-graders walking home after school. There was a path that ran through the woods behind London Elementary School to Butler Street. A lot of kids took it. The muddy ground was covered in footprints and bike tire tracks. It was a goddamn thoroughfare. So how is it that no one had seen or heard a thing?

The girl's name was Kendra Thompson. The kids who'd found her recognized her right away, in spite of the condition she was in. Her face was intact, but her body . . . it looked . . . like it had fallen into the lion pit at the zoo. Jason had never seen anything like it. Not even in those zombie movies he watched. That stuff—that was nothing.

"Where's Louisa?" a woman called. Jason turned. It was Mrs. Buffum. She'd worked in the front office since Jason was a kid, and it was clear she'd be there till she died. Mrs. Buffum was part of the school, like the brick outside and the cracked porcelain bathroom fixtures. Her well-padded rear end had earned her the unimaginative nickname "Mrs. Buttum" back when Jason was a kid. He wondered if anyone called her that still.

"Louisa?" Jason asked. He was the nearest officer, the one who was supposed to be controlling the crowd, keeping the people back, while the state crime-scene guys did their job.

"Louisa Bellavance. Or 'Lou,' I guess she calls herself. She came in to school earlier today. I was surprised to see her—I thought she was taking some time away. But I looked out at the playground during morning recess and there she was, playing with Kendra. They were sitting together on the swings, laughing."

"You're sure?" Jason said. "You're sure it was Lou you saw her with?" Jason's heart slammed in his chest.

"Positive. I thought how nice it was that Louisa had come back, that she was playing with her best friend. It seemed like just what she needed after all that horrible business with her family—to be a normal kid again, playing on the playground."

Jason jogged over to the group gathered around the body, and tried to keep his face composed while he delivered the news. "Hey, Chief Bell, a school employee just told me the victim was last seen with Lou—Louisa Bellavance. The kid from the motel."

"Jesus," said Tony Bell. "So maybe our guy kills Kendra and grabs Louisa."

"Or maybe she ran?" one of the state cops suggested.

"Quite a coincidence," Tony said. "Louisa's whole family being slaughtered a couple days ago, now her school friend."

"What if . . ." Jason said. "What if Louisa was

the target all along? The other girl just happened to be with her?"

He thought of Margot's insistence—and his own gut feeling, if he was being honest—that Amy hadn't killed her family at the motel. What if they were right, and the real killer was out there still? But he'd left a survivor, a potential witness.

Then he remembered his visit with Rose Slater.

"Do you believe in monsters, Jason?" she'd asked.

"No, ma'am," he'd told her.

"Neither did my daughter. And look what happened to her."

And now look what had happened to little Kendra Thompson. Jason wondered if she'd believed in monsters.

"We need to find Louisa Bellavance," Tony barked. "Now!"

Rose

The girl kept interrupting, asking all the wrong questions. She didn't understand. Once the evening med cart came around—and it would any minute now—they'd watch her take her pills, and twenty minutes later she'd be out. At least, that was the case when she actually swallowed the pills, which she usually did. The next thing she knew, it would be morning, and the day nurse would be coming in to pull back her curtains and give her her morning pills and talk about the weather. They'd put an alarm on her bed last week (which Rose allowed them to think she couldn't disable, though of course she could, just like she could tuck her sedatives into her cheek and spit them out into a Kleenex once she was alone, when she so chose—she wasn't an idiot, despite what they thought).

They weren't going to lose her again. It looked bad for the staff to have a resident go missing, as Rose had, time after time, for hours.

Sure, folks wandered. It's what people with dementia did. They confidently waltzed into the wrong room, and cried out in alarm at the stranger in their bed. They went into the closet thinking it was the john, or down to the day room at midnight to soothe the baby they thought they heard crying. Many of them were just looking for the way out, the way home. But the staff always found them somewhere on the locked ward right away. Not Rose. Rose's disappearances had confounded them. They always took place at night. She'd be discovered missing during rounds, some time after midnight. They'd search all night and into the morning for her. Then, inexplicably, there she'd be, back in her bed, by daylight, wondering what all the fuss was about.

"I've been here all along," she'd tell them.

"Well, you must have been invisible," a nurse once snapped.

Rose had smiled at that. "That's me," she said. "The Invisible Woman."

The one nobody sees for what she truly is.

The staff all called her that from then on: "How's our Invisible Woman doing today?" Not to her face, but to each other. Sometimes they called her "our Houdini."

She liked the air of magic it gave her. She didn't like how they always prefaced it with "our," but she knew it was the truth. She was theirs. Their prisoner. Their problem.

Only they didn't know the half of it. Could never have guessed.

Eventually, the staff decided enough was enough: Rose might hurt herself, and the facility would be at fault. They installed the bed alarm and began giving her enough sleeping meds at night to tranquilize a cow.

This suited her fine. For the first time she could remember, she'd wake up feeling rested.

Rose was pulled back to the present as Piper pushed open the heavy curtain and looked outside. It was dusk, and the clouds were thick and threatening, making the sky darker still. "I went down to the room below the tower," Piper said. Rose squinted at her, tried to picture the woman before her now as the little girl she'd once been: the girl who'd roller-skated with her Amy, flying around in cut-off shorts, with the little radio they carried cranked up as loud as it could go. Piper had never met Rose, but Rose had seen Piper plenty. She'd watched her that summer. Spied from the trees, from the tower. A few times, she'd been nearly caught—by that silly boy who was always hiding in Room 4, and then by Amy, who would awaken in the night and catch her mother watching her from the shadows.

How many nights had she spent like that, hiding in the shadows of her daughter's room, waiting, watching, seeing if she might change—if Amy was a mare, too?

"Shh," Rose would tell Amy. "Go back to sleep. You're dreaming."

"I was there today. The twenty-ninth room," Piper said now, leaning in, and speaking more loudly than she needed to. "Someone's been down there recently. Someone's been using it."

Rose nodded.

"Tell me, please," Piper said. "Is she back? Sylvie? Did she have something to do with what happened to Amy and her family?"

Rose looked at Piper, but was listening to the noises in the hall outside. Through the din of voices and bells, she heard the unmistakable clacking of the med cart's wheels rolling down the hall, but there were still a good four or five rooms before hers.

"Listen carefully," she said. "I am going to tell you the truth, but we haven't got much time. You mustn't interrupt."

"Okay," Piper said, leaning even closer.

"It wasn't Sylvie being kept down in that basement. Sylvie is dead. Has been for over fifty years."

"Dead? Are you sure?" Piper gave her an am-I-dealing-with-a-poor-senile-old-woman-after-all look.

"Of course I'm sure, silly girl," Rose hissed. "I'm the one who killed her."

1961

Mr. Alfred Hitchcock
Universal Studios
Hollywood, California

October 2, 1961

Dear Mr. Hitchcock,
I think there is something wrong with me. At least, I hope there is. I sincerely hope that I am delusional.

Because, Mr. Hitchcock, I believe my sister Rose wants me dead. I think there is something wrong with her, terribly wrong. She has always been jealous of me, but these days, it seems so much more than that. There's an icy hatred in her eyes.

I wake up in the night sometimes and find her bed empty.

Worse still is when I wake up and find her standing over me, staring down.

Once, I woke up and she had her hands around my throat.

Though I know I will sound insane, I must tell you the worst of all: One time I swear I saw a creature crawl into her bed in the middle of the

407

night. I thought at first it was a dog, or a small bear, but it wore human clothes: Rose's dress. As I stared at it in the moonlight, it burrowed under the covers, and I closed my eyes in horror. When I dared to look a moment later, there was my sister, her head on the pillow, appearing peacefully asleep.

In the morning, there was dark, coarse fur on Rose's pillowcase. And her sheets had the rank stink of a wild animal.

What is my sister?

And what is she capable of?

Yours truly,
Miss Sylvia A. Slater
The Tower Motel
328 Route 6
London, Vermont

Rose

Even though Sylvie had disappeared, they made Rose go to school, pretend that everything was normal.

"There's nothing you can do moping around at home," Mama said; she packed a tuna sandwich for Rose in a paper sack, tucked it into her school bag, and sent her on her way to meet the bus. Mama, who never cried, had been crying all morning. She wouldn't look Rose in the eye; she seemed eager to get rid of her.

Daddy called the police, Rose learned later. Sylvie was reported as a runaway. Daddy went down to the train and bus stations, flashing a picture of Sylvie, asking if they'd sold her a ticket or seen her. Nobody had.

"Probably headed for Hollywood," Mama kept saying. "That girl has stars in her eyes. Has since the day she was born."

Sylvie's friends were all shocked to hear the news; they denied knowing anything about a plan to run away. They did say she'd been acting strange lately, and they'd guessed that she might have a secret boyfriend. When asked for any details about this boyfriend, none of them knew a thing—it was just a feeling they all had.

Her closest friend, Marnie, suggested that

Sylvie would go straight to Universal Studios to look for Alfred Hitchcock. When the police followed up, Mr. Hitchcock's assistant told them that he did not know anyone by the name of Sylvia Slater from Vermont, and Mr. Hitchcock had never received any letters from someone by that name. But, yes, the assistant would certainly contact the police if any girl fitting that description should show up at the studio.

Rose checked that all Sylvie's letters, the ones she'd stolen from the mailbox and opened over the years, were carefully hidden. She didn't want anyone to find them. For years, they'd been her secret view into Sylvie's world. But there would be no more letters.

That night, after her parents were fast asleep, Rose sneaked out of her bedroom and went to the workshop, where she grabbed the flashlight she'd carefully unpacked from the bag last night. She went down to the tower. She thought of the night before, of Sylvie speaking to her from the shadows: "What is it you want from me?"

Rose's head began to ache as she entered the tower, flicked on the light. She went all the way up to the top floor and shone her light around, half expecting Sylvie to be there, hiding in the shadows.

She remembered their fight, which had been so like a dance, and the expression on Sylvie's face just before she fell backward off the tower: utter horror.

Rose turned off her flashlight and sat with her back against the cold stone wall. She looked up at the stars and wondered what the night sky looked like in faraway places, places like Hollywood, where Sylvie wanted to go.

There were footsteps below, on the ground floor of the tower.

"Sylvie?" Rose called, half hoping it really was her sister. Not the least bit frightened anymore by the idea of her being a monster; of what she was capable of. If only it *was* Sylvie; if only Rose was all mixed up about Sylvie and Fenton and mares and luna moths.

Someone was climbing the ladder.

Rose heard breathing. She froze. Listened to footsteps move across the second floor and then steadily up the final ladder. She stood, holding the metal flashlight over her head like a club.

Hands came into view, gripping the rungs of the ladder, reaching out to the floor.

Familiar hands.

Not Sylvie's.

Mama's hands.

"What are you doing up here?" Mama asked, as she pulled herself off the ladder and stepped gracefully onto the floor.

It was odd, seeing Mama in the tower. Even though Daddy had built the tower for her, Rose couldn't remember ever seeing Mama inside. She seemed, now that she thought about it, to avoid it.

"I couldn't sleep," Rose explained. "I thought maybe I'd come down here and find Sylvie. She used to come here sometimes. At night."

Mama looked at Rose a minute, considering. It was the first time Mama had looked her in the eye all day. But her expression was strange, unfamiliar, apprehensive. It was as though Mama was meeting a person she didn't know (and wasn't sure she liked) for the first time.

At last, Mama stuffed her hands into the pockets of her wool coat and said quietly, "I heard you and your sister fighting up here last night."

There was a bright flash of pain in Rose's left eye. She pushed her thumb into the socket, trying to massage it away. She desperately wanted to climb back down the ladder, go up the driveway and into the warm safety of the house, crawl into her bed, and sleep. Maybe, if she went back to sleep, this whole day would disappear.

"You did?" Rose asked.

Mama nodded in the darkness. "Can you tell me what happened?"

Rose closed both her eyes. "I followed Sylvie to the tower."

"With a backpack full of traps and chains?"

Rose swallowed hard, wondering how Mama knew about the backpack.

"I wanted to catch her. I knew you would never believe me—you'd never see her for what she really was unless I showed you."

"What was she, Rose?"

"A mare—at least, I think so. I'm almost sure. 'Cause they *do* exist, Mama, just like in the stories Oma told me when I was little. And I know the reason she told me so much about them. She knew that Sylvie was one. She was trying to prepare me. To teach me all about them so that I would know what to do, how to stop her if I had to."

And she *had* stopped her, hadn't she? Rose's head was pounding ferociously now, the pain shooting through her left eye like an icicle.

She clearly recalled the walk back to the house last night, the heavy knapsack thumping and clanging on her back; in her hands, she'd carried the luna moth in the net. It had struggled at first, then held still, resigned to having been captured.

Mama stepped closer to Rose. She settled on the floor beside her, leaned against the cool stone wall, and sighed deeply.

"Oh, Rose," she said sadly, softly. "You've got part of it right: Mares *do* exist. Your grandmother was one herself."

"No," Rose said, "she couldn't be!" It didn't make sense. Oma had told her such horrible stories about these creatures and the things they were capable of.

Mama continued. "My mother never used to remember what happened once she'd transformed." Mama's expression was one of pity now. And remorse. "She'd come home, clothing torn, blood under her fingernails—she would never have any idea what she'd done."

Rose's head swam. "But . . . wasn't she dangerous? Weren't you afraid she might hurt us when she came to visit?"

She remembered the safe feeling of being in Oma's arms, the smell of horehound candy, the lulling sound of her voice.

Mama shook her head. "I wasn't too worried, no. My mother had learned to control it quite well—apparently, better control comes with age. As an extra precaution, there were pills she took at night, sleeping pills that kept her from transforming when her guard was down."

"But, still . . . to invite a"—Rose thought the word "monster," but could not say it aloud—"someone who could do those things, here, to stay with us . . ."

"Mares have a way of recognizing one another, of sniffing each other out, you could say. That is why I invited her, to spend time with you girls, so that we would know if either of you was a mare. She told me she was sure neither of you were, that we were safe."

"But that wasn't true," Rose said.

"No, it wasn't true. I believe my mother knew it, even then, and lied to me."

"When did you figure it out?" Rose asked.

"I started to worry when you told me Sylvie

had been sneaking out of bed at night. I watched her carefully, looking for signs. When I discovered Fenton's body in the tower, I blamed myself; I knew that I could have stopped it. But even then, I had it all wrong. I hid the body, cleaned every-thing up, and started to watch Sylvie. Finally, yesterday, I confronted her."

"Did she know? Did she know what she was?"

Mama was silent a moment, studying Rose in the moonlight.

"Sylvie wasn't the mare, Rose." Mama looked into Rose's eyes. "You are. It's been you all along."

"I don't understand," Rose said. She dropped to her knees now, head in her hands, the pain a great wave washing over her. She was sure she would be sick, her stomach was churning so.

Mama's words hung in the air, bright sparkles that only intensified her pain. Her mother looked small and far away, like she was speaking to Rose from the end of a long tunnel, her words small and echoey.

"I ran down to the tower last night when I heard you girls fighting. But then I heard another sound, a snarl and a growl, and I got there just in time to see Sylvie fall. I believe she died instantly, thank God."

"No!" Rose said. "She transformed! She fell, but she turned into a moth and fluttered back up!"

"As I told you, that moth you captured was not your sister. She broke her neck. I saw there was nothing I could do and knew I had to hide the body—what if your father woke up and found us? I quickly carried her into the woods." Mama paused here, took a deep breath, rubbed at her eyes. "When I looked back through the trees, up at the tower, I saw a dog's shiny black head peering down from the top."

"No," Rose breathed.

"I don't believe you meant to hurt her. I believe it was an accident. You were fighting, you started to transform, your sister was frightened, and in her struggle to get away from you, she fell over the edge."

"But Sylvie," Rose croaked out, "she's the one. She was the mare. I saw her. . . ."

Rose thought of the nights she'd wandered off from her bed. The strange dreams she'd had, dreams of claws and fangs and blood. How she'd found fur on her pillow. She'd opened her eyes and felt like her body was not her own. She'd believed there was a mare sleeping beside her each night, but it was worse than that. The monster was inside her.

That's what Oma had been trying to warn her about, to prepare her for. That was why she'd spent so much time with Rose, why Rose was clearly her favorite. They were two of a kind, she and Oma.

Rose had dropped the flashlight. It shone on the wall and dimly illuminated the space she and her mother sat in. Her mother continued to speak, even though Rose wanted to beg her to stop, not to say any more.

"My mother said it usually skipped a generation, that I shouldn't have children of my own. But then I met your father, and he wanted children so badly."

"Does Daddy know? About mares?"

Mama shook her head. "I never told him; I've never told anyone and prayed I would never have to. When he told me about the tower he intended to build, I asked that it have an oubliette, thinking that if either of you girls turned out to be a mare, I would have a place to keep you safe, to keep the world safe from you. I told your father a secret dungeon would give the tower an air of authenticity. I asked him to do it as a special, secret favor for me.

"I'd like to take you there now, to show you the room. You wouldn't have to stay there all the time, only at night, only until we find some other way to help you . . . control this."

"A hidden room?" Rose asked. She thought of the story of Rapunzel, locked away in a tower by an evil witch. But Mama was no witch. And this was no fairy tale.

"I showed it to Oma when she came to visit. She was horrified. Said it was no place for a child. I

417

suppose it's my fault she lied to protect you. I only wish . . ."

Mama was crying now: soft sobs that shook her whole body. "I blame myself for what happened to your sister. You can't help what you are. I should have stopped you. There are two dead now, and I can promise there won't be any more."

Two dead.

Two.

"Fenton?" Rose whimpered.

Her mother nodded.

"No," Rose said, inching away. "It can't be me. It was Sylvie. I followed her to the tower. I *saw* her transform."

Mama shook her head. "Don't you know what Sylvie was doing in the tower? Don't you? She was meeting Fenton."

"Fenton? Why?"

"She believed she was in love with him. She confessed the whole thing to me, when I confronted her about her nighttime wanderings, thinking she was the mare. She told me she'd been meeting Fenton in the tower at night for years now. They'd even discovered the secret room, but had no idea what it was for. She asked me about it during our talk yesterday, and I denied knowing it even existed. Anyway, in the beginning, Sylvie and Fenton would hide out down there and just talk late into the night. But as time went on and their feelings grew, they became . . . *romantic.* They were planning to run away together. To California."

"But Sylvie—"

"Sylvie is gone, Rose. I took care of her body. Gave her a proper burial where no one will ever find her. The last thing we want is an investigation. If our secret was uncovered, I would never be able to protect you."

Rose dropped her chin to her chest and began to sob. Mama moved forward and stroked Rose's tangled hair with tentative fingers.

"I know it doesn't seem like it, but it's going to be all right. Like I told you, my mother discovered she was able to keep herself from transforming by using sedatives at night. We can start trying them on you. We'll find a way, Rose."

Everything Rose thought she knew fell away from her then.

"You can have a life. A normal life. I've lost one daughter. I won't lose both."

Rose looked up at her mother, who looked at her with eyes that simmered with fear, regret, and something else—loathing. She knew, knew that, try as she might, her mother would never forgive her. Sylvie would always be the good daughter: the beautiful moth with pale-green iridescent wings. Rose, even locked in a dungeon or cured by medicine, would always be the monster.

2013

Piper

Piper sat in shock as the nurse came bustling into Rose's room, pushing the med cart. "Rose," the nurse said, "time for your evening pills."

Rose nodded, and dutifully took the tiny paper cup of pills and the cup of water with a flexible plastic straw from the nurse. She tipped the cup of pills into her mouth, took a sip of water, and swallowed.

"Good girl," the nurse said. "You ring if you need anything."

She nodded politely at Piper and said, "The pills can make our Rose a little groggy."

"I understand," Piper said.

And she did. They kept Rose medicated to keep her from disappearing. But what they didn't know was that it wasn't Rose in human form they were looking for when they found her bed empty at night—it was Rose in mare form, Rose as a black dog, or even an insect. She'd told Piper that it really wasn't that hard for her to change into whatever she wished. It was a skill, like any other, something a mare develops over time. She'd also learned to transform at will when wide awake, and was able to keep a good part of her human consciousness—and conscience—once she'd changed. Mostly, however, she'd learned, over the years, to control it—to take just the right amount of muscle relaxants every evening to keep her from changing in her sleep, unaware.

The nurse wheeled the cart out of the room and turned left, making her way down the hall.

Rose stared at the jar on the bedside table with the luna moth inside.

"Charlotte showed us that jar that summer," Piper said. "She told us you always believed it was Sylvie."

Rose shook her head. "For about twenty-four hours I did, yes. But then I learned the truth: my sister died in that fall, and my mother covered it up; she hid the body so there wouldn't be any investigation that might reveal our family secret."

"So why did you keep the moth?"

Rose smiled bitterly. "I suppose as a reminder of how we all trick ourselves into believing what we need to believe."

"Was it *you* Amy saw that summer? You who left those notes in the typewriter? Not Sylvie's ghost?"

"Yes," Rose said. "My mother and I agreed that it wouldn't have been safe for me to live at home. What if I slipped up and Amy saw me transform? Or what if, God forbid, I hurt Amy by accident when I was a mare?"

"So you just left her?"

"I never went far. We allowed the story of my supposed drinking problem to flourish; my mother made references to me being far away, 'getting help.' But I mostly stayed around Vermont; I rented squalid little rooms and apartments, and got by however I could, working at supermarkets and Laundromats. I even stole a bit here and there if I needed to—never enough to call attention to myself, of course. And at night sometimes I came back to the motel and checked up on things. Like I did today." She smiled at Piper.

"It was you? You left me the note this morning?"

Rose nodded. "Wednesday mornings are busy here. We've got Bingo; then the children from the elementary school come to visit and sing songs with us. It's not so hard to slip away in the chaos. No one notices a little bird flying out through an open window; in no time, I can be across town at the motel."

"And back then, you never let Amy see you. You let her believe it was Sylvie's ghost."

"It was easier that way. I knew I should just stay away, but I couldn't. I'd come back and watch Amy while she slept, just to make sure I hadn't passed it on to her."

"And was she?" Piper asked, hardly believing she was even asking the question. "Was Amy one, too?"

"No," Rose said. "Like my mother told me—it usually skips a generation."

Piper sprang forward in her chair. "Lou? She's a mare?"

Rose nodded, licked her lips. Her eyelids started

to close. Fast-acting medication, whatever it was. Or maybe she'd just worn Rose out.

"Did Amy know?"

"Didn't want to believe it. That's why I came back, why I moved back into the house with them. I tried to help them, like Oma tried to help me. I sensed it right away with Lou, but of course I needed to be sure before I could warn Amy. Once the transformations began, I tried to tell Amy, but it was too late. She called me crazy, and her stupid husband backed her up.

"Then, last week, she came to me, hysterical. She'd seen Lou transform. She wanted to know what to do. I told her about the medicine. I told her to take Lou to the twenty-ninth room and try to keep her down there until she figured out how to get the medicine, what the right dosage would be. Lou was stronger than I ever was. She had quickly learned how to transform at will—to change in the daytime, even, and take whatever form she wanted. And, like any young mare, she was impulsive . . . dangerous. She wasn't always able to control her actions once she turned."

"Wait a second—are you saying it was Lou? That she killed her family?"

The old woman's eyes were shut now, her voice trailing off into sleep. "A mare can't help what it is. Can't help the things it does."

"Oh my God," Piper said, grabbing her bag and running for the door. "Margot."

Margot

Something was wrong and Margot knew it, had known it all day. She'd been uncomfortable since breakfast, but she had told herself that the cramping she felt was brought on by too many crêpes.

"I think I need to take a little bathroom break," Margot told Lou. The girl looked disappointed. She'd won four hands of Crazy Eights and was well on her way to another victory. They'd already taken one long break when Lou had gone into the kitchen to bring back a snack—saltine crackers with globs of jelly, something that had somehow taken her nearly twenty minutes to prepare.

The cordless phone on the nightstand rang, and Margot picked up.

"Hello?"

"Margot? It's me," Piper said, sounding out of breath. "Is everything okay?"

"Yeah, we're fine," Margot said.

"And Lou, she's still there? And she's . . . she's okay?"

"Yes, Lou is right here and she's fine. We're both fine." Margot smiled at Lou, who was watching her intently with a small frown. "She's killing me at Crazy Eights! Why all the concern?"

427

"Is that Piper?" Lou asked. Margot nodded and held up a finger—one minute. Lou stood suddenly, knocking the cards off the bed, and left the room.

"It's something Rose told me," Piper went on. "Margot, I know this is going to sound crazy, but I think Lou might be—" The connection went dead.

"Piper? Hello?"

Lou returned and plopped herself down beside Margot on the bed, another jelly-smeared saltine in her hand.

"Is everything okay?" Lou asked.

"Yes, fine. Piper just wanted to check in. We had a bad connection. Now, I'm going to run to the bathroom, and then you and I can get back to cards. Why don't you go ahead and pick them up, then deal us a new hand?"

Margot began the slow process of dragging her huge body out of bed. She did what the doctor told her: sat for a minute with her feet on the floor before standing. Still, when she did rise to her feet, she felt dizzy.

"Are you okay?" Lou asked.

"I think so," Margot said, black spots swimming in front of her eyes. She sat back down on the bed, hard.

When she hit the mattress, she realized her pajama pants were soaking wet.

It took a few seconds for her to realize what

had happened: her water had broken. This was normal. Everything was fine.

She picked up the cordless phone and dialed Jason's number. Nothing happened. The line was dead. Maybe the battery was drained?

"Lou?" Margot said with all the calm and clarity she could muster. "Could you hand me my cell phone, sweetie? It's over on the other nightstand."

Lou crawled off the bed and dug around on the nightstand on Jason's side of the bed. "I don't see a phone," she said.

"It was right there," Margot said, panting a little as a huge cramp came on.

Not a cramp. A contraction.

The baby was coming.

"Well, it's not here now," Lou said cheerfully.

Odd. She could have sworn she'd just seen it. But she must be mistaken. Maybe Piper had picked it up and put it somewhere else? Or maybe she'd even mistakenly thought it was hers and taken it with her? No problem. There was another cordless phone in the kitchen, plugged into the base. She'd call Jason, then Piper, and tell them the baby was coming. She wouldn't tell them how dizzy she was, how the black spots were swimming in front of her eyes. No need to worry them. She just needed to get the wheels in motion. Get to the hospital. The doctors and nurses would know what to do. They'd take care of her and the baby.

"Okay," she said, voice calm and assured. It was her mother voice. Her woman-with-a-plan voice. "There's another cordless phone in the kitchen. Could you bring that to me, please?"

"Sure," Lou said, skipping out of the room.

From here, her footsteps in the hallway sounded almost like—like scrabbling, like a dog's nails running on wood. What kind of shoes was the kid wearing?

In a minute, Lou was back, phone in hand, her feet bare. But there was something funny about her feet: they were terribly long, the toenails pointed. Margot blinked. Her blood pressure was affecting her vision.

"Thanks," she said, taking the phone from Lou. She pressed the keys to speed-dial Jason's cell. Nothing happened. She hung up, pushed another button. There was nothing. No dial tone.

"It's dead," she said lamely. They kept it plugged into the base to charge. How could the battery be dead?

Lou had picked up the framed wedding photo of Margot and Jason that they kept on their dresser. "Jay Jay," Lou said, smiling at the picture.

"That's my husband," Margot said, flinching at Amy's old nickname for Jason.

Lou smiled placidly. "It's Mommy's friend Jay Jay."

The spots in front of Margot's eyes grew larger,

wavier. Another contraction rolled over her. She tried to breathe through it.

"What else did Piper say when she called?" Lou asked. "Did they find Aunt Crystal?"

"No, sweetie. Not yet. I'm sorry."

"Good," Lou said. "She was mean. I don't like it when people are mean to me."

"There's another cordless phone in the office," Margot said, panic starting to creep over her. "Could you go get that one for me?"

"Yup," Lou said; she put the photo back down and bounded out of the room. For a second, Margot thought she saw feathers woven into the back of Lou's braid. But then Lou was back in a flash, holding the second phone in her hand. Or was it a claw? No, she didn't have four reptilian digits where her fingers should be. She couldn't.

"Your hand," Margot said. There were definitely sharp talons at the ends of Lou's fingers.

"What?" Lou asked, smiling, holding up her other hand, which was normal.

Margot knew, even before she took it, that this phone was dead, too. She knew it from the way the girl smiled at her, her teeth strangely pointed, her eyes distinctly *wrong* now—the blue irises huge, covering any trace of white, the pupils vertical slits.

It was as if a curtain had been dropped: everything got dark and quiet except for a strange buzzing sound in Margot's ears. And Lou's voice.

"You and Piper, you've been so nice. You wouldn't do anything mean, would you?"

"Of course not," Margot said. "I promise."

The girl's face was dark now, more animal than human. Margot shook her head, sure she was seeing things.

"Mama promised, too," Lou said quietly, regretfully.

"I need . . ." Margot said, trying to stand, but too dizzy to manage. "Help," she mumbled, sitting back down. "I need you to go get help."

"But I'm here," Lou said, sitting beside Margot on the bed, putting her hand on Margot's thigh. The claws poked through Margot's cotton pajama bottoms, drew blood that came in little pinpricks, blossoming once they hit the fabric. "I'll help you."

Piper

Neither Margot nor Jason was answering their cell phones. The house number rang and rang, too, after her conversation with Margot had been cut off.

Piper thought of calling 911 and saying there was an emergency. But they would ask what emergency, and what would she tell them? That she had left a ten-year-old child who was actually a monster playing cards with her sister? Then she'd be the one the cops would come after, ready to lock her up and give her a heavy dose of antipsychotic medication.

Was she crazy for being frightened, she asked herself as she rolled through a stop sign, for actually believing the possibility that Rose's stories were real?

A mare can't help what it is. Can't help the things it does.

"Damn it," she said, hitting the speed-dial number for Margot's cell phone. "Pick up the damn phone!"

Voice mail again.

She threw her phone down on the passenger seat in frustration. The rain had picked up. It drummed heavily on the roof, blurring the windshield even with the wipers at full speed

433

and the defrost fan blowing. She was on Main Street now, heading away from downtown. Up ahead, she saw the wrecked Tower Motel sign, faded and leaning. And beyond it, looming like a monster of stone and cement, the tower.

And at the bottom, Clarence's oubliette.

The twenty-ninth room.

Built to keep Charlotte's children safe.

But it hadn't, had it?

She continued on, speeding in spite of the weather, hydroplaning a little when she turned corners. At last, her sister's house came into view. It wasn't in smoldering ruins, nor was it surrounded by police and the SWAT team.

But it should be.

Piper shook the thought off. Nonsense. She's just a girl. They're probably still playing Crazy Eights. Margot's laughing at all the rules Lou keeps making up as she goes along.

The kings mean you have to take a card from another player. And the aces turn you into a monster.

Piper put the car in park, cut the ignition, and ran toward the house.

"Margot? Lou?" she called before the front door was even halfway open. She was pumped up on adrenaline, hand trembling as it gripped the knob. "I'm back. I was running late, so I didn't stop for pizza. I can go pick one up, though. Or we can get it delivered." She kept talking, waiting for a response as she moved down the hallway, into the kitchen. "Hello?"

A box of crackers and jar of grape jelly had been left on the table. Smears of purple covered its surface, like dark, coagulated blood.

She headed for Margot's room. "You guys still playing cards?" she asked, straining to keep her voice light and chipper.

Please. Please let them be.

But no.

The room was empty. The covers were on the floor. The fitted sheet covering the bed had a large wet spot, like someone had spilled something. The cards were all over the floor, along with a cracked plate still sticky with jelly.

She heard Jason's stern warnings: "She's not to leave the bed. We've got to keep her calm. If her blood pressure shoots up again, it would put both her and the baby in danger."

"Margot!" Piper shouted, voice shrill with panic.

She tore out of the room and down the hall, throwing open the doors to the bathroom, guest room, and laundry room—all empty. She flipped the basement lights on and trotted down the stairs, to find only the furnace, water heater, chest freezer, and an old Ping-Pong table.

Where the hell were they?

Then she heard it: a piercing cry from outdoors, somewhere in the backyard.

Margot, screaming.

Jason

"Looks like an animal attack," one of the state boys said. "Those have to be claw marks, right? No knife did that."

"But what kind of animal could do something like that?" Tony asked, his flashlight aimed down at the body.

They'd gone to Crystal's trailer to try to locate Lou, and had found Crystal while searching the grounds. Her body was sprawled between the Dumpster and a cinder-block wall out back, behind the row of trailers. She was wearing sweatpants, a T-shirt, and slippers. A bag of trash was spilled everywhere. She'd been taking out the garbage when the attack occurred; you didn't need a fancy criminal-justice degree to see that.

"A bear?" one of the men suggested.

"Uh-uh, a black bear wouldn't attack a person like that," Jason said.

"So—what? A catamount, maybe?" Tony said.

"Maybe," Jason said. "But we haven't had a big-cat sighting in years. They just aren't around anymore."

"Maybe one is," Tony said, pointing the beam of his flashlight out into the woods behind the trailer park. "I want this whole area searched. Whatever we're looking for, man or beast, may have left something behind. A paw print, maybe. Let's get on it."

Officer Malcolm Deavers came out of the trailer holding a piece of paper. "I think I know where the girl is," he said.

"Where?" Tony asked.

"She's at Jason and Margot's."

"What?" demanded Jason, snatching the note from Deavers and blinking down at his sister-in-law's handwriting in disbelief. He turned to hurry back into his cruiser and head for home, muttering, "Goddamn it, Piper!"

Piper

"Margot!" Piper called, looking out the open back door into the rain. She flipped on the floodlights that lit up the backyard and stepped out onto the patio. In front of her was the in-ground pool, its cover off; Jason had begun to scrub it down in preparation for the summer. The blue-painted cement reminded her of being twelve, of Amy and her chasing Margot around the pool in circles.

She saw no sign of her sister or Lou.

Piper started out across her sister's neatly landscaped yard—perennial beds, vegetable garden, perfect green lawn. Beyond the lawn, the woods.

"Margot?" Piper called again.

"Piper!" It was Margot's voice—somewhere in the dark woods. Then a guttural groan.

Piper broke into a run.

As soon as she left the ring of light cast by the outdoor floodlights, it became impossibly dark. She blinked, willing her eyes to adjust, but could make out only the vague outline of trees close by. And darkness. Pure darkness. The rain pelted down on the canopy of leaves above, a percussive din that seemed to drown out all other sound.

She heard a low moan up ahead and to the left.

"I'm coming!" Piper called. She was doing an awkward stumble-run now, a zombie shuffle, with her hands outstretched in front of her. Her own breath was loud in her ears.

At last, she saw a form in a clearing ahead, a pale shape there on the ground. Margot in her flannel pajamas. She was curled on the forest floor in a fetal position, arms cradling her pregnant belly.

"Margot!" Piper cried, moving through the trees faster now. She dropped into a crouch beside her sister. It was brighter in here, the cloud-filtered moonlight illuminating everything with a bluish glow. "Jesus, are you okay? What are you doing out here?"

Margot was breathing hard and fast. But it wasn't just Margot that Piper heard. Something else was breathing, too. Soft, snorting breaths coming from somewhere not far behind them. Twigs snapped. Something was moving among the trees, just out of sight.

Margot was shaking her head, huffing and puffing. "Something's wrong with Lou. She . . . she changed. Into an animal or something."

"Are you hurt?"

"No, but I'm in labor, and the phones . . . I just wanted to get away from her. I thought maybe I could cut through the woods to the road. . . ."

Even in the dim light, Piper could make out enough of Margot's face to see that she was terrified.

"Let's get you to the hospital," Piper said in the

most confident voice she could muster. She slipped an arm under her sister's shoulder. "Can you stand?"

Margot shook her head again, hopeless.

"I'm too dizzy. When I sit up, everything gets blurry. You need to go. Find Jason."

"I'm not leaving you," Piper said firmly, just as a terrible snarl tore through the darkness behind her.

It was close—close enough that she could smell it now, its dank, musty animal scent. Slowly, Piper turned, keeping herself protectively in front of Margot as she braced herself for the sight of a horrible nightmare creature. She was almost relieved to see it was an animal she recognized, not something out of a horror movie. About ten feet away from her, a black panther crouched low, watching Piper. Its coat was black and sleek from the rain, and its pale eyes glinted in the moonlight.

"Hello, Lou," Piper said, hardly believing this animal was the little girl she'd left just hours ago, but somehow knowing it to be true.

The panther snarled, bared its teeth.

Piper took a half-step back, then stopped, determined to stand her ground and protect her sister.

"I don't want to hurt you." Piper raised her hands up in a gesture of surrender. "And I don't think you want to hurt me and Margot, either, do you?"

The panther watched her, seeming to listen, to consider what Piper was saying, as it held itself perfectly still. It could have been made of obsidian.

"I'd like to help you, if you'll let me. I helped your mother once, when we were girls. I didn't understand what was happening then, but I do now."

Suddenly the panther's head swiveled, eyes locking on the darkness behind Piper. Something was padding through the woods. Piper turned around to see a huge, shaggy black dog step out of the trees. It had a big blocky head with a shortened, graying muzzle, and small upright ears. Under other circumstances, in the dim light, Piper might have mistaken it for a small bear. Piper remembered Amy's story of the ghost dog that visited her while she slept. Now she understood.

"Rose," Piper said.

The dog approached, its head down, its hackles raised. Piper understood then that Rose was ready to defend herself. To defend her family. She held still and tried to remain calm, tried to remember that this was still Rose, that there was a piece of her inside—a rational being who only wanted what was best for her grandchild.

"I think we both want the same thing . . ." Piper began, but she was interrupted by a small voice.

"Grandma?" Piper turned back and saw that the panther had become a little girl once more. Lou was naked, on all fours on the forest floor. Her eyes had a strange glow, and her hands . . . didn't look like hands at all, but dainty black paws. Piper blinked, and watched as they turned back to a child's hands. Piper could now see the faint shadows of bruises around the girl's pale wrists.

Bruises from being shackled under the tower, her mother trying to keep her safe.

> When Death comes knocking at your door,
> you'll think you've seen his face before.

Lou, fully human now, rose to her feet.

The dog let out a sharp bark and trotted over to Lou; it circled her once, then darted toward the thick line of trees, and back again. Rose was coaxing Lou to follow her into the woods.

"Lou?" Piper said, looking into the little girl's eyes, which were once again those of a human child—blue, like her mother's. "You don't have to do this. You can learn to control this. You can have a normal life."

Lou shook her head. "That's what Mama said. But she locked me up like I was an animal at the zoo. Made me take pills that made me sleep all the time."

The dog came back to Lou's side, nudged her hand.

"We can figure it out," Piper said. "I'm sure there's a way we can fix this."

If you hold up a mirror, you shall see
that he is you and you are he.

"Maybe I don't want to fix it." Lou stroked the dog's head as she spoke. "Maybe I like the way I am. I'm good at it. Better than anyone in my family ever has been."

She looked down at the dog, who gave a little woof of agreement, then nudged hard at Lou's hip, still trying to lead her away.

"I can change into whatever I want just by thinking about it," Lou continued. "A bird, a bee, even a panther."

She said this last part with a smile that showed her teeth, still pointed.

"But, Lou, *can* you always control it? Don't you sometimes change without meaning to? Hurt people you don't mean to?"

The little girl stopped moving and blinked at her. "I—"

"What happened that night? With your family?"

"I didn't . . ." Lou stammered, voice cracking. "I didn't mean it. She locked me in that room. It was so cold. Dark. I couldn't move. I was strapped down to a bed. I was calling for her and calling for her, begging for her to come let me out. Then, the next thing I knew, I was up in the house. My mama, she . . ." Lou's voice faltered, and she began to cry. She may have been a monster, but she was also a little girl who had lost everything. A creature who had destroyed those she loved most.

Piper looked at the dog. "Rose, you have to know this isn't what's best for Lou. It's not what Amy would have wanted."

The dog gave a low, disapproving growl and wrinkled her lips, baring gleaming fangs.

"Margot!"

A man's voice, coming from the direction of the house—Jason. Margot moaned.

"She's here!" Piper called back.

"No!" Lou said angrily. "Don't call him over here! He doesn't understand, and he's a police-man. If he finds out . . ."

Piper turned back to Lou. The little girl's face was frantic.

"It's okay," Piper told her, voice soothing. "I'll take care of Jason. I can help you—I know I can," she promised.

The beam of Jason's flashlight was bouncing through the trees, and they could hear footsteps crashing through leaves.

"That's what Mama said, too," Lou said, her voice suddenly not that of a child, but flatter, deeper, more guttural. And then Lou dropped down into a crouch. It could have been a trick of the eye at first—a cloud passing over the moon that made Lou's body go from pale to dark. But as Piper watched, the dark skin became fur glistening in the moonlight, black and shiny. Her body elongated, her hands grew into great paws. Supple muscles rippled under the creature's glossy coat. And where, only seconds before, there had been a little girl on her haunches, a sleek black panther stood, eyes yellow, teeth bared, as it let out a loud, threatening snarl.

Jason

The cruiser's tires squealed as Jason pulled into the driveway. All the house lights were on, and the front door was open. He bolted inside, calling for Margot and Piper. No answer. The kitchen was a mess, and the bedroom was worse. Signs of a struggle.

"Shit," he mumbled, heart hammering. "Shit, shit, shit."

He thought of the doctor's warnings, how Margot needed bed rest. If anything happened to Margot or the baby . . .

"Margot!" he bellowed, charging through the house. The sliding doors leading to the patio were open, and all the lights out there were on, too. Suddenly he heard voices: Piper's, he thought, and someone else's—a child? They came from the dark woods behind the yard. Stepping outside in the rain, he ran the beam of his flashlight back and forth over the dense wall of trees.

"Margot!" he called.

"She's here!" Piper's voice called back from somewhere deep in the woods.

He started running, illuminating the way with his flashlight. He crossed the yard and plunged into the woods. Tree branches scratched his face, grabbed at his arms, trying to hold him back. He tried to imagine what on earth Margot was doing out here. It must have to do with that girl, Lou. Did the killer come for Lou, chase Margot and the girl into the woods? Were they hurt? Was the killer still out there?

More voices from up ahead. Then the snarling growl of a big cat.

He drew his gun. "Margot!" he cried, hurling himself forward, no longer watching the ground, tripping, stumbling, terrified of what he might find. He reached a clearing, illuminating a nightmare scene with his flashlight. It was nothing like what he'd imagined.

Margot was curled up on her side on the leafy forest floor, head tucked, eyes squeezed closed, panting.

In front of Margot, no more than five feet away from her, a sleek black panther stood. It gave a screeching hiss when he shone his light on it. Beside the panther, an enormous black dog with its teeth bared.

Jason knew immediately that this cat was the animal that killed Crystal Bellavance, the little girl behind the school, and, somehow, Amy and her family. He raised his gun, and took aim.

"No!" Piper yelled, stepping directly in front of his gun, the barrel inches from her chest. "Put it away," she said. "It's just going to scare her more."

The panther had flattened its ears and lowered

itself to the ground so it was lying down directly in front of Margot. Margot let out a small, fearful whimper. The dog moved a few steps forward, a deep, menacing growl rumbling in its throat.

"Step aside, Piper," he ordered. This was not the time for an animal-rights speech. How could Piper not understand the danger they were all in? When Piper refused to move, Jason side-stepped, then again trained his gun on the large black cat.

"Jason, for God's sake, listen!" Piper moved in front of the gun again, hands up, talking fast. "You aren't going to believe this, but—"

Suddenly Jason lost all interest in the panther, in Piper's frantic speech. Margot's body had started to twitch strangely. Her eyes rolled back in her head, her jaw clenched, and her back arched. She began to convulse, as if she were being electro-cuted.

"Margot!" Jason cried, lowering his gun as he ran to his wife. The panther sprang away, into the safety of the woods, the dog bounding behind it. Jason dropped to his knees and put the flash-light down, its beam illuminating Margot's horrific face: eyes bulging, tongue protruding, everything contorted and all wrong.

Piper was instantly at his side. "Oh my God, is she having a seizure? What do we do?"

Jason pressed his gun into her hands. "Take the gun. Shoot them if they approach."

"Jason. They're gone."

He glanced up and saw she was right. The animals were nowhere to be seen. In the back of his mind, he knew they should stay on guard, though he couldn't tear his attention away from Margot.

"Take it anyway," he grunted. Piper complied.

Jason cradled Margot's head as gently as he could, trying to keep her from hitting it too hard on the forest floor—all he knew to do from his basic training. And timing—he knew he should be timing the seizure to report to the paramedics, but he couldn't count seconds, couldn't even think clearly, could only hold her head and murmur, "It's okay, Margot, it's okay, just relax, it's okay," mindlessly, knowing it was not okay, not at all. She needed to be in a hospital, with equipment and medication and doctors. Now.

When Margot stopped seizing at last—it had been less than a minute, but it might as well have been eternity—her body went limp and still, her breath coming shallow and rapid. Jason scooped her up from the ground, staggering a bit.

"We have to go. We've got to get her to the hospital."

Piper led the way out of the clearing, sweeping the beam of the flashlight through the trees. There was no trace of the panther or the dog. It was almost as if they'd never been there at all.

Piper

Piper paced back and forth in the waiting room, her soaking-wet shoes squishing with each step. Although Margot had regained consciousness in Jason's cruiser, when they arrived at the hospital it was clear that Margot and the baby were in imminent danger. Jason had radioed ahead to the ER, and she was immediately surrounded by nurses, doctors, and techs. In a flurry of controlled chaos that took only minutes, oxygen was started, an IV was placed, medications were given, labs were drawn, and she was attached to monitors of all sorts. Then they were rolling her down the hall for an emergency C-section. Piper had time to give her a quick kiss and say, "I love you, you can do this," and then Margot was off, Jason at her side, holding her hand.

Now it had been nearly two hours, and still no word. Piper took a sip of the cold, sour coffee she'd poured herself some time ago.

Jason came in, disheveled but beaming.

"They're okay," he said, his voice breaking. Piper ran to him and threw her arms around him.

"We have a healthy baby girl!" he said in her ear. "And Margot's blood pressure has stabilized. She's awake and alert—the doctor says she's going to be fine. And, oh, Piper, the baby is so beautiful."

He was crying. They both were. They held each other tight. Piper realized, in that moment, how much Jason loved Margot. Everything else fell away: Lou, Amy, all of it. There was only the sweet relief that Margot and the baby were going to be fine—that was all that really mattered.

When they pulled apart, Jason said, "When they were prepping her for surgery, she was saying the craziest stuff. I don't know if the meds they gave her were making her loopy or what. She said that she saw Lou turn into some kind of monster, and that's why she ran out into the woods—to get away from her. Then, somehow, Lou became a panther? And she said it was Lou who killed her family. She even said that big black dog in the woods was Rose Slater. . . ."

He trailed off when he realized that Piper wasn't laughing.

As Piper looked at Jason, she remembered when they were kids, how he'd always been on the outside. It was time to let him in.

"I know it seems crazy, I really do," Piper said. "But it's all true. Let's sit—I want to tell you everything."

And she told him everything. She began with finding the suitcase that summer and worked her way forward, leaving nothing out. She told him about the room in the tower, the skeleton, how

Rose killed Fenton and Sylvie, and Lou killed her family. She explained about mares, how they appeared human but could turn into something else, how this ability or curse or whatever you wanted to call it ran in Amy's family. She told him about trying to help Lou, how she felt like that's what Amy would have wanted, but Lou had chosen to stay with her grandmother, to go on being a mare. When Piper was finished, Jason stared at her, glassy-eyed.

"Piper, I just can't . . . I'm just not able to believe all that."

"I don't expect you to believe me. A part of me even wonders if I'm actually insane, if this is all part of a complicated paranoid delusion." She laughed weakly. "But I know it's the truth, and I know it was time to tell you. No more secrets. Okay?" She reached out and took his hand, gave it a squeeze.

He nodded, but he looked completely over-whelmed and baffled. Piper was fairly certain he thought she was crazy, and just didn't have the energy to argue.

"No more secrets," he said after a moment. "Now, come on. I want to introduce you to your niece."

Piper held the swaddled baby in her arms—little Ella. Ten perfect fingers, ten perfect toes. Grayish-blue mermaid eyes, in a funny little wrinkled face.

Margot was propped up in the hospital bed, looking exhausted but blissful, as she watched Piper cooing at Ella. The nurse had just come in to check vitals, to peek at the dressing on Margot's belly, and to ask about her pain.

"Doing well, Mom," the nurse said with a quick smile. Jason was on the other side of the bed, holding Margot's hand. He gave it a squeeze. The nurse bustled out.

"Mom," Jason said, kissing Margot's cheek.

Ella started pecking at Piper's collarbone. "I think she's hungry."

Piper brought the baby over to Margot and settled her into Margot's arms.

"I can't get over how beautiful she is," Piper said, standing right beside Jason now, her arm around his waist as they both gazed down at the baby, one little starfish hand peeking out from beneath the blanket, her tiny perfect mouth opening wide, looking for nourishment.

Margot caught Piper's eye, and shot her a look—*What did you say to him? What happened?* Piper smiled and shook her head ever so slightly—*Everything's okay. We'll talk later.*

Margot nodded, looking down at Ella as she nursed. "Perfect," she said. "She's just perfect."

Jason

Jason called the station the next morning, while Margot and the baby were sleeping, to see if there was an update on the whereabouts of Lou. McLellan told him, "No sign of the girl yet, but we've got half the state out looking. Now it seems her grandmother, Rose Slater, has disappeared from Foxcroft Health and Rehab—last time anyone saw her was at evening bed check."

"Weird," Jason said, biting his lip, remembering what Margot and Piper had told him—how that big dog had been Rose Slater.

"Yeah, but you haven't heard the craziest part of it all," McLellan went on. "Call just came in. The Tower Motel is burning. The whole damn thing is up in flames. I'm on my way there now."

Jason hung up and filled Piper in.

"You should go to the motel," she said. "See if they need you there. I'll stay with Margot and the baby."

The driveway was full of fire trucks and various EMS vehicles, so he parked along the street, pulled over right by the old motel sign.

He'd seen the smoke billowing as he drove through town. Here it was thick and black, a great cloud covering them; it was rising and spreading, soon to cover all of London. It didn't smell like cigarettes or a campfire; it smelled dangerous, full of chemicals and melting plastic.

The house was burning, as were the two rows of motel units and the old crumbling tower. His eyes went to Room 4, where he used to spend his afternoons imagining he was grown up, living some other life. Flames shot through the roof, which crumbled down.

The entire London Fire Department was on-site, dousing the flames with high-powered hoses, but it was clear that the place was beyond saving. The goal now was to protect the woods behind the house and motel. If they went up, the condos might, too.

"Any idea how this started?" Jason asked the fire chief.

"Place was soaked in gasoline," the chief said, hurrying off to talk with some firefighters from Barre who'd just arrived to help out.

Jason stood in the driveway, in the place he'd stood a thousand times, staring up at the window of the house, Amy's bedroom window. Smoke poured out of it. Flames shot through the roof.

Once upon a time, there had been a boy who'd loved a girl. He followed her everywhere, like a sad dog. Some part of him, he knew, had gone on following her, chasing her through his dreams, calling her name.

Amy, Amy, Amy.

For whatever reason, he'd never really let her go. He'd known it that day last week as he sat across from her at the kitchen table—known it and hated himself for it.

But now it was time.

Time to let go, once and for all.

Jason turned back to the house and watched the smoke rise and take shape: first a phantom, then a bird, a many-headed monster, and, finally, a beautiful girl with streaming hair and the longest legs he'd ever seen. He felt the smoke enter him, tasted it on the back of his tongue, acrid and ruined.

He remembered that long-ago first kiss at the bottom of the pool; the teasing way she'd called him Jay Jay; the crushed cigarettes he'd left her in the tower. He imagined each memory leaving his head, drifting up with the thick black smoke: up, up, up, until it was all just a ruined blur and his eyes burned and he wanted, more than anything, to leave this place for good.

He turned and started back down the driveway, his eyes on the tower. There were no hoses spraying water on it, no firefighters paying it any attention whatsoever. It stood, like a great black, crumbling chimney, flames shooting out the top.

The wooden floor was gone now, as were all the joists. Without the strength of the wooden framing, the tower began to shift, to fall in on itself. The walls of stone came crumbling down in huge clumps of rock and concrete. The fire roared like a great hungry beast.

He thought of Piper's insane story. Of the secret room that she said was down at the bottom of the tower—the twenty-ninth room, built to chain up monsters, to keep them safe and the world safe from them.

It sounded like a story Amy would have cooked up back when they were kids. He remembered her showing him the blurry Polaroid, telling him it was a ghost, begging him to believe her, to say he'd seen it, too. And then he thought of what she'd been trying to tell him that day last week: how, of all people, it was him she had turned to—him she chose to tell that she now believed the monsters her mother spoke of might be real.

Jason looked up through the smoke and flames, through the ghosts of memories, and saw movement just beyond the tower. There, behind it and to the right, where the yard turned to woods, two sets of eyes were watching.

It was the big black dog and the wild cat. Jason looked up the driveway at the firefighters and police rushing here and there, eyes on the burning buildings. No one seemed to see the animals at the edge of the yard. No one but him.

He moved toward them, slowly at first, but then, when they turned and trotted off, he began to jog.

He drew his gun and followed them into the woods, up behind the pool, across the long-overgrown path that he had taken a thousand times as a boy, running from his house to the motel.

He was running now, clumsily stumbling over tree roots, dodging pine trees. The animals were too quick for him, moving with the grace and dexterity of wild things.

At last, the animals paused, and turned back to look at him once more. He raised his gun, took aim at the panther.

The big cat caught Jason's gaze and held it, with strange but somehow familiar blue eyes. Blue eyes?

He blinked in disbelief.

"Lou?" he called out hesitantly, lowering the gun.

The dog nudged at the panther, then sprang into the brushy woods. The panther stayed a moment longer, eyes still locked on Jason. At last, it turned away slowly and followed the dog deep into the shadows, until the two beasts were nothing more than shadows themselves.

Mr. Alfred Hitchcock
Universal Studios
Hollywood, California

April 14, 1961

Dear Mr. Hitchcock,
Sometimes I can see it so clearly: my future in Hollywood. My mother shakes her head, laughs, asks why I would want such a thing. But still, I picture myself there, under the Hollywood sign, my own name in lights and on the front of every industry paper: Sylvia Slater, star of the big screen.
I will be bright and shining.
I will be larger than life.
I will live forever.
Who wouldn't want a thing like that?

Sincerely Yours,
Miss Sylvia A. Slater
The Tower Motel
328 Route 6
London, Vermont

Acknowledgments

Some books come more easily than others. This one had a great many challenges in store for me, and I have a lot of people to thank for helping me find my way through it.

Dan Lazar, I've said it before and I'll say it again: I couldn't ask for a better agent, and I really couldn't have pulled this off without you. A thousand thanks.

Andrea Robinson, who said at one point that this book was like a puzzle, for diligently (and oh so cleverly!) working to help me figure out which way the pieces might fit together.

Anne Messitte, for all her editorial insight, guidance, and tremendous support in all things book-related.

The whole team at Doubleday, for each and every thing you do, whether it's correcting a spelling error, putting together a brilliant cover, or getting me home from an event when I'm stranded in a snowstorm.

Karen Lane and all the folks at the wonderful Aldrich Public Library in Barre, Vermont, for helping me with the microfilm machine (which I was pretty sure I broke until Karen fixed it!) so I could research Alfred Hitchcock's visit to Barre.

Paul Heller, for his tremendous help with painting the picture of the evening Alfred Hitchcock and Shirley MacLaine came to Barre.

(It is true that *The Trouble with Harry* was filmed in Craftsbury, Vermont, and the world premiere was held at the Paramount Theater in Barre. Being a novelist, I took some pieces of that truth and wove them into my story. If any of the facts are not historically accurate, it's due to my choices, and not the information I received from Paul or any of my other sources.)

Sara Baker, for giving me the lowdown on what it was like to grow up in a family-run motel in Vermont, and for all the wonderful feedback on an early draft (and for the delicious iced coffee!). I couldn't have created the Tower Motel without you.

My father, Donald McMahon, for his unfailing support, and for helping me learn all sorts of facts about the aircraft of World War II, which unfortunately never made their way into the book.

Drea Thew, as always, for living through every one of my freak-outs over the book, helping me edit each draft, and always being my first and most trusted reader. Remember when you asked if I was sure I really wanted to write a book about shape-shifting monsters? Turns out I did.

And, finally, to Michaela and Keelin Needham, and to Zella McMahon, who taught me a great deal about monsters, and helped me envision this story while we ate lots of gelato. Next time I'm stuck with an idea, I know just the girls to go to, to help me work it out (and, yes, more gelato will definitely be involved).

About the Author

Jennifer McMahon is the *New York Times* bestselling author of seven suspense novels, including *Promise Not to Tell* and *The Winter People*. She lives in Vermont with her partner, Drea, and their daughter, Zella.

Center Point Large Print
600 Brooks Road / PO Box 1
Thorndike, ME 04986-0001 USA

(207) 568-3717

US & Canada:
1 800 929-9108
www.centerpointlargeprint.com